PRAISE FOR
ASHES

"[H. R. Howland's] debut novel has a plot that moves with jungle cat speed. Watch out!"   —Thomas F. Monteleone

"*Ashes,* by H. R. Howland, is what horror and suspense fiction is all about—a hard-driving story with plenty of thrills along the way, and characters you come to care about deeply . . . especially when the tension ratchets up until you can barely stand it."   —A. J. Matthews, author of
The White Room and *Looking Glass*

"H. R. Howland writes with crisp, classic style, a lot of heart, and the constant, uneasy feeling of twilight—when the light is slipping away and the night is coming on. Expect great things."   —Christopher Golden

"[Howland] keeps the action swift."   —*Hellnotes*

"*Ashes* starts like gangbusters and rarely lets up. The writing is excellent and briskly paced, with strongly detailed settings and crisp dialogue. [His] ability to paint a word-picture of violence even made a hardened horror fan like myself squeamish at times."   —Cinescape.com

H. R. HOWLAND

THE
EPICURE

BERKLEY BOOKS, NEW YORK

THE BERKLEY PUBLISHING GROUP
Published by the Penguin Group
Penguin Group (USA) Inc.
375 Hudson Street, New York, New York 10014, USA
Penguin Group (Canada), 90 Eglinton Avenue East, Suite 700, Toronto, Ontario M4P 2Y3, Canada
(a division of Pearson Penguin Canada Inc.)
Penguin Books Ltd., 80 Strand, London WC2R 0RL, England
Penguin Group Ireland, 25 St. Stephen's Green, Dublin 2, Ireland (a division of Penguin Books Ltd.)
Penguin Group (Australia), 250 Camberwell Road, Camberwell, Victoria 3124, Australia
(a division of Pearson Australia Group Pty. Ltd.)
Penguin Books India Pvt. Ltd., 11 Community Centre, Panchsheel Park, New Delhi—110 017, India
Penguin Group (NZ), Cnr. Airborne and Rosedale Roads, Albany, Auckland 1310, New Zealand
(a division of Pearson New Zealand Ltd.)
Penguin Books (South Africa) (Pty.) Ltd., 24 Sturdee Avenue, Rosebank, Johannesburg 2196,
South Africa

Penguin Books Ltd., Registered Offices: 80 Strand, London WC2R 0RL, England

This is a work of fiction. Names, characters, places, and incidents either are the product of the author's imagination or are used fictitiously, and any resemblance to actual persons, living or dead, business establishments, events, or locales is entirely coincidental. The publisher does not have any control over and does not assume any responsibility for author or third-party websites or their content.

THE EPICURE

A Berkley Book / published by arrangement with the author and Sweet Nightmares, Ltd.

PRINTING HISTORY
Berkley mass-market edition / December 2005

Copyright © 2005 by Holly Newstein and Sweet Nightmares, Ltd.
Cover art by AXB Group.
Cover design by Rita Frangie.
Interior text design by Stacy Irwin.

ISBN: 0-425-20717-X

BERKLEY®
Berkley Books are published by The Berkley Publishing Group,
a division of Penguin Group (USA) Inc.,
375 Hudson Street, New York, New York 10014.
The name BERKLEY and the BERKLEY design are trademarks belonging to Penguin Group (USA) Inc.

PRINTED IN THE UNITED STATES OF AMERICA

10 9 8 7 6 5 4 3 2 1

ACKNOWLEDGMENTS

The authors would like to thank Dr. Nancy Mest Gordon for her help with medical procedures and with the layout of Hahnemann Hospital. Without her we would have made even bigger fools of ourselves.

We would also like to thank our beta testers, especially the "real" Becky, Jessica, and Susan. You know who you are.

Finally, a big thank you to Rick Hautala; Colin and Andrew Newstein; Cheryl, Shawn, and Melissa Bieber. We love you.

Epicure, *n*: one devoted to sensual pleasure: one with sensitive and discriminating tastes, esp. in food or wine.

—*Merriam-Webster's Collegiate Dictionary*,
10th Ed. 1993

ONE

Susie Troutman opened her eyes.

"Jessie-ka! Is *Miss Becky* on yet?" she called. Her bed was so warm and comfortable that she didn't want to get up.

"It's almost five, little Pickle," Jess called from the living room downstairs. "I was just going to wake you up." Jess always insisted that Susie take a rest after school was out and her homework done. Even on Fridays when she had no homework. Susie hated being treated like a baby. After all, she was six and a half years old and in first grade. But it was funny—she always seemed to fall asleep.

"Oh, *no! Miss Becky's* coming on! Gotta hurry!" Susie leaped from the bed, comfort forgotten, her plaid skirt and long thin legs flying. She grabbed her best pearl necklace that Grandma had given her and put it over her head. She jammed her feet, in their navy blue school socks, into a battered pair of white satin mules with a few shreds of ostrich feathers still waving wearily on the instep. She smoothed her rumpled green-and-blue plaid jumper with the crest of St. Laurence's School embroidered on the chest. Then she looked wildly around her cluttered little room. "Jessieeeeee! Where's my Miss Becky? I *can't* watch my show without her!" Susie wailed. "Blessed Saint Jude, help me find my Miss Becky. Hallelujah and amen."

"I'll help you and Saint Jude find her," Jess said. She chuckled as she came up the stairs.

They rummaged through Susie's untidy room, searching for the Miss Becky doll. Susie was nearly frantic.

"Miss Becky will be *so* mad if we miss her show!" Susie's eyes welled with tears.

"She's got to be here somewhere, Suz. You didn't leave her outside, did you?"

Susie frowned. "Miss Becky doesn't go outside. She's got gorey-phobia. Like Mrs. Franey." Mrs. Franey lived across the street from the Troutman-Grasia duplex and never left her house.

Jess laughed. Her eyes fell on a small denim-clad doll's leg peeking out from under the bed. She lifted the dust ruffle. "Here's Miss Becky! She was under your bed, you silly." Susie grabbed the doll and bolted from the room, raced halfway down the stairs, and stopped.

"Blessed St. Jude, we thank you for favors received," she muttered quickly and made the sign of the cross. Then she ran down the rest of the stairs and threw herself onto the sofa. She arranged the sofa pillows carefully around the doll, making sure Miss Becky was comfortable, and settled back to watch her show. Jess followed, smiling at Susie's eagerness, and sat down next to the little girl.

"Aren't you getting too old for this show, Pickle?"

Miss Becky and Friends was the hottest children's show on public television. Miss Becky was a little girl who lived on a farm and had all kinds of educational adventures with her friends Henry the Horse, Matilda the Cow, and Chucky the Chicken. The characters were all puppets. Susie's doll was a stuffed toy, soft and cuddly and an exact replica of the Miss Becky puppet on TV. Miss Becky had beige plush skin, brown eyes, and curly raven-black hair. She wore overalls and a red-and-white checked shirt, and a straw hat tied down with a red bandanna. It was Susie's favorite toy.

Susie clutched her doll tighter. "Am not too old, either, Jessie-ka. Miss Becky is my very favorite."

The show was over-sweet and over-cute, with jingly little songs that children sang endlessly after the show was over—the kind of show that made adults leave the room. But Jess actually enjoyed watching the show. A part of her longed to disappear into a magic world where everyone was happy and problems were solved in twenty-five minutes. She could lose herself in the show and in Susie's delight with it, and forget for a while.

As the opening scenes rolled across the TV screen, Susie's gray eyes were as wide as saucers. Jess stroked her long, straight golden-brown hair. Susie was not a pretty little girl—she was thin and gawky, with a narrow face and pale skin—but Jess suspected that Susie would be striking when she grew up. Not a beauty, but a real head-turner nonetheless. Right now, her intense rapture over *Miss Becky and Friends* was endearing.

Today's theme was baby animals—Miss Becky had found a baby bluebird that had fallen from its nest and wanted its mommy and daddy. Of course there was a little song to go with it:

> I want to go home
> To my nest in the tree
> Where it's dry, safe, and warm
> That's where I should be
> Oh, where is my mommy

And my daddy, too
Why did they leave me?
I feel so blue.

Jess thought of Ramon—his deep laugh, his warm
strong hands. Her throat tightened, and tears began spilling
over her cheeks. Susie noticed Jess's tears and cuddled
closer to her. She used the Miss Becky doll to wipe away
the wetness from Jess's face.

"Don't worry, Jessie. They'll come back."

Jess hugged the little girl tightly. *No, they won't. And
you'll find out too soon that they don't, Pickle.* A few more
tears, this time for Susie, rained down on the girl's head.

"The baby bird's parents will too come back," Susie
said in a reproving tone as she wiped the top of her head
with her hand. "I know that already. You're thinking about
Uncle Ramon and Mommy."

"You did it again, Pickle. Quit reading my mind."

"I can't help it if I know stuff," Susie said impatiently.

"It's going to get you in trouble someday. *I* know that
much," Jess replied, wiping her eyes on the back of her hand.

An odd expression came into Susie's eyes. "Know what
else? You're going to get in trouble with me. Big trouble."

"C'mon, let's watch the show. You're creeping me out
here," said Jess.

"Okay." Susie was instantly absorbed again.

Jess clicked up the volume on the TV with the remote.
Forget it, just forget it, she told herself.

The rain poured down in silvery sheets on the cobblestones
in Old City Philadelphia. There were no tourists wandering
around on this soggy late afternoon. No one gawking at the
brick-fronted, historically certified "trinity" homes on tiny
Ashland Street. Nobody trying to get a glimpse of what
was behind the curtained windows of the houses. From

these windows, yellow incandescent light filtered through, making watery, pale gold reflections in the gray puddles on the sidewalks. The few people that were out walking moved quickly, hunched under umbrellas.

On fine October evenings, Philadelphia's famous Society Hill would be alive with people. The brick-and-wood homes that lined the streets dated back two hundred years and more, and the simple clean lines of the Georgian Colonial style were pleasing to the eye. Tall trees lined the streets, blazing with the reds and oranges of fall color. There were almost-hidden little alleys where the original cobblestones and brick sidewalks still paved the street. There was a feeling of entering a time warp back to the Colonial city—which could be spoiled only if someone decided to park a car illegally on the narrow street.

There would be voices and laughter and, later, the raucous noises of late partiers stumbling home after an extended happy hour in one of the trendy bars by the Delaware River. For now, there was only the sound of driving rain and the splash of the cars rolling through the rush hour. Suddenly a stray cat yowled in the street. It carried over the splash and thrum of the rain, an eerie sound that made a man who lived in one of the homes on Ashland Street shudder.

Dr. Bennett Sykes was hunched naked in a chair in the corner of his bedroom. In front of him was a computer, the monitor casting its pale glow on his face. He was checking his e-mail. He had just come out of the shower, and his wavy dark-blond hair curled damply on the back of his neck. He had one new message.

He clicked it open and sat staring at the jumble of letters on the screen. After a minute or two, a smile touched his lips. He closed his eyes for a moment, as if in prayer. Then he deleted the message. He squared his shoulders, like a person beginning a large and complicated task.

He began to type out a reply.

* * *

Across the narrow street, a curtain in an upstairs window flicked almost imperceptibly. A thin woman stood next to the window in the darkened room. She lifted a pair of binoculars to her eyes. Each lens had been carefully hooded to insure that there would be no telltale glare. She focused on Bennett Sykes's bedroom. Bennett's sheer white curtains made it seem like she was peering through a mist, lending the scene a dreamlike quality. A sigh escaped her as her eyes took in the broad, bare shoulders, the strongly muscled back, and the slender, nimble fingers dancing over the keyboard. She took no notice of what he was typing. She took one hand off the binoculars and slid it slowly down her body, over her small breasts and flat stomach, and let it come to rest between her thighs.

Bennett finished his e-mail and sent it. He linked his fingers and stretched out luxuriously in his chair, like a cat. Then he rose and began to dress for work.

The woman across the street moaned.

It had been a long, lousy day. More like a Monday than a Friday. First, the kids woke up cranky and miserable.

"*Mom!* Where's my Taz shirt? I gotta wear it today!"

"*Mom,* I *hate* Frosted Bran Flakes! Can't we have waffles?"

"He hit me!"

"She started it!"

"You are such a moron, you jerk!"

"Blow it out your ear, butt-head."

"*Mom!* Sam called me a butt-head!"

Kasidy herself couldn't find a pair of panty hose without a run. She decided to wear a pantsuit, but the jacket had a grease spot on the sleeve. Finally Kasidy got them and herself fed, dressed, and into the minivan. And she was only ten minutes late. During the drive to school in the pouring rain and the snarled-up Center City traffic, Sam and Karen kept up a constant barrage of whining, sniveling, and complaining.

I'm going to go freakin' postal, she thought. She turned the radio up in a futile effort to drown them out. Even the anesthetic melodies of the "smooth jazz" station couldn't cut it.

When she pulled up sharply in front of Friends' Middle School with a squeal of brakes, she yanked on the parking brake, turned to them, and glared at each one in turn. Finally, they were silent.

"You two have used up your daily allowance of tattling and whining, and it's not even eight A.M. yet. I don't want to hear any more of this crap when I come to pick you up. Got it?" Kass spoke through gritted teeth.

Sam and Karen sighed. "Okay, Mom."

"And I don't want to hear any tomorrow or Sunday, either. Understood?"

"But, Mom, aren't we going to see Dad this weekend?" Sam asked anxiously.

Now it was Kasidy's turn to sigh. "Honey, I don't know. He hasn't called."

Sam stared at Kass for a long moment. Then he snorted. "Geez. What a jerk. Well, bye, Mom." He leaned over the seat and kissed her. Then he got out and slammed the door, just a tad too hard.

"Hey, Karen, this is your stop, too." Kass looked at her sullen daughter.

Karen was silent. Then she reached for the door handle.

"You know what? Divorce sucks. Bye, Mom." Karen also slammed the door hard.

Kass pressed her lips together and drove on to work.

* * *

Kasidy Rhodes was a newly divorced, single mother struggling with a career and two preteen children. Her husband, Herb, had left her abruptly six months ago, after eleven years of marriage, and entered a midlife affair with one of the paralegals at the law firm where he was a partner. He had been so anxious to get out of the marriage that he let Kass keep the town house on Spruce Street and almost all its contents. He'd taken only his personal belongings. He'd also ripped the very heart out of Kass's world and taken that, too.

Kass looked in the rearview mirror at the traffic behind her. *Sam, I think your father is a jerk, too, but I'll never tell you that,* she thought. Herb was the only man Kass had ever really known, biblically and otherwise. He had lived up the street from her in Drexel Hill, and they had begun to date when Kass was fifteen. Herb was six years older than Kass, and seemed so mature and sophisticated to her.

Herb had been a junior at Temple University, and Kass had been a senior in high school when they discovered she was pregnant with Karen. Kass had married Herb one week after graduation and had gone to work for an advertising agency, first as a secretary and then as a junior copywriter. They lived on her salary and loans from their in-laws until Herb graduated from Temple Law School. He was hired by Edwards, Elliot and Rubin in Philadelphia. By that time Sam had made his appearance. Herb quickly made partner, and Kass gratefully retired to become a stay-home mom. To all appearances, they were an upscale yuppie family—successful, upwardly mobile, with active happy kids—until Louisa came along.

She had met Louisa only once, at last year's Christmas party, before the affair had begun in earnest. Louisa was a skinny girl with mousy brown hair, glasses, and protruding front teeth. But she had a pair of the biggest, perkiest breasts Kasidy had ever seen. She remembered how Herb had hovered protectively around Louisa at the party, stealing glances down the V-neck of Louisa's tight, metallic gold sweater.

She glanced down at her own body. Kass was round all over—small round breasts, round belly, round thighs. Years of working out at the Y had taught her, finally at the age of twenty-eight, that she would never be tiny-waisted and flat-bellied like some of the other spandex-clad women there. She made up for it by dressing in tailored clothing that made the most of what she did have.

What really set Kass apart was above her neck. She had thick, glossy chestnut hair, which she wore in a smooth shoulder-length cut that flattered her face. She had round amber eyes and a full mouth that curved into a lovely smile when she was happy. But these past few months the smiles had been few and far between.

Her former employer, Holmes Fein & Company, hired her back as a copywriter after Herb left and she realized that his support checks were not going to cover all her expenses. As much as she disliked the daily hassle of getting to and from work, the work itself was much better than staying home, crying over the soaps, and brooding about Herb's desertion.

She parked her car in the garage across the street and ran into the building. No time to grab a cup of coffee from her favorite vendor on the corner. She pushed her way onto an already crowded elevator, ignoring the frowns and cold stares from the other passengers. She got off at her floor and hurried through the plush, opulently furnished lobby with the big brass letters on the wall proclaiming HOLMES FEIN & CO. Finally she made it to her little desk in the back of the offices.

The copy for Chez Chiennes Noir, a trendy and expensive restaurant, lay on her desk with a yellow Post-it note stuck in the middle of the page. Mitchell had written in sprawling red letters, "Hate it. Try again." Kass had worked on it for hours, slaving over each word. Just then, Mitchell walked by.

"Late again, Kass?"

"Sorry, Mitchell." Mitchell was tall, dark, and gaunt. He was impeccably dressed in an Armani suit. Everything was perfectly pressed, and his shoes had nary a scuff. He looked like he just stepped out of a glossy magazine ad. His black eyes fixed contemptuously on the grease stain on her jacket. Kass reddened with embarrassment. Mitchell always made her feel like she was an unmade bed.

"You saw my note? I want new copy by ten o'clock this morning. Dieter and Raoul are coming by for a lunch presentation at noon and I want to show them a killer ad for *Philadelphia Magazine.*" Dieter and Raoul were the owners of Chez Chiennes Noir. Kass suspected Mitchell had his eyes on Dieter. Mitchell's eyes flicked over Kass. "Do a good job on the copy and clean up your jacket, and maybe I'll have you join us."

"I'll do my best, Mitchell," Kass replied. She wanted to scream.

"Good girl," he said, and continued on down the hall. His over-spiced cologne hung in the air behind him.

Kass's phone rang. Gritting her teeth, she picked up the receiver.

"Kasidy Rhodes."

"Kass, it's Herb."

"Hello, Herb," she replied coolly. "Are you picking up the kids today or not?"

"That's what I wanted to talk to you about. Lou and I have decided to get married in the Virgin Islands. Lou wants to have Sam and Karen come with us. Isn't that great?"

Kass was speechless for a moment.

"You there, Kass? Damn these cell phones . . ."

"I'm still here, Herb. How nice for you," Kass said. She hoped she sounded as icy-cold as she felt.

"We leave next Friday. The kids will be out of school for a couple of days, and then I'll send them home, okay? So that means I'll have them for two weekends in a row, this weekend and the next weekend. I went ahead and got the plane tickets for the four of us."

The bastard didn't even ask me if it was okay, Kass thought. She closed her eyes as it abruptly sunk in that the "four of us" no longer included her.

"Who's paying room and board for this . . . excursion?"

"I am. Jeez, Kass, all you do is think about money." Herb sounded injured, as if he couldn't believe his ex-wife was such a money-grubber.

"It's okay with me, Herb." *Like I had a choice, you ass-hole.* "I assume you want me to call the school and let them know."

"That'd be great, Kass. Don't tell the kids, though. Lou and I want to surprise them. Hey, aren't you going to congratulate me?"

"I'll see you tonight, Herb. Gotta go." Click.

Married. Herb was actually going to marry his little Barbie doll. The realization slammed into her like a punch in the solar plexus. She ran to the ladies' room before Mitchell could see her cry.

Mitchell had read over the copy Kass put on his desk promptly at ten.

"Now that's much better," he said. " 'The tranquil atmosphere of the streamlined, pastel-shaded Art Deco décor'— Dieter will love it. You'll have to join us for lunch."

Kass could not believe that he liked the copy she threw together in twenty overwrought minutes better than the copy she spent a full day on yesterday, but Mitchell was the boss.

Lunch was not a pleasant experience. They went to Le Jardin, an alfresco restaurant near Rittenhouse Square. Since it was pouring rain, the sidewalk tables had been crammed into the tiny, steamy dining room, and it was so crowded and noisy Kass couldn't hear herself think.

Mitchell and Dieter were immediately engrossed in conversation, leaving Kass to talk to Raoul. The only thing Raoul was eloquent about was food, and he tasted every dish that was served to them, reaching rudely across to take forkfuls from other people's plates. Then he would describe in excruciating detail how he could make it better, bringing his face so close to Kass's as he spoke that she could see the remains of what he'd just tasted in his moustache.

Kass was bored to tears. She was no gourmet, and she thought any meal that she didn't have to cook or clean up after was just fine. Raoul's monologues were nearly as intolerable as his breath, so she drank a bit too much wine in an effort to endure him without screaming. By the time they returned to the office, Kass had a raging headache. She spent the rest of the afternoon in Mitchell's office, strategizing the ad campaign for Chez Chiennes Noir. Mitchell's potent cologne didn't help her headache at all.

The day's hard rain had made the city streets into dirty brown rivers, and when she left the office at five, traffic was worse than usual. A fifteen-minute drive took forty-five, and when she got home Herb had picked the kids up from their after-school program and brought them back to the house to pack for the weekend.

The big town house, built in the 1820s, had been Herb's pride and joy. Marble steps, worn down in the middle by over a century of feet entering and leaving, ran up from the sidewalk to the redbrick three-story home. Grecian marble pillars, gray with age, framed the tall wooden door with the important-looking brass door knocker in the form of a lion's head. There was a tiny courtyard to one side of the steps, enclosed by an elegant wrought-iron fence.

The house looked warm and welcoming, with white shutters and doors and the multipaned Colonial windows. As Kass drove by, in search of a parking spot, she was overcome by self-pity. *Herb just walked away from his precious*

house—and me—as if we were a couple of used Kleenexes.
She parked on the street and came in through the front door,
shaking off her umbrella. As she came in, she could hear excited shouts and laughter.

Herb was sitting on the chintz-covered sofa. From the
flushed and sparkling expressions on the kids' faces, she
guessed Herb had told them about his wonderful wedding
plans.

"Mom! Mom! Guess what! Dad's taking us to the Virgin Islands next weekend!" cried Karen excitedly.

"Yeah, and we get to miss two days of school!" Sam said.

"I've never been to a wedding before! This is going to
be *so* cool!" Karen was dancing around the living room
like a prima ballerina. Herb sat back on the sofa with a
self-satisfied grin.

Kass's head throbbed painfully. The day's anger and
frustrations burst inside her like a warhead, blasting away
her last shreds of self-control. She glared at her children
and her ex-husband, her face flushed with rage.

"Hey! What happened to 'Hi, Mom. How was your
day?'" she snapped.

The kids stopped and just stared at her. For a moment,
Kass felt like the Grinch who stole Christmas, but then the
anger swept in again. The last time she'd seen the kids so
happy was before Herb left. Nothing she had done with
them since had produced this kind of delighted reaction.
Now Herb was going to marry his bimbo, and the kids
were in ecstasy. *Go to hell, all of you,* she thought.

Herb looked at her. "Aw, Kass, lighten up. They'll have
a great time. Lou is really looking forward to having them
there. We'll take good care of them."

"Oh, they'll have a *wonderful* time. You'll play with
them and buy them whatever they want—all the things you
never did while we were married—and then it's back to reality and boring old Mom who's tired all the time from
busting her ass to keep them fed and clothed. Well, fine.

Go!" Kass ran to her room, sobbing, and slammed the door. After a few minutes of hushed conversation, the kids left with Herb and didn't even try to say good-bye.

Later, when she had cried herself out and her headache was gone, Kass was mortified at her outburst. She thought about calling the kids over at Herb's, but she was sure Herb had told Louisa all about his bitch ex-wife's temper tantrum. *I simply can't face speaking to that woman right now,* she thought. *Not even for Karen and Sam.*

She microwaved a diet dinner and ate it without tasting it. She took off her work clothes and threw them into a pile on the floor of her room. She put on her sweats, which made her look twenty pounds heavier. *It's not like there's anyone around to see me, or to care what I look like,* she thought.

The person she wanted most to talk to would only see her words on a computer screen.

Kass went into the tiny den that used to be a pantry and turned on the computer. It beeped and blinked and hummed as it went through its start-up routine. Herb had gotten it as a Christmas present for himself, about two months before he moved out. Kass had been uninterested in it, but the kids liked it and used it.

It was Karen who had introduced Kass to the wonders of cyberspace. Kass had come in one evening, after listening to Karen click away for about two hours.

"What are you doing there, sweetie?" she had asked.

Karen jumped, a little guiltily. "Um, this is a chat room, Mom. I'm talking to my friends."

Kass had read all the bad press about chat rooms. How dangerous they were, and how nobody but sex-crazed perverts hung out in them. Her first instinct was to scold Karen and turn off the computer. But she looked at the screen and saw at least ten different names. There were all sorts of odd abbreviations Kass didn't understand, but as she read what people were typing, she realized it was a fairly innocuous conversation. Typical ten-year-old-girl stuff. One person named "Cybergrrrl" was fervently singing the praises of Justin Timberlake.

Kass was drawn to it in spite of herself. Karen fidgeted as her mother stared at the screen.

"Mom, it's a monitored chat room. For kids. I know all the rules about not giving your real name and personal information and stuff. Please don't make me turn it off. *Please?*"

Kass looked at the screen and at her daughter's face. "Show me how this works," said, surprising herself with her sudden interest.

As Kass explored the Internet, she found a chat support group for divorced parents. People aired their gripes, heartbreaks, and rage over their ex-spouses, their kids, and life in general. Kass became a regular in the group and found chatting online with like-minded people a cheap and easy kind of therapy. It helped her to adjust to a life she hadn't chosen.

She needed badly to chat tonight. When the computer finished its beeping and blinking routine, she logged on.

"You've got mail," said the cheerful electronic voice. Kass clicked the mouse to open the note.

> **TO:** mamakass
> **FROM:** DR.B
> **RE:** where have you been?
>
> Hey {{{{{{{{{mamakass}}}}}}}}}}I missed you this week. I'll be online Friday until about 8 or so. Look for you then.

Kass had to smile at all the hug symbols B had put around her screen name. With a few more mouse clicks, Kass quickly found her chat room.

"Please be there, B," she whispered. "God, do I need to talk to you." The chat room was nearly full to capacity, which surprised her. "But then, what else do lonely people do on rainy Friday nights? Jeez, it would be nice if somebody went out once in a while so they could tell the rest of us if there's still life out there," she muttered as she checked the list of people in the room. She sighed with relief when she saw the name she was looking for.

Hi all, she typed. *Hey there B.*

DR.B responded *HEY THERE {{{{{MAMAKASS}}}}. How are you tonight?*

Lousy, Kass wrote. *Really lousy. Louisa lousy. LOL.*

DR.B used the "whisper" icon to respond to Kass so no one else could read what he wrote. *Tell me all about it. You must be really down.*

DR.B was Kass's favorite online friend. He had been married to a woman named Sylvia, who had left him for a ski bum fifteen years her junior that she met when they vacationed in Colorado last year. Syl and her gigolo were living on the hefty spousal support checks he had to send each month. He could be bitingly funny about Sylvia and Trent and the money, but he never whined about his ex-wife like some of the other men in the room did. Part of DR.B's charm was his humor and wit. And he always seemed genuinely concerned about her and her happiness. She often thought, *If only people were like this in "real life," the world would be a much better place. More good warm hugs to be had, too.*

Kass typed furiously, whispering back to Dr. B about her bad day, her jealousy of Herb and Louisa, how the kids she loved so much were so happy about their father's wedding that it just killed her . . .

When Kass had finished her long paragraph of griping and sent it, there was a long pause. No reply.

Still there, B? Sorry if I bored you, she typed.

ZZZZZZ, came the response.

LOL, she typed. She really did laugh out loud.

Where do you live, MamaKass?

Kass paused a moment. *Oh well, what could it hurt*, she thought.

Fifth and Spruce Streets in Philly, she typed back.

You're kidding!! I live on Ashland Street in Society Hill. Just a few blocks away!

Kass was astonished. This man, whom she'd confided in, developed a friendship with, and wished so hard was "real," lived within walking distance of her. The coincidence was mind-boggling. Her fingers flew over the keyboard as she replied.

WOW! Who would have guessed? I've been talking to you for all these months & I never knew you lived so close! Ashland Street—we're practically neighbors!

What would you think about meeting F2F? I've often wondered what you look like.

I don't look like much. 5 ft. tall, reddish hair, hazel eyes, 135 lbs.

Sounds good to me. I'm 6 ft. tall, brown eyes, blond hair, 170 lbs.

You sound yummy. Surprised no one's snapped you up yet.

Well, the wrong one did.

LOL, B.

Haven't found the right girl yet. Working nights doesn't help.

A voice inside Kass's head said he probably was really short, fat, and bald. But if that were true, then why would he want to meet face to face? And he had been thinking about her. Wondering about her. Nobody thought about her anymore. In her loneliness, Kass forgot all about the rules she so strictly enforced on Karen.

After a minute or two, *So what do you think?* flashed onto Kass's screen.

Kass took a breath. *OK*, she typed. *When and where?*

Dinner. Tomorrow. There's a new restaurant, Chez Chiennes Noir. I'm one of their regulars. Know where it is?

Yes.

OK. Seven o'clock. Meet me in the bar.

How will I know you?

You'll know me.

I can't believe I'm going on a date. But I feel like I've known you forever.

Me too. I can't wait. This is going to be fun.

OK. Seven at Chiennes Noir.

You got it. Gotta go get ready for work. See you tomorrow.

Wait! What's your name? In case I need to ask for you.

Bennett.

Kass stared at the screen for a long time after Bennett logged out.

I have a date. A real live dinner date with a man. A man I've never met, but who is one of my closest friends. Well, hot damn! She smiled for the first time that day.

She noticed that another of her cyber-friends was trying to get her attention.

WAKE UP MAMAKASS, Merry had typed.

Jeez, don't shout. Hurts my ears, replied Kass.

LOL Mama. You and Dr. B were whispering about something, weren't you? Are you OK?

Very OK. Merry—turns out he lives near me & he asked me for a date!!

Merry typed nothing for a minute or two. Kass checked the lag time.

You there, Merry?

Merry suddenly left the chat. *She must have moofed,* thought Kass. Kass logged off also.

As she got ready for bed, she decided to go to Strawbridges' tomorrow and buy a new dress. Maybe some new shoes and perfume, too. *I'm acting like a teenager,* she realized. *But it's been twelve years since I was on a real date.* She looked in the bathroom mirror and smiled at herself. Her eyes shone, and her cheeks glowed.

Part of her mind whispered that she could be making a big mistake, but she ignored it.

"Fuck you, Herb, and your bimbo bitch, too," she said to her reflection.

Her reflection laughed back at her.

On Ashland Street, a woman slammed her fist down on her computer keyboard. A few of the keys popped off and flew to the floor.

"Goddamn you, Bennett Sykes! If I can't have you I'll be damned if that little slut will!" Hysterical laughter filled the room as the woman yanked the keyboard from the computer and began smashing it against the desktop.

A young couple strolled down the historic street, under the shelter of a single umbrella. Even with the splash of the rain and the windows closed they could hear the unsettling sound of the high-pitched laughter and of splintering plastic being pounded mercilessly. They paused for a moment to listen.

"Wonder if it's domestic violence if you're beating up your appliances?" asked the young man in a feeble attempt to be witty.

"Maybe it should be. Weird, huh?" the girl replied. She shivered a little and clung tightly to her boyfriend's arm. "Let's get moving."

They began walking a little faster down to Pine Street, escaping from the noise.

When Susie's mother got home from work, Jess crossed the front porch and unlocked the front door of her own house. She turned on the lights, illuminating the shabby

furniture, the old console television, and the worn carpe
with its matted pile. The only pictures on the yellowed liv
ing room walls were two photographs—Jess's First Com
munion portrait and her high school graduation portrait
There was a whiter rectangle on the wall where anothe
picture had hung until recently.

Everything in the house was almost as it was before he
father died. Jess looked around the depressing little room
and sighed deeply. She missed him so much.

Jess's mother had disappeared when she was a year old
Her father, Ramon, tended to his single-parent duties with
a fierce devotion. He adored his daughter, and she took
great pleasure in living up to his every expectation. She
made straight A's in school, became the star of the swim
team, and was a soloist in the school choir.

Ramon Grasia was a stocky, homely man who had emi
grated to Philadelphia from Puerto Rico when he was
teenager. He worked as a bus driver for SEPTA, getting b
on his salary, but he wanted more for Jess. He gave up smok
ing when Jess was five, and used the money he no longe
spent on cartons of cigarettes to buy lottery tickets. H
would pull her close to him and let her hold the tickets
"Querida, when we win, I will take you all over the world.
He would have her get out her geography book, and the
would plot a trip around the world. They spent hours dis
cussing each country they would visit—the languages, cus
toms, terrain, cuisine—enjoying the fun of learning togethe

Or he would say, "I will build you a beautiful house,
and Jess would run for her colored pencils and paper. The
would sit at the kitchen table, drawing pictures of homes
Ramon clutched stubs of pencil in his big fist, scribblin
away as enthusiastically as his little girl, making grand a
chitectural creations that would have been impossible i
real life. Years went by and Ramon never won the jackpo
but he and Jess didn't mind. It was so much fun just t
dream together.

When she entered high school, he would tell her, "When we win, you will go to college." That would spark a discussion of which college Jess would attend and what she would major in. Jess brought home college catalogues from school, and they would pore over the glossy pages. Ramon compiled lists of the best-paying jobs for college graduates. Jess hoped for a scholarship, so Ramon encouraged her in her athletics and music, losing a lot of overtime in order to attend Jessica's concerts and swim meets, but it didn't matter. He had to be there for her.

But in the end, there was no scholarship. There was only enough money for Jess to go to vocational school. She became a medical technician and went to work in the pathology department of Hahnemann Hospital in Philadelphia.

And then it happened. That summer, Ramon's lottery numbers finally came up. He was the sole winner of a two-million-dollar lump-sum jackpot. He and Jess had their pictures in the paper. Susie's mother tipped one of the local TV stations off to her neighbors' lifelong dream-come-true tale, and they sent a reporter and cameraman to cover their trip to Harrisburg to collect the lottery check. Ramon looked into the camera and grinned, his strong arm around his fair-haired daughter's shoulders—a bit of a reach for him. "Harvard Medical School is very expensive," he gravely informed the invisible audience. "When my daughter goes there, she will need this money." The reporter and lottery officials laughed.

"Man, those two look so different," muttered the cameraman, focusing on Jess's shy, lovely face. "Day and night. Definitely her mother's daughter."

Ramon invested his winnings carefully and continued working for SEPTA. Jess spent her afternoons filling out college applications. A month after the trip to Harrisburg, a man boarded Ramon's bus. The skinny man's brow was beaded with clammy sweat. His ragged clothes were filthy, and his hair was matted. The pungent aroma of unwashed skin preceded him aboard the bus. He was shaking like a leaf in the July heat.

His eyes rolled crazily as he stared at Ramon. "Hey, man! I saw you on TV! You're the fucker won the lottery! Well, you can pay my fucking fare!" He began staggering past Ramon toward a seat. Ramon shot out a burly arm and grabbed the man's grimy shirt.

"That'll be a buck twenty-five. Or you can get the hell off my bus."

The man wheeled around. He reached into the pocket of his baggy jeans, but instead of bus fare, he pulled out a pistol and fired several shots into Ramon's face. Blood and brains splattered all over the windshield. People began screaming. The skinny man was hit in the face with a pulsing spray of blood from Ramon's severed carotid artery. He was blinded just long enough for a heavyset woman, a nurse at Einstein Hospital, to level him with a flying tackle. The gun flew from his hand and was picked up by another passenger, a student at Central High School. The boy was green-faced and trembling, but he carefully held the gun by the barrel so as not to smear fingerprints on the gun's handle.

The other passengers fled the bus and the stench of blood, and milled around outside the bus shouting at each other in fear and excitement as the police arrived. Several passengers vomited on the sidewalk. The nurse sat placidly on the skinny crackhead until the police waded up the bus steps through a shiny red-and-black river of gore.

An hour later Jess stared up at an image of her father as he lay in a drawer in the morgue at Einstein. The closed-circuit camera focused sharply on Ramon's features, in a gruesome close-up. Half his face was smooth and perfect, as though he were sleeping. The other half was a mess of clotted blood and tissue, and there was a huge hole in the side of his neck.

"This man is your father?"

She turned to the pathologist, who was awaiting her positive identification.

"I'm a tech in the path department at Hahnemann, and I want to see my father myself," she said in a tightly controlled voice. "Not on some monitor. With my own eyes." Her blue eyes narrowed.

"Only hospital personnel are allowed in the morgue area," he said.

"I'm hospital personnel, and I want to see my father." Jess's voice rose. She got up from her chair and ran through the door into the cold room. An orderly was waiting to close the drawer and turn off the camera. He looked up in surprise as Jess burst in. The pathologist followed her, signaling to the orderly to relax.

Jess bent down over her father's body. Her long hair fell into the jellied dark mass that used to be his head. She smoothed her fingers over a lock of blood-encrusted hair that was sticking to his forehead.

"Oh, Daddy," she whispered.

The pathologist put his hand on Jess's shoulder.

"It is your father, then?"

She nodded.

He moved his hand down to her arm. "Come on, then. You're really not supposed to be here. Let's finish filling out the papers, okay?" He used his best soothing voice.

"*No!*" Jess screamed. "No! I'm not leaving him alone in here. Let go of me!" She threw her arms around her father's corpse, pressing her cheek against the unmarked side of his face. "Daddy! Daddy! *No!*" Her voice rose high and piercing, like an animal's howl.

Then her knees gave way under her, and the pathologist helped her up. He put his arms around her shaking body and half-led, half-dragged her from the morgue, wincing at her shrieks of agony.

The orderly turned off the camera and slid the drawer closed.

* * *

Jess was devastated. Her father, who had been everything to her, was suddenly gone. She sat through Ramon's funeral Mass at St. Laurence's, pale and stony-faced, as clouds of incense billowed around her and the priest intoned the ancient words of comfort and promise in his soothing baritone. Susie sat with her mother, Heather, in the front pew with Jess, but seemed strangely afraid of this stiff and silent version of her baby-sitter and neighbor.

"Why can't you hug Jessie?" Heather hissed as Susie cringed back.

Susie, five at the time, had whispered "Jessie-ka is sharp and prickly right now."

"Oh, she is not," her mother replied impatiently, but she knew better than to force the child. Susie had odd ways of expressing herself.

After the funeral, Jess came home and took the picture of Christ off the wall in the living room. She threw it to the floor and stomped on it again and again, listening to the crunch of breaking glass and splintering wood, hearing the paper picture in the frame tear with a rasping sound, grinding the remains into the carpet with her heels. Then she stopped. She stood stiffly and held her breath for a long moment, waiting.

She exhaled noisily. "There, I knew you didn't exist. It's a lie, it's all a big fat lie, and my daddy is dead." She picked up the spoiled picture and clutched it to her, ignoring the glass shards cutting into her hands and the rivulets of blood flowing down her arms.

Jess sat down heavily on the floor and rocked back and forth, like a frightened child, for the rest of the night. Afterward, she refused to attend church. She continued working at Hahnemann. She stayed in the home she had lived in all her life, not changing a single thing in it. She continued to care for Susie after school. And she never thought about the future. Dreaming about the future made no sense to her when she had no one to share the dreams with.

The lottery jackpot remained invested in the securities Ramon had chosen. Jess lived on her modest income and Ramon's pension from SEPTA.

Jess had only three people that she was willing to reach out to. Two of them were her neighbors. Heather was an unwed single mother and Jess's self-appointed guardian, and Susie was like the little sister Jess never had. The third person who kept Jess going was her boss, Dr. Bennett Sykes. He was head of the forensic pathology department at Hahnemann, one of the best forensic pathologists in the city, and Jess was his medical technician.

Jess looked down at the carpet that had been in the house as long as she could remember. She absently rubbed the toe of her sneaker over an ancient cigarette burn.

"Time to go to Forensics Land," she said aloud. Her voice sounded small in the empty house. Loneliness bit into her, and she sighed again.

She went up the stairs and got dressed for work.

Hahnemann Hospital was built at the corner of Broad and Vine in Philadelphia in the mid-1920s. The original building's Art Deco façade had darkened with city grime since then, and the surrounding neighborhood, once grand and residential, had commercialized and then deteriorated. A mid-city expressway had been built along Vine Street, and the roar of traffic was constant. In spite of its forbidding appearance, it was a premier teaching hospital, with an international reputation.

In the 1980s a new building was added behind the hospital to increase classroom space and research facilities. The clean modern lines of the new building were in direct contrast to the blackish-brown stone of the building that faced Broad Street. During the day the buildings swarmed with people dressed in smocks, lab coats, and scrubs. But in the evenings, the complex was nearly deserted.

The Broad Street Subway trains rumbled beneath the noisy streets, screeching to a stop under the corner of Broad and Vine. On this rainy evening, a slender blonde woman ran lightly up the reeking steps that led from the subway station to the street. Even the cold, drenching rain could not wash away the stench of urine that had penetrated the concrete after years of drunks and homeless people using it for a public toilet.

Jess wrinkled her nose and put up her umbrella.

"You think you'd be used to it after all these years," she muttered to herself. She rode the Frankford El and the Broad Street Subway to work every day from Upper Darby, through some of the ugliest neighborhoods of Philadelphia. Somehow she could never manage to ignore the filthy smells and the dirty homeless people, who were a constant presence in the dim warrens of the subways. She walked quickly past the front of the hospital and turned down the narrow alley that ran alongside Hahnemann, past the emergency room entrance to a service entrance a few feet farther down. She shook out her umbrella and slipped through the automatic doors. Halfway down the slick, polished linoleum hallway was the elevator. She rode the elevator down to the basement.

As the doors opened, another kind of stench assailed her nostrils.

"Oh, jeez, we've got a floater," she muttered to herself. She found her locker and put her umbrella, raincoat, and dinner away. Then she hurried down to the morgue.

"Hi there, Jess. Hope your stomach is strong tonight." A tall, moustached man with longish blond hair looked up from the clipboard he was holding and smiled at her. The pungent stench of rot was almost palpable.

Ugh, she thought. *I'll have to take a long shower when I get home tonight to get this smell out of my hair and off my skin. Yuck.*

"Hello, Dr. Sykes." She smiled, even as her stomach quivered. "I guess I won't feel much like eating tonight. What do we have?" She walked over and stood next to him, peering at the notes on his clipboard.

"We have a white male, thirty-four years old. They pulled him from the river down by South Street. He's been in the river for a while. There seems to be a bullet wound in the head."

"Any ID?"

"Yeah, he had his wallet in his back pocket. His name is Frank Stewart. The cops tell me he used to be one of them until he was fired last year for conduct unbecoming."

"What did he do?"

"Allegedly, he had a drug habit. Taking bribes from the dealers in exchange for looking the other way, and he was taking crack out of the evidence lockers."

Jess nodded. "I think I read about him in the paper. I thought they arrested him."

"He was out on bail. The cops who brought him in said he was due to go on trial next week."

"So we'll have to do toxicology tests."

"Yepper." He looked at her and smiled. "Just another fun day in Forensics Land. They're still getting the autopsy room set up, and I'm waiting for Radiology to send down the X rays. Dr. Gordon and Dr. Carlsen will be joining us." Doctors Gordon and Carlsen were two of the residents.

"So, Miss Grasia, if you want some coffee, I'm buying."

They walked down the hall and entered Dr. Sykes's cramped but impeccably tidy little office. Bennett whistled tunelessly as he poured the coffee.

"You sure are in a good mood tonight, Doctor."

Bennett Sykes laughed. "Well, I'll have three lovely ladies working with me tonight. And I know at least one who won't get sick on me." He handed Jess a heavy white mug, fragrant steam rising from the top. "I had some good news before I came in tonight, too. The Epicurean Society is having their annual meeting, and I'm in charge of the dinner menu. So I'll be planning the entire meal, soup to nuts."

"Ugh, how can you think about food now?" Jess groaned. She put her nose down close to her coffee, letting her lungs fill with the steam, trying to crowd out the stench from the floater. Dr. Sykes could not abide the coffee Hahnemann provided—which tasted, he insisted, like dirty sneakers boiled in Schuylkill River water—so he kept his own private, expensive Braun coffeemaker in his office, along with a selection of gourmet coffees.

Bennett Sykes had worked hard to turn Jess into a coffee connoisseur. She took a sip and looked up at him. "Mocha Java, right?"

He grinned. "Very good, Jess, very good." His brown eyes twinkled at her. She returned the grin, her spirits lifting as she looked at him leaning back in his chair behind his desk.

Dr. Sykes was a comfortable, steady presence in her life. He seemed truly concerned for her feelings and well-being, and was never too busy to make her coffee, or make her laugh. He didn't patronize her in spite of her youth, treating her as an intellectual equal in a place where medical technicians were among the lowest of the low. His kindness to her in her lonely grief inspired affectionate respect—an emotion she had once given to her father.

His handsome, almost rock-star looks appealed to her as well. Where her father was dark and stocky, Dr. Sykes was tall and slim, with longish dark-blond hair and a neatly trimmed moustache. Half the women in the hospital had a crush on him, which was a source of amusement for her—and occasionally an irritation. There were some who manipulated her friendship in order to get closer to her boss.

She noticed a card propped up on his desk. It had a black-and-white photo of a buxom, sexily disheveled woman on the front, apparently just rescued from being tied to the train tracks or being ravished by a monster. Under it was the caption "How Can I Ever Repay You?" Jess was sure there was something suggestive inside.

"Who sent you the card? A little old lady you helped cross the street?" She giggled at her own joke.

Bennett smiled, a little ruefully. "No, it's from Meredith. I helped her out with some pathology stuff for one of her patients." He picked up the card and tossed it in the wastebasket.

"Oh." Jess shrugged. Dr. Meredith Shirk's obsession with Dr. Sykes was an open secret in the hospital.

"So, what's on the menu for your Epicurean thing, Chef Doctor?" asked Jess.

"Haven't decided yet." A strange quizzical expression came over his face as he looked at her. She noticed and fidgeted in her seat a little.

"What?" she asked.

"Nothing," he replied absently. Voices came from down the hall. "Ooooh, ick!" "God, what a stink!" Exaggerated retching noises. His expression changed again, much to Jess's relief.

"Guess our residents are here. Ready, Jess?"

"As I'll ever be," she replied with a grimace. She gulped down the rest of her coffee, scalding her throat a little, but she knew she'd need it.

They left the office together.

The basement of Hahnemann Hospital was a maze of ugly corridors, harshly lit by fluorescent ceiling fixtures. The walls were lined with lockers. Pipes were visible along the upper walls and ceilings. The brown-and-green linoleum was scuffed and worn. It was easy to get lost there—and easy to believe that there was no way out of such a creepy and depressing place.

The autopsy rooms were located near the morgue. Each one had a table and bright overhead lights, similar to an operating room, but none of the life-support equipment normally found in an OR.

It was not necessary.

When Dr. Sykes and his assistants entered Autopsy Room Three, gasping a little at the stench, the body of Frank Stewart was lying on the table, covered with green drapery. The cloth was already stained with the river water soaking out through the waterlogged skin. A technician from Radiology was clipping the head X rays to the light boxes along one wall. He was young, and his face was ashen. He was obviously struggling to keep the contents of his stomach where they belonged.

"Will that be all, Dr. Sykes?" he asked. His teeth were clenched.

Bennett Sykes laughed as he walked over to the films and looked them over. "Looks good to me. Go get some fresh air, okay?"

"Yes, sir." The young tech almost ran from the room.

Bennett, Jess, and the two residents were gowned like surgeons. This was more for their protection than the victim's. They wore no masks, and the gloves they pulled on were heavy rubber ones, not the light latex gloves used in surgery.

Jess wheeled a cart laden with instruments over to the table. She picked up a metal basket of Vacu-Tainers and pulled the drapery down from the corpse's face and arms. She needed to get blood samples for the tests.

Frank Stewart was swollen to almost twice his normal size with water, putrefaction, and gas. His flesh was sickly white and spongy because of its long immersion in the Schuylkill. She fitted a needle onto one of the Vacu-Tainers and began probing for a vein in the corpse's left arm.

"We'll open the belly first, take a look at the CVS and respiratory systems," Bennett said to the residents. "You can see over there in the X rays that there's definitely a bullet in the brain—see, in the left frontal lobe—but we need to determine if the bullet wound was the cause of death, or if the poor bastard drowned."

He picked up a scalpel and began to make the cuts. Soon Frank Stewart had a Y etched onto his torso, from the shoulders and traveling down over his belly. Black blood mixed with clear, yellow fluid and oozed down over his distended rib cage. As Bennett began to cut deeply through the muscle tissue, opening the perineal cavity, Jess took a deep breath. She knew what was coming.

With a rush like a loud sigh, the gases that had accumulated inside Frank Stewart as he rotted under the surface of the Schuylkill escaped into the autopsy room. They all jumped back from the table as the horrible stench intensified a thousand times over. Dr. Carlsen put her hands to her face, covering her nose and mouth. Cold sweat broke out on her forehead.

"Excuse me, Doctor," she said in a strangled voice and bolted from the room. Jess's strong stomach held fast, but even she felt the Mocha Java she'd drunk churn a little. Dr. Gordon stood her ground, a little pale but otherwise all right.

"Glad I skipped lunch," she said, with a weak laugh. She straightened up, ready with the retractors.

Only Bennett seemed unaffected by the ungodly stink. "Jess, you ready?" he asked.

Jess picked up a clipboard and a pen. "Ready, Doctor."

Bennett cut through the sternum as Dr. Gordon placed the retractors to hold back the muscle tissue. He inserted a rib spreader and plunged his hands into Frank Stewart's chest.

Bennett began cutting the heart free from the chest and dictated the notes to Jess as he worked. "Pericardial sac normal, no effusions or adhesions. Heart appears slightly enlarged." He scooped it from the chest and dropped it on the scale with a wet thud. Jess dutifully recorded the weight.

"Note that the lungs are free of water. Subject was dead before he was dumped in the river. Esophagus and bronchial tubes somewhat inflamed, a possible effect of heavy crack smoking. It does do that to you, Jess, so let this be a lesson." He grinned at her, and she smiled back as much as her quivering stomach would allow. He continued, "Lungs have a nodular appearance with some areas of discoloration." His hands worked quickly, scalpel flashing and cutting deep in the corpse's belly, removing the liver and putting it on a scale, running lengths of intestines through his gloved fingers.

"Okay. Liver 1.2 kilograms, smooth external appearance, cut surfaces appear normal. Stomach and intestines show no signs of gastritis, ulceration, or diverticulitis. Stomach empty, no food content." In between her note taking, Jess helped Dr. Gordon take tissue samples for examination.

Dr. Carlsen had returned, pale and shaky, but bravely began cutting the scalp and peeling the skin away from the skull.

"Powder burns and scorched hair visible on the forehead," Dr. Carlsen said. She began measuring Frank Stewart's face, to record exactly where the entry wound was. Jess picked up the autopsy-room camera and photographed the wound from several angles. When Jess was finished, Dr. Carlsen resumed cutting. She peeled the skin back, and Frank Stewart's face folded neatly down around his neck. A bullet hole, round and smooth, was drilled in his skull.

They opened the skull, removed the brain, and weighed it. They retrieved the bullet, a .22 caliber. "Not too much hemorrhage or tissue destruction," Bennett commented. "If it had been a nine millimeter slug, his brain would have been liquefied. I hear organized crime favors the small-caliber bullets. Neater that way. Mr. Stewart here must have had some interesting friends."

As she worked, Jess wondered what Frank Stewart's life had been like before he was enslaved by his addiction.

He had been a police officer, sworn to uphold the law. He must have had a family, who had once been proud of him. Now he was a rotting corpse, just another victim. Like her father. She gritted her teeth and struggled to stay in control of her emotions. Finally the autopsy was completed.

"Okay, we're done here. Let's sew him up and get him back to the morgue," said Bennett. He looked closely at Jess, who looked drawn and pale. "Let's go get some fresh air. You can come back in a bit and help them finish."

They took the elevator up and stepped outside. It was still pouring rain, but the air smelled clean. Jess breathed deeply. Suddenly her eyes filled with scalding tears again. Bennett put his arm around her, and she leaned against him, sobbing.

"You're not sick, are you?" he asked.

"No," she choked out between sobs.

"Is it your father?"

She nodded, pressing her face into his shoulder. He laid his cheek gently against her silky hair, fragrant with the herbal shampoo she used. He loved her freshness—her fair hair, her perfect skin.

"Don't cry, Jess," he said, patting her back soothingly. In his own way, he was as attached to her as she was to him. Into these subterranean hallways full of the stench of death and formaldehyde, she had come, fair and light. She radiated promise. He had spent most of his life probing the mystery of death. Now, in this girl-woman, unfolding like a perfect rose, he saw the richness and power of life. He tightened his arm around her ever so slightly as she sobbed freely in the rain.

When he first met her, she had been fresh out of school, shy and quiet—and beautiful. He had seen the intelligence and curiosity in her eyes, and he alone had glimpsed her potential. After her father died, he worried that her grief would extinguish her zest for life—or, worse, propel her into a relationship with some young man who knew nothing worth knowing. He had made a conscious decision to become her mentor, to teach her about the secrets separating death from life. And soon, he knew, he would become much more than her mentor. He smiled into the darkness. Jess, her face hidden against his shoulder, did not see.

The need to spend more time with her at this critical juncture was one of the factors in his decision to work nights, an unusual move for a chief pathologist. Slowly and carefully, he had manipulated himself into her affection.

In a year or two she would be ready for her first Epicurean Society meeting, he decided. He had, earlier tonight, briefly considered another role for her in the Epicurean Society. She was the right age, for sure. All the necessary attributes. But she was too special. Selfishly, he wanted her for himself.

Death is an experience to savor, he thought. *You'll find out, my girl.*

"Don't cry, Jess," he repeated. "It's okay." He felt her hot tears soak through his lab coat onto his own skin. His smile widened in the darkness.

TWO

Dr. Bennett Sykes liked to think of himself as a man of many interests. He loved good food and fine wine, as well as cheesesteaks and beer. He enjoyed going to concerts by the Philadelphia Orchestra. He also loved professional hockey, and held season tickets to the Flyers games.

He collected books, most notably cookbooks and rare editions of the works of Edgar Allan Poe. Poe's fevered tales of premature burial fascinated him, as did death in all its manifestations.

When he was two years old, his parents had had a fight one evening after too many cocktails and too much wine with dinner. Bennett had cowered in the living room of their elegant high-rise apartment, with its view of the brightly lit city skyline, and wished he could escape into the television. At least the talking horse on the TV didn't scream at Wilbur.

"That's it, Mildred! I don't need to listen to this shit! I'm going for a drive," his father yelled. He had headed for the door, then stopped. He swept the pajama-clad little boy up from in front of the television.

"Hey, Ben, my little cowboy. Wanna go ridin' with Daddy?" Bennett looked into his father's flushed face. He could smell the wine and Scotch fumes on his father's breath. He nodded enthusiastically. Anything was better than sitting here trying not to listen to his parents' angry voices.

Ignoring Mildred's protests, he had taken Ben down the elevator to the garage and plopped him into his Alfa Romeo two-seater. Little Ben was excited at being allowed to join his father on this late-night ride. If he had been old enough to understand how drunk his father was, he would have been terrified.

Bennett's father turned onto the East River Drive, which wound along the banks of the Schuylkill River, past Boathouse Row and the entrance to Fairmount Park. Ben had chortled with glee as he watched the lights streak past his window. The engine roared as his father upshifted, and the little car leaned hard into the turn, tires squealing. He slid over the smooth leather seat. Daddy had forgotten to fasten his seat belt. Sliding was lots more fun than being strapped down.

"Having fun, cowboy?" Bennett's father had grinned crookedly at him.

"Whee, Daddy!" The little boy had grinned back at his father. This was lots better than watching *Mr. Ed.* It was good that Daddy was smiling instead of yelling at Mommy. Bennett was happy.

Then he glanced up through the windshield. "Daddy, look out!"

It was too late. The car smashed into a bridge abutment at a sickening rate of speed. Bennett's father was killed instantly, his body as twisted and mangled as the wreckage of the Alfa. Bennett was thrown twenty feet out of the car, landing in a tangle of shrubbery by the roadside.

Bennett's first conscious memory after the accident was of floating near the ceiling in a strange room, crowded with anxious doctors and nurses shouting commands at each other and handing shiny, cruel-looking things back and forth. Machines were hooked up to a little boy on a gurney. The machines hummed and ticked and hissed. Bennett realized that the little boy, covered with blood and dirt, his arm canted at a strange angle, tubes dangling from the tiny body, was himself. But he was unaffected by all the chaos below, feeling no pain. He felt detached from the world.

He looked up and saw a glowing white light at the end of what looked like a tunnel. Voices, beautiful, comforting voices, whispered to him. He thought he could hear his father's voice. Gentle hands lifted him up, up into the light. He heard faint music and felt a radiant warmth envelop him. An intense happiness filled and excited him. He knew he was on his way to a place where there were never any yelling parents or icky whisky smells. No hurts, and nothing to be scared of. It was home. He was going home.

He stretched his own broken, chubby little arms out to the light, trying to embrace it with all his strength.

"Look at that!" one of the nurses cried.

Suddenly Bennett was jerked from the warmth and light and sweet beauty back down into the crowded room, back down into his own tiny, crushed, pain-racked body. He tried to scream in a primeval rage, only to choke on the tube in his throat. He could hear his mother's high-pitched sobs, and the doctor was pulling up his eyelids and shining a harsh bright light into them. A nurse was tying down his arms and legs, from which hung several IV needles.

"My God," breathed one of the doctors. "The kid might make it after all."

Tears ran down Bennett's cheeks. *I want to go home,* he whimpered to himself.

Much later, after all he had to show for the experience were scars on his arms and chest and legs, which faded over time and became barely noticeable, he realized that he had had a near-death, or out-of-body experience. But the overwhelming sensation of perfect peace and beauty persisted in his memory. He decided to devote his life to the study of death, to discovering exactly what happened at the moment when life ceased and death began. To see if he could recapture, or at least understand, what he had known for only a second or two.

He decided to become a doctor and found himself attracted to pathology. Perhaps in autopsies he could discover the chemistry of life and death. Forensics seemed to offer the best opportunities for studying the countless ways life could be abruptly ended. He would be able to see what would kill one person, yet another one would be able to return to life much as he had. Life was so fragile, yet so tenacious.

His father had been a vice president of finance at First Pennsylvania Bank. Bennett had inherited a nice trust fund, which paid for his medical school tuition. While Bennett was in college, his mother died suddenly. She had been receiving treatment for heart trouble, but Bennett suspected an accidental overdose of alcohol and tranquilizers was the true cause of death. He felt no grief for her—she had always been remote and aloof from him, drifting in her own hazy, Valium-insulated cocoon. Upon her death, he had more than enough money to pursue his other consuming interest.

As a teenager, he discovered Edgar Allan Poe and thought he recognized a fellow traveler in Poe's dark poems and harrowing tales. His interest persisted through college and medical school, and he read and reread everything he could find by Poe. Once Bennett had become a pathologist at Hahnemann, he sought out antiquarian book dealers. They were happy to track down rare copies of Poe's books and writings for him, and he was willing to pay handsomely for them.

On this sunny early fall afternoon, Bennett walked the twenty blocks up to Rittenhouse Square, where his favorite book dealer lived in one of the elegant old apartment buildings on the south side of the square. He walked past the tall sycamores, just beginning to show their fall colors of pale yellow and brown. Several children were feeding the remains of a doughy soft pretzel to the sparrows in the square, screaming in delight and fear when flocks of pigeons flew in around them like feathered kamikaze pilots. The old men and women, who were the chief tenants of the apartment buildings, sat on the benches and watched the fun. The sidewalks were full of shoppers, tourists, and students who were enjoying the warm sunshine, a last remnant of summer.

Bennett entered the lobby of the building, blinking in the sudden absence of light. He nodded to the doorman.

"Hey, Clyde. How goes it?"

The doorman grinned, his white teeth a bright flash in the dim lobby.

"Hey yourself, Dr. Sykes. Fine day today, ain't it?"

"It sure is that, Clyde. Would you buzz Mr. Israel Vega for me, please?"

"G'wan up," said the doorman. "Mr. Vega's expectin' you."

Israel Vega's apartment door was hospitably ajar. Bennett pushed it open and stepped inside. The apartment was small and cluttered, the furniture overstuffed and filled with old brocaded pillows; motes of dust moved lazily in an amber shaft of sunshine streaming in through a smudged window. It smelled of dust, old leather, and mildewing paper, overlaid with the delicate floral aroma of fine Darjeeling tea. Every wall was lined with floor-to-ceiling bookshelves, all filled with lovely, leather-bound, gold-tooled books.

To Bennett, Israel's apartment felt almost holy, like entering a church. He breathed deeply, soaking up the exotic atmosphere of the place.

Israel Vega came from the kitchen. He had a porcelain teapot, two cups, and a saucer of lemon wedges balanced on a silver tray.

"Hello, Bennett. It's just time for tea. Join me."

"With pleasure, Israel." Bennett sat down on the cushiony old sofa, pushing a mound of pillows to one side. The sofa seemed to swallow up his lanky six-foot frame in a warm, soft embrace. Bennett sighed in content.

"What a perfect place to read—or nap," he said.

Israel Vega chuckled in agreement. He was a small man, with curly white hair and olive skin that indicated his Sephardic heritage. His eyes were wide and dark—Spanish eyes, thought Bennett, and he had the full rich mouth of the voluptuary even at the advanced age of seventy. He put the tea tray down on the inlaid coffee table and sat down next to Bennett. He poured two cups of tea into cups of porcelain so fine as to be translucent. He placed a slice of lemon in the saucer and handed it to Bennett. His hands were graceful and sure.

"What have you found for me, Israel?" Bennett asked. He took a sip of the tea. It was hot and exquisitely delicious.

Israel put down his cup and reached under the coffee table, pulling out a heavy cardboard box. Inside was an oversized book wrapped in linen. He handed it to Bennett.

"What is it?" asked Bennett. His eyes glittered with excitement and curiosity.

"A remarkable edition of *The Raven*—*Le Corbeau*—in French, illustrated by Edouard Manet."

Bennett unfolded the linen covering. The slender book was bound in rich wine-red leather, the lettering stamped in gold. He opened it. He could smell the sweet fragrance of old rag paper, perfectly kept and preserved. The book was in marvelous condition. Manet's magnificent color-plate illustrations were a perfect complement to the haunting poem, translated into French.

"The French were the first to truly appreciate Poe's tales as fine literature," Israel said. His voice was soft and slow, slightly husky, with a Mediterranean lilt to it. "The Americans allowed such a genius to live in poverty and to die in the gutter." He sighed deeply. "The French have such superb taste."

"Israel, this is beautiful," said Bennett. He turned the book over and over in his hands.

"Such a book, Bennett. Such a book helps Poe lie in peace finally, with Annabel Lee in her tomb by the sounding sea," Israel replied.

"You're sentimental today," said Bennett, smiling.

"It is the beauty of the book and the charm of the company. More tea?"

Bennett accepted another cup of tea. He placed the book on the table in front of him and carefully wrapped it back up in the linen. "How much are you asking?"

"Not as much as the manuscript I sold you a couple of years ago." Israel Vega's eyes twinkled.

Bennett smiled and was silent for a moment.

"I see you are remembering the manuscript, too." Israel's soft voice, so well suited to a bibliophile, interrupted Bennett's thoughts.

"Yes, I was. And I am indebted to you for introducing me to the Epicurean Society," replied Bennett.

"You did not look very grateful when we pulled up to that old house in Strawberry Mansion," chuckled Israel. "Years ago, it was a wealthy neighborhood. Many Jewish merchants settled there and built those elegant homes, with slate roofs and three-story turrets and carved scrollwork. It was so beautiful. Now it's a slum. A slum full of addicts and thugs." He shook his head sadly.

"I didn't know what to think," said Bennett. "That ramshackle old abandoned mansion, surrounded by vacant lots and trash. And the rats were everywhere. But when we went in . . ."

"Yes," said Israel. "The crystal chandelier sparkling in the candlelight. The mahogany table laid with fine china and silver. And the food! A wonder to please the gods!"

The memory rose up in Bennett's mind as if it had just happened yesterday. He and Israel had driven through North Philadelphia, the streets looking as if a war had been fought in them. The lovely old homes were in heartbreaking disrepair. Israel had turned on Diamond Street and pulled up at a home standing alone in the middle of the block. The homes on either side had been torn down, and the rest of the homes across the street were boarded up and dark. The street was empty. One window of the huge home was unboarded and unbroken, and Bennett could see candlelight glowing inside. He got out and walked up the steps as Israel knocked on the door.

They were ushered into a hallway that led to the back of the house. Bennett saw the kitchen and dining room, cleaned and restored to a substantial shadow of their former glory. All the rest of the rooms were closed off. Bennett had suspected they were as ruined as the exterior of the house. But the dining room's parquet floor glowed dully in the dim light, and the expensive hand-painted wallpaper had been scrubbed where it was not torn. From the high, richly patterned painted-tin ceiling, a miraculously intact chandelier had cast quivering rainbows on the walls. And the rooms were full of the savory scent of dinner, which almost but not quite masked the smells of rotting plaster, mildewed wood, and rat feces, which permeated the decaying house.

"I had never seen anything like it," Bennett said.

"It was perfect, wasn't it? Melmoth outdid himself." Israel smiled. "You see, dear Bennett, that transcendence can take place in the most unusual places."

Bennett was silent for a few moments. "I am going to host next week's meeting."

"I know," Israel replied. "I suggested it. Your enthusiasm for our little Society makes you an excellent choice. Here, I have something else for you." He got up and left the room. Bennett finished the last of his tea, enjoying the astringent, lemony taste on his tongue.

Israel returned with a dusty, plain black book in his hands. He handed it to Bennett.

"This is a journal kept by past hosts of our little banquets. We ask that each host record his impressions and ideas in order to assist future hosts in their preparations. You will find it helpful."

Bennett rose. "I have some ideas. I can't promise such an elegant setting as Melmoth's, but I am sure you will be pleased."

"The sacraments are what matter most, in any case." Israel looked at Bennett, his large dark eyes deep as an abyss. "Take care to choose wisely, my friend."

Bennett nodded. He pulled out his checkbook from his back pocket, wrote out a check, and handed it to Israel, who looked at the amount and smiled.

"That French book will be a nice addition to your collection," he said softly.

Bennett smiled. "Too bad I can't read French."

"Does it really matter?

"No," said Bennett. "See you a week from Monday."

Bennett decided to take a taxi home, rather than risk walking home with his new acquisition. As he stared out the window, rolling past the stores that lined Chestnut Street, his thoughts returned to that fateful manuscript Israel had sold him.

It had been an unpublished manuscript of Poe's, written on yellowed foolscap, the ink fading to a dark sepia, complete with cross-outs, inserts, and blots. The edges were beginning to crumble. Bennett pulled a pair of cotton gloves over his hands in order not to damage the paper further. He touched it gently, almost reverently.

"You are sure this is authentic?"

Israel had nodded.

"What is it? A first draft of one of the stories?"

"No," Israel replied. "It is a description of a banquet, given by a secret society."

Bennett leaned closer to the pages, trying to read the fading, old-style writing with all its flourishes and quirky spelling. "So it's fiction, then?"

"No," repeated Israel. "Remember, Poe wrote newspaper articles and edited journals. His poems and tales were his avocation." Israel paused.

"The society he wrote of still exists today." His voice was lower than normal, almost a whisper.

"Really?" Bennett asked. He looked up and his eyes met Israel's. Israel's eyes were blank, his face smooth and impassive, giving nothing away. "You are a member of this society, then?"

"Yes. As a matter of fact we are meeting next month."

"A literary gathering, I assume?"

"It is a theological society of sorts, devoted to questions of death and life, and what is left in the body and what departs," Israel had replied.

Bennett was immediately intrigued. He carefully placed the pages in their cloth-lined box on the table and leaned forward in his chair. "Tell me more about this society," he had said eagerly.

Israel had smiled and pointed at the yellowed pages. "Take the manuscript home and read it. I am afraid it is not complete. The last page is missing. Then, after reading, if you would like to know more, I will arrange for you to attend the banquet next month. I think you would enjoy it."

Bennett had paid more than he could really afford for the manuscript and taken it home. The account, written as if for a newspaper column, but with Poe's unerring style of building suspense, detailed an exquisite meal, with magnificent wines and fascinating conversation. Bennett read avidly until he came to the point at which the narrator was about to reveal a profound secret—then the manuscript broke off.

Bennett had called Israel Vega the next day and accepted the invitation.

The taxi stopped at the corner of Ashland Street. Bennett got out and paid his fare. Then he walked briskly down the little alley toward his house. He went in and put the book down gently on the coffee table. Then he hurried up the stairs. He had a date to get ready for.

From the Journal of the Epicurean Society
May 1915

Well, I imagine this was inevitable. It's a damned inconvenience, I don't mind telling you, but not totally unexpected. After all, when a gentleman's been a member of this society as many years as I have, one will be selected to host the banquet. This journal arrived by special delivery courier this afternoon, notifying me that I've been selected to be this year's host. In point of fact, it is quite the honor. The timing is a bit inopportune, however.

My traveling dental clinic and carnival—a unique and successful venture, I may add—leaves Philadelphia tomorrow morning to begin its summer travels, which will make this task a burdensome challenge, to say the least. I'll need to come up with a plan and make as many preparations as possible while on the road, then return to the city in time for the banquet. For now, I must occupy myself with tomorrow's departure. I feel obligated to point out that I'm a dentist, not a writer. I don't expect this journal to be a literary work, and neither should the reader. What I hope it will do is serve the purpose of instruction for the next banquet, and the next, et cetera.

One thing is certain, though. Whatever entrée idea I select must be prepared with relative ease and be astounding. I want this particular meal to be an unusual and memorable one, and I will make every effort toward that end.

Dreadful news from the Great War in the Philadelphia Inquirer *this morning. The evil Huns have sunk the* Lusitania, *with a loss of at least a thousand lives, including a much-admired member of our Society. Those bloodthirsty Boche will stop at nothing—a very few weeks ago they used poison gas in France on our valiant boys, and now they stoop to the murder of innocents. Have these animals no shame, no conscience? No finesse?*

However, I was charmed by dear old Charlie Frohman's last words. He stood bravely on the deck as the sea rushed up to pull him into its icy, wet embrace and proclaimed "Why fear death? It is the most beautiful adventure in life!"

Truly, a credit to our Society and an inspiration to myself.

We arrived in Pottstown without mishap and spent most of the day setting up the clinic and carnival. The carousel I purchased in Philadelphia works beautifully, and I will write Mr. Denzel and tell him how pleased I am. I'll begin seeing patients tomorrow, and commence my search for a suitable young lady.

We have now been in Pottstown, Pennsylvania for three days. A very profitable three days, I must say. Today alone

*I extracted over one hundred teeth at two bits a yank, for a
gross profit of twenty-five dollars. Not bad for a day's work.*

*I dispatched a telegram to my good friend Salvatore,
who calls himself the sultan of steak. He just opened his
own steakhouse on Passyunk Avenue in South Philadelphia. I inquired about popular new ideas for serving meat
at large parties. As we are moving the show to Reading in
the morning, I requested his response be telegraphed there.*

*Sal's reply to my inquiry arrived with some very exciting
news. It seems that he is developing a new entrée himself.
He said that a large number of people could be fed with relative ease and at minimal cost. He asked how many people
would be attending my party, and said that I would need approximately six ounces of thinly sliced meat per guest.*

*Reading is a beautiful city. From a distance, the town
looks so peaceful, resting at the base of Mt. Penn. Up
close, it's prosperous and busy. The huge rail yard and tex-
tile mills are the core of the city's success, but additionally
the four local breweries and five bottling companies make
fine local beers. This has helped to keep the unemployment
levels well below the average, and the employed much more
cheerful.*

*I think it would be wonderful to serve ice-cold Reading
lager at the banquet, so on the way back to Philadelphia
I plan to stop back here and procure a keg (or two). I
telegraphed Sal today accepting his generous offer and
providing the entire tour schedule. I made it clear to him
that I would provide the meat and beverage for the banquet. He now understands that I will be returning to
Philadelphia quite soon, and he will be apprised of any
change in schedule as quickly as possible.*

For now, we're off for Allentown.

*Today I pulled so many teeth that I actually lost count. I
would guess the sum to be in excess of three hundred and*

fifty. I've been pulling so many teeth that, to expedite services, I've started depositing the extracted teeth into a wooden bucket that I keep next to my dental chair. People are finding this a fascinating attraction, and are returning simply to see how full the bucket of teeth is. I am considering making the bucket a paying attraction, perhaps placing it in a tent of its own.

I've extracted teeth from many pretty young girls since this excursion began, but parents, siblings, husbands, or boyfriends always accompany them. I know that I will eventually find the girl that I'm looking for, but it's imperative that she comes to me alone. This is becoming an arduous task, locating a solitary girl in her early twenties that I would consider remotely close to Epicurean standards.

Our next stop is Aronston. Perhaps fate will be kinder there.

The bucket of teeth is filling quickly, and bringing in substantial revenue as an attraction. We are set up just outside of the Aronston city limits, and the turnout has been exceptional, thus far. Apparently, times are good here as well. The town's main industry is candy production. A dentist's dream or nightmare, depending on one's point of view. The smell of chocolate fills the air.

I recall the lore of this town that was told to me by my father back in Philadelphia. Apparently two brothers, "The Murdering Mennonites," were hung in the town square for the murder of their sister's killer, the son of the town's founder. It was a badly botched, grisly event that hastened the demise of public hangings as a form of entertainment in Pennsylvania. I rather think they should bring them back—for their deterrent effect, of course.

I found it impossible to rest last night. I was filled with anticipation as if some important event was about to occur. I decided, after hours of sleeplessness, to dress and take a predawn walk into Aronston.

I was pleased that I had dressed warmly. The air was chilled. A distant train whistle was the only sound that broke the silence of the night as I entered the city limits. I stayed to the main street, not wishing to get lost. The aroma of cocoa filled the air, even at this ungodly hour.

I went a good distance into the town. I looked into the dark storefronts and passed the local Odeon, where the marquee announced that D. W. Griffiths's Birth of a Nation *was now playing. Another aroma startled my senses. Smoke. I stopped walking, trying to decide from where the smell originated. It wasn't the smoke from a fire. Of that I was certain. This smell was different, sweeter. A smoke-house perhaps!*

My heart was racing as I continued along the main street. Within minutes I arrived at the front entrance of a small meat processing plant. The sign out front read:

Mama Angelina's Quality Meats.

There was an employee announcement board next to the front entrance, and I went over to examine its contents. As I expected, there was no advertisement posted for the dental clinic and carnival. Fortunately, I had a few in the inner pocket of my overcoat, and posted one.

Somewhere in the distance a rooster crowed announcing the dawn of a new day. A new day that I hope will find me able to advance my scheme for the Society banquet.

Late this afternoon, a middle-aged gentleman came into the clinic along with his wife and seven children. He said that his name was Samuel Schwartz, and that he works at the meat processing plant. He saw the advertisement and thought he'd bring his family into the clinic since he couldn't afford to take them all to a regular dentist. I suggested to him that certain payment options were available. I went on to offer free dental work for himself and his entire

*family if he agreed to help process and deliver a parcel of
meat to me in the near future. He eagerly agreed and told
me how to contact him when I was ready.*

Today, I found her. I knew it as soon as she walked into
the clinic. Tall, slightly muscular, and young. Obviously
she was a farm girl—none too cleanly, and she had the
smell of a farm about her. Most important, she was alone.

Once she was seated in the dental chair, I began to notice
her features. Blonde hair braided tightly and coiled around
her head, a weathered face, slim waist, flat stomach, and
ample breasts. Below the grime of the farm was an attractive young girl.

I knew before I had her open her mouth that what I'd
find would be a horror, and I was right. All of her teeth
were rotten. Some half-gone, some more than half. What
teeth remained were black with decay. Her breath was noxious. I explained that the work that was required would
take a long time, and I asked if she could possibly come
back after the carnival closed. She hesitated, but then
agreed after I said I would arrange for her to have safe
transportation home. She said that her mouth has pained
her for as long as she can remember, and a few more hours
of discomfort wouldn't make any difference. She said that
her pa couldn't afford a dentist, and she worried about how
much all this was going to cost. I told her to enjoy the day
at the carnival because her pain would end soon, and that
there were options for payment. After she left, I paid a
young boy a nickel to take a note to Mr. Schwartz at Mama
Angelina's.

She came back after the carnival closed. She must have
been waiting close by because I only waited a short while
for her arrival. I escorted her inside the tent, making certain that no one was lingering about to see us. Once she
was seated comfortably in the chair, I asked her to open her
mouth. I cursorily examined the remains of her teeth for a

short time, and told her I needed to sterilize my equipment, and that I would return, anesthetize her, and commence the extractions. I instructed her to remain in the chair, close her eyes, and relax.

It was a simple matter to douse a handkerchief with ether and clap it over her nose and mouth while she lay resting in the chair, muttering soothing phrases about how it would be over soon. Once she was unconscious, I picked up the big feather pillow I had brought along for the purpose and straddled her in the chair, pressing it tightly down against her face. After a minute or two, I could hear her choking. Her strong young body thrashed a little but then was still. I continued to press for at least another ten minutes, then slowly released her.

I lifted the pillow from her face. She looked like she was sleeping, except for the trickle of blood from her nose. I checked for a pulse to make sure she had expired. Once I was satisfied she was dead, I turned the light off and departed the clinic, in case there were questions later that required an alibi. I went to a local tavern and ordered supper, eating it in a leisurely fashion and chatting up my neighbors at the bar counter.

When I returned sometime later, my first task was to undress the body. I adjusted the chair so she was lying as flat as possible. I started by removing her sturdy shoes and socks. Her feet were heavily callused, the toenails dirty. Obviously she wore shoes in the summer only to church and on special occasions—such as carnivals.

Next I took a pair of scissors and cut her dress down the front from hem to collar. Same with the sleeves. The dress fell away, and I then cut off her chemise and underpants. I covered the corpse with a clean sheet, and went to retrieve a wheelbarrow, a bucket, and my razor.

When I returned, I loaded the body into the wheelbarrow and covered it with the sheet. I set the bucket on top. I had briefly thought of using a motored vehicle to transport the body, but was afraid that the noise would arouse unwanted attention at this time of night. I pushed the wheelbarrow outside and around the clinic. I headed toward the pool that we use for the carnival animals. Once there I immersed her completely in the cold water. I washed her as best I could, placed her back into the wheelbarrow, filled the bucket, and returned to the clinic where I placed her on a table that I had prepared earlier.

With great care I spread her limbs as much as possible, draping her arms and legs over the sides of the table, and shaved her from the neck down with my straight razor, one appendage at a time. The leg hairs were not thick, which leads me to believe that she never shaved them before. The underarm and pubic areas were thicker. I used the water in the bucket to keep the area I was working on moist.

When the shaving was completed, I took a minute or so to examine her. There was no discoloration or bruising. Her skin was now pink and soft to the touch. The area between her legs was enchanting.

Once back on the dental chair I secured her feet tightly to the bottom of the chair with rope and pushed her head back, exposing her throat. I then went outside to empty the water from the bucket and assure again that nobody was about. When I was satisfied, once more I entered the clinic, reclined the chair so her feet were in the air, and slit her throat with the straight razor. As the blood drained from the open wound and into the bucket, I gathered a scalpel, a saw, and a spade. Surprisingly, it only took a few minutes to bleed her white, after which I took the bucket outside to dispose of the blood.

Keeping her in the same position I opened her belly with the scalpel. After removing all of her internal organs and placing them in the bucket, I leveled the chair once more and untied her feet. I moved her back to the table where I removed her feet, hands, and head, using the saw. Once these body parts were in the bucket, I took them and the shovel out beyond the carnival grounds and buried them in a shallow grave. The last thing that I placed into the earth was her head. Before internment, I picked her head up by her pigtails, kissed her forehead, and thanked her.

After washing the bucket again in the animal trough, I went back to the clinic and used the saw to separate the arms and legs from the torso. I then centered the open sheet in the wheelbarrow, placed the body parts inside, and covered them up with the rest of the linen. I stopped briefly to wash the parts off before heading into town to the meat processing plant.

Samuel Schwartz met me at the front of the plant as we had previously arranged. He looked curiously down at the wheelbarrow, and I needed to remind him that our arrangement included no questions. We reviewed the order: no bone, no skin, thinly sliced.

I pulled the sheet back to show him what he'd be working with. I watched closely for a reaction. All the blood drained from Samuel's face, and he gasped but managed not to make too much of a fuss. I closed the sheet, gathered the corners, and lifted the bundle out of the wheelbarrow. I handed it over to him, reminding him that I'd be by the next evening to pick up the package. He took the parcel and silently nodded his agreement.

I then rushed back to the clinic and drafted a telegram to Sal. The sky was beginning to redden in the east.

That evening after dark I met again with Samuel. He handed me three fairly large packages and said all of the meat was inside, and to keep it at a temperature of no less than thirty-four degrees. He also said that I don't have to be concerned about any leftover by-product. He claimed that he put all of the leftovers through the grinder, which would be used in animal feed. I set the packages down for a moment. I extended my hand and offered thanks for his assistance. As he reached to accept the handshake, he inquired about the taste of the meat. I told him that it tasted like pork, and that it was referred to as long pork in the Society in which I'm a member.

Then, in a trembling voice, he asked me if I knew who she was. I put my arm around his shoulder as if to draw him close to whisper a secret, then pulled the straight razor out of my coat pocket and slit his throat. I left him in a clump of bushes by the front steps of the plant. By the time anyone finds him, I'll be long gone. I will return to Philadelphia posthaste, leaving the carnival to travel on to Harrisburg without me. I will rejoin them after the banquet. In the meantime the troupe will have a few days to rest. This was a very popular idea, particularly when I assured them they would receive half-pay for the idle days, since it was I who inconvenienced them all. With the money I've made on the new attraction of the tooth-filled bucket, it will not inconvenience me in the slightest.

Sal's telegram arrived literally moments before I departed Aronston. He says that he has reserved the Arch Street Meeting House for the date and time that I had specified. He also stated that he took the liberty of purchasing the other ingredients that we require for this entrée. The list includes soya bean oil, cheese, Spanish onions, sweet red and green peppers, mushrooms, and Italian rolls. I can't begin to imagine what he has in mind.

After stopping briefly in Reading to pick up a barrel of lager, I arrived safely back in Philadelphia late in the afternoon. I took the parcels of meat and keg of lager over to Sal's restaurant. We briefly discussed what side dishes I wanted. He suggested sliced dill pickles and French fries. I left the side dishes up to Sal's discretion, which seemed to please him. I repaired to my room at the Bellevue Hotel and began work on a project I'd conceived—and *brought a goodly handful of specimens from the tooth bucket for . . .*

Sal and I arrived at the Arch Street Meeting House more than two hours before the Society members were scheduled to arrive. Sal had reserved the east wing for our gathering. Among the dioramas chronicling the history of William Penn, we set up tables and chairs, serving tables, the keg of beer sitting in a large vat of ice, and a small stove for the frying of the meat. I put on the necklace of teeth I'd strung the previous evening and felt quite festive.

Sal began to sauté the onions in an iron skillet. Once the onions were finished, Sal put them into a large bowl, covered the bowl with a cloth, and put them on the back of the stove to keep warm while he repeated the process with the red and green peppers. As the Society members began to arrive, Sal added the remaining oil to the pan, and started frying the slices of meat. The cooking only took seconds for each slice.

As the Society members entered the hall, they were directed to immediately obtain a plate. A line quickly formed in a cafeteria style, as each platter was prepared. Sal took a plate and a roll. He sliced the roll horizontally, and placed the meat into the roll. He then added the onions and the cheese on top of the meat. The sautéed peppers went on top of the cheese. Each platter was garnished with a dill pickle and spiced fried potatoes. The beer, cold and foamy, was a perfect accompaniment.

Sal served himself last. After he finished his sandwich he said that the pork made a good sandwich, but he thought steak much better in this particular combination. My fellow Society members were delighted, of course, and complimented Sal lavishly on his interesting new culinary ideas. Sal ate a second sandwich and thought it over. He declared that even so, in the future he would stick with beef. A wise choice, we all said, as long pork can be troublesome to find

*and expensive to procure. Someone mentioned that a new
processed cheese, just introduced by J. L. Kraft in Chicago,
would be delicious on the sandwich. Opinion has it that Mr.
Kraft will do for cheese what Mr. Bardwell did for chocolate. Sal promised to look into it.*

*In the fall, when the carnival returns to Philadelphia to
winter over, I plan to venture to the Sultan Of Steak on
Passyunk Avenue, and try another one of these wonderful
sandwiches that Sal calls the "Philly Cheese Steak."*

Edgar "Painless" Parker, 1915

South Street was still the hippest street in town, thirty-
some years after the song that immortalized it was a hit.
Trendy restaurants, expensive boutiques, head shops, and
espresso bars lined the fourteen blocks from Broad Street
to Front Street.

Chez Chiennes Noir was a renovated storefront/apart-
ment building near the corner of Eleventh and South. On
the ground floor was a bar, done in dark mahogany with a
shiny brass rail. Mirrors and original, pastel-shaded art-
work hung on the cream-colored walls. The second and
third floors were the dining rooms, done in the pastel
shaded Art Deco style Kass had labored to describe. Fresh
white tablecloths covered the small tables, which were
adorned with a centerpiece of white roses in a crystal bud
vase and floating candles in a brandy snifter half-full of
water.

Since it was a very new restaurant, on this Saturday it
was crowded with young urban professionals and Main Line
cognoscenti, all eager to be among the first to dine there and
to decide if Chiennes Noir would become the new chic
place to see and be seen. Waiters and bartenders scurried
among the elegantly dressed couples, anxious to impress
and please and earn a spot on the "Best of Philly" list.

Kasidy Rhodes timidly pushed open the door to the bar. Her cheeks were flushed as she looked around the packed, noisy room.

"This is such a mistake," she muttered to herself. "How could anybody find anyone in this crowd? What a fool I am."

She eased her way through the bar crowd, fighting the urge to turn around and walk out. "He probably really is short and fat and bald, and if he isn't, he's probably going to stand me up. Serve me right, too, meeting perfect strangers on the Internet."

Her eyes fell on a man sitting alone at a tiny table by the window. He was holding a single long-stemmed red rose, twirling it slowly between his fingers. He looked over at her and smiled, raising his eyebrows to ask an unspoken question. He had wavy dark-blond hair. His eyes were brown and crinkled at the corners when he smiled. He had a straight nose and a well-shaped mouth partly hidden under a neatly trimmed moustache.

Kass could not believe this man could be waiting for her. "He's gorgeous," she whispered. She stared back at him, a look of surprise and disbelief on her face.

The man chuckled. He got up from the table and threaded his way through the crowd. He stopped in front of Kass and held the rose out to her, grinning.

She returned the grin but was still unable to speak. She reached out and took the rose, holding it to her nose to breathe in its faint, sweet fragrance. Finally she found her voice.

"Hello, Dr.B," she murmured, color blazing in her cheeks.

"Hello, Mamakass," he replied. He looked down at her. "So you think you're nothing much, eh? Well, I disagree." His eyes moved up and down her body.

Kass had on a new, chic black shift that skimmed her body and made the most of her curves. Her hair shone like burnished copper in the low light from the bar. She lifted her eyes to Bennett's and was almost shocked by the appreciation in his face. It had been a very long time since a man had looked at her like that. She felt her skin tingle, as if she had just stepped out of a cold shower.

"I think you'll be pleased with the food here," Bennett said with a smile. "The chef really knows what he's doing, and since I am something of a gourmet myself, you can take my word for it."

"I'll know that for myself in a little while," Kass said. Food was a welcome and benign topic at the moment.

"Yes, you will," Bennett replied, chuckling.

He took her hand and led her over to the staircase leading up to the dining rooms. Dieter was the maitre'd this evening.

"Good evening, Dr. Sykes. It's so nice to see you again. Hello, Kasidy Rhodes." He bowed gravely.

"We're ready for our table now, Dieter," Bennett said.

"Of course," Dieter said and turned immediately to a white-shirted, bow-tied waiter standing a step or two above him. "Andrew will show you to your table."

Bennett took Kass's hand and tucked it into the crook of his arm. They followed Andrew up the stairs.

Jess was chopping vegetables for her dinner in her tiny kitchen when she heard the knock at the back door.

"It's open, Heather," she called.

Heather Troutman walked into the kitchen. Susie's mother was a tall, thin woman with mousy brown hair, pulled back into a ponytail. Lines of exhaustion cut deep around her mouth and eyes, and her skin was gray from too much caffeine and nicotine—and something else.

"How are you feeling?" Jess asked.

"Shitty," Heather answered. She opened the kitchen window, and Jess placed an ashtray on the windowsill. Heather lit a Marlboro and looked at Jess.

"We got an appointment with the lawyer Monday at noon. I told him I only got an hour for lunch, and he said that'd be no problem. Shit, girl, is that all you're gonna eat for your supper? Veggies?"

"And tofu." Jess laughed.

"Shit, Jess. It's fucking Saturday night. You should be out on a date, not home alone eating rabbit food." Heather frowned at her. "If I'd've had your looks, I sure as hell wouldn't be hanging around here."

"I don't want a boyfriend." Jess said shortly. "What do I need a boyfriend for, anyway?"

Heather slammed her hand down on the windowsill, and Jess jumped. "Goddamn it, Jess, you can't hide in this house forever. You got a life to live, and you should get out there and live it." Heather narrowed her eyes. "If Suz and me didn't need you so bad, I'd fucking kick your skinny little ass out the door." She took a deep pull on her cigarette.

Jess smiled. Heather had grown up in the streets of South Philly and laced her speech liberally with four-letter words. They no longer shocked Jess. It was just part of Heather.

Then her face grew serious. "Heather, are you sure this is what you want?"

"I should ask you the same thing. Hell, Suz's father don't want her, even though he might pretend he does. Him and his bitch wife just like to piss me off. Susie hasn't seen him for over a year. My mother's too old to have another kid running around the house. I wouldn't let my no-good brother have her if he were the last guy on earth. Dumb fuck can't hold a job for more'n a month before he drinks himself out of it. You're nineteen years old. You got looks. And money, too. You sure you want Susie? You know the kid'll tie you down. Guys your age, they don't want no girls with kids."

Jess walked over to Heather and kissed her cheek. "Susie's like a sister to me. And you've always been so good to me. Like a mother. I don't know what I would have done when Daddy died if it wasn't for you and Susie."

"You gotta promise me one thing, Jessie."

"What's that, Heather?"

"If you want to bury yourself alive in this house, there's not a whole lot I can do about it. But don't you go hiding Suz from life just because life bit you in the ass. You know Ramon would never have wanted this for you. He loved you. He wanted you to have it all."

Jess's eyes filled with tears, remembering her father. "I *do* want Susie. More than anything. I love her to pieces. I'm . . . I'm just not ready to make any changes right now."

"Yeah? Your dad's been dead a year now, and I bet you still got his clothes in the fucking closet upstairs." Heather blew a cloud of smoke at Jess. "Am I right or what?"

"Actually, I got rid of them. Last week Purple Heart came and got them." Jess looked at the floor.

"Well, it's a start," said Heather. "Shit, I got a six-year-old crazy about a TV show and a nineteen-year-old who's just plain crazy." She smiled thinly at Jess.

Jess raised her head and looked into Heather's eyes. "I'll be okay, Heather. I'll take good care of Suz. I know it'll make you happy."

"Yeah, I'll die in peace." Heather sighed. "When I saw Dr. Shirk the last time, after the lumps came back, she said it's only a month, maybe two, before I'll have to quit work. You said she's the best fucking cancer doc in the city, so I guess she should know. Already the painkillers don't work as good as they used to. I got to see her again next week. I'll tell Susie when I quit work." She looked sharply at Jess and blew cigarette smoke through her nostrils. "You haven't said anything to her, right?"

"Not a word," Jess said solemnly. "And don't you worry about money. You should quit work now, save your strength. Heather, if it's money you need . . ."

Heather crushed out her cigarette. "And let that shithead father of hers know something's wrong? Hell, no. I want this all done up nice and tight and legal before he finds out. Instead of being happy that he doesn't have to pay me support by signing full rights over to me, the bastard'll sue for custody just to fuck with me if he knows I'm sick. And you keep your money. I don't want no help from you. You're helping me enough as it is."

"Susie'd never agree to live with her father. She doesn't even know him," replied Jess.

"Yeah, but the damn courts these days. You can be a flaming crackhead with a criminal record a mile long, and the fucking judges will give you custody if you're the real parent. Believe me, Jessie, I can see it clear as day. There would be Mr. Shit-for-Brains in front of the judge with his bitch wife, crying to the judge about how he'd make a happy home for his precious little daughter who he's seen maybe six times since she was born." Heather gestured angrily. "Then there would be you, single girl, young, no family. No, you only baby-sat for Suz every day of her fucking life, and you love her like a sister. Guess who'd get custody? Not you. And the fucking judge wouldn't give a good goddamn what Suz wanted, wouldn't care what was best for her."

Heather's face was grim.

"No, Jessie, I ain't stopping until I know for sure that Susie's gonna be okay." She lit another cigarette, and Jess frowned at her.

"Heather, those things are probably what got you in trouble in the first place. At least you could cut down."

"Hell, I'm already dead. What difference does it make now? Like I said, I'm gonna die happy." Smoke curled from Heather's nose again. "Jessie, just promise me you'll beat Susie's brains out if you ever catch her smoking."

"No problem there," Jess replied firmly. She leaned down through the smoke and put her arms around Heather.

The older woman leaned against the younger one for a moment, her face drawn and tired. Then she patted Jess's arm and gently released herself.

"That damn show's about over now, so I'll head on back. What does she see in that Miss Becky anyway? Dumbest thing I ever saw."

"Susie loves it. And it's educational, too."

"Yeah, but sometimes I think I'll go nuts if I hear that asswipe 'Friends Forever' song one more damn time." Heather got up slowly, wincing a little and rubbing her back. "Time for another Percocet. Damn things don't even make me high anymore." She smiled wryly at Jess. "See you Monday then, Jess."

"I'll be there."

"I know you will. And find yourself a boyfriend, willya?"

"*Heather . . .*"

"Shit," replied Heather.

Heather Troutman was tough and profane, but she loved her daughter fiercely. When the doctors diagnosed her with non-Hodgkin's lymphoma two years earlier, she was furious.

"I'm gonna raise her, goddamnit," she had told Jess and Ramon. "No fucking cancer is going to stop me. Shit, Suz'll probably kill me with ulcers in about ten years anyway."

She endured chemotherapy, which made her sicker than she had ever been before, but she hung tough, always ready with a smile for Susie. Nine months later, the lumps in her groin and armpits returned, and she went through a second round of chemo with the same gritty determination.

When the lumps in Heather's groin and armpits returned for the third time, she knew that she wasn't going to beat the cancer. Dr. Shirk, her oncologist, recommended another round of chemotherapy, but Heather refused.

"I'm not going to spend my last months on earth throwing my guts up and feeling like a fucking truck's parked on my chest," she had told Jess. "I want to enjoy whatever time I got left with Suz." Dr. Shirk prescribed painkillers, for the cancer had invaded Heather's spine, and promised to keep her comfortable until the end.

Heather began planning Susie's future with the same determination she used to battle her disease. First, she convinced Susie's father to renounce his parental rights. Susie's father had begun dating Heather right after separating from his wife. Six months later, he reconciled with his wife, leaving Heather pregnant with Susie. Heather wasted no time crying over him, but began planning her unborn child's future with bitter determination.

Heather did not tell Susie's father she was pregnant until after Susie was born, when she promptly sued him for child support. The wife was furious, as Susie's father had neglected to mention anything about his dalliance with Heather to her. Paternity was established, and after a few shaky months the wife stayed on. Susie's father did his best to forget about his daughter. He succeeded so well that he often forgot to send the support checks. Heather never let him get away with it.

"You'd think that fuckhead would send the checks just so he wouldn't have to listen to me while I ream him a new asshole," she had fumed to Jess one day.

When Heather knew that the lymphoma was going to win this time, she realized that the last person she wanted to raise Susie was her father. He was a cowardly bastard, and his wife had never even met Susie. She decided she had to get full parental rights to Susie just in case. That way, any subsequent guardianship decisions would be entirely Heather's. The trick was not letting him know why she wanted the rights.

He was suspicious at first when Heather suggested he give up all rights to Susie. But when she mentioned that it meant he could quit paying support, he became much more receptive to the idea. His wife approved, and the agreement was drawn up.

Then she approached Jess about becoming Susie's guardian. She knew that Jess loved Susie with a love that equaled her own, and she knew Susie would force Jess to get back to the business of living. She was relieved when Jess agreed. Now everything was in place. It was a perfect situation.

Too bad I won't be here to see how it all turns out, Heather thought, sighing.

Heather walked into the living room. Her daughter sat raptly in front of the television, wearing the pearls and old slippers she always put on to watch *Miss Becky and Friends.* The Miss Becky doll was cuddled in her lap. The closing theme song was playing. The puppet characters held hands and looked lovingly at each other as they sang:

> Friends forever
> We'll always be
> Me for you
> And you for me
> Rain may fall
> But it's sunny weather
> When you call me
> Your friend forever

Heather made a gagging noise deep in her throat. Susie looked over at her mother and smiled. Heather returned the smile. *Watch yourself,* she thought.

"How's Miss Becky tonight, hon?" Heather came over and stroked Susie's hair.

"Good, Mommy. It was the one where Chucky got lost and scared, and Miss Becky and Matilda and Henry looked and looked until they found him. But then Chucky wasn't so scared anymore. He knew they'd find him 'cause he's their friend forever." Susie put her arms around her mother's neck. "Where'd you go, Mommy? Over to Jessie's?"

"Yeah, I had to tell her something." Heather's face contracted for a moment.

"Time for your pill, right, Mommy? Miss Becky and me will get you some sugar water to help the medicine go down." Susie ran to the kitchen and got a glass of water, put three heaping spoonfuls of sugar in it, and brought it back into the living room. Heather put the pill in her mouth and grimaced as she washed it down with the sickeningly sweet water.

Susie peered anxiously into her mother's face. "How come those pills aren't making you better yet? I always get better when you give me that yucky pink medicine."

"I'll be better soon, sweetie. Real soon."

Susie's eyes narrowed. "You don't mean it, Mommy. At least not like I get better."

Heather hugged her daughter and was silent for a few moments. Then she pasted a smile on her face.

"What do you want for your dinner, Suz?"

Susie put her head down to her doll's for a moment. "Me and Miss Becky want macaroni and cheese. Please."

"Such nice manners. Where'd you learn them? From Jessie?"

"No. Miss Becky says please and thank you are magic words that make good things happen."

"You and Miss Becky," groaned Heather. But she was still smiling. It could be worse, she thought. It could be that show about the purple dinosaur, which everyone said was much worse than *Miss Becky*.

Heather got up and went into the kitchen. She wiped up the sugar water Susie had slopped on the tiny kitchen table and put water on to boil.

"Shit," she muttered. She looked into the living room, where Susie was playing with her Legos and keeping up a one-sided conversation with Miss Becky. Heather's eyes filled with tears.

"Yeah, Suz, I'll be okay soon. And so will you." Heather turned back to the stove.

"The lady will have the medallions of beef, and I will have the poached salmon. We'll share an order of the stuffed mushrooms, and please bring another bottle of Pouilly-Fuisse with the mushrooms."

"Very good, sir," said Andrew. He took the menus and left.

Kasidy smiled at Bennett over the roses and the candles. She took another sip of the excellent wine. "*Two* bottles of wine? Are you trying to make me drunk?"

Bennett smiled back. "We have all night to finish it. You're not in any hurry to get home, are you? I'm really enjoying this."

"Oh, no," Kass said. "I'm having a wonderful time. I hope the food is good."

"It's much better than their French," said Bennett. "The name should be 'Chiennes Noirs.'" He emphasized the *S*.

"Dieter is from Austria, I think. That probably explains it," said Kass.

"That's right, Dieter knew you when we came in. How did you meet him?"

As she made small talk with Bennett, Kass was powerfully drawn to him. He was so handsome and attentive. Herb had never been this good-looking, even before he began getting bald and paunchy. Herb had never smiled at her the way Bennett did, or made Kass feel so pretty. It seemed as if Bennett couldn't take his eyes from her.

Watch it, Kass, a warning voice said. *Don't get in too deep too fast.*

Kass dismissed the voice. It wasn't as if she didn't know Bennett. She'd spent hours chatting with him online. They were comfortable with each other, like old friends. But it was exciting, too. Exciting to see, finally, what each other looked like and sounded like. She wondered what he felt like and tasted like, and blushed at the thought.

Bennett grinned at her as if he could guess what was on her mind. He reached over the table and squeezed her hand. "We have all night, Mamakass. All night," he said.

Jess hadn't needed to think twice about raising Susie. She had lost both mother and father, and now was going to lose her dearest friend. Little Susie was now the only link she had to the past, and she couldn't bear to lose her, too. The two of them were as close as sisters. Susie was a sensitive and thoughtful child. Her intuition about things seemed almost psychic. Jess wondered how the practical, realistic Heather could have given birth to such a child.

Jess's thoughts strayed to her own mother. She had only one photograph of her, a framed snapshot that her father had kept on his bedside table. But Ramon had told her the story many times.

Jess's father had been a bus driver for SEPTA, Philadelphia's transit authority. Twenty years ago he had been driving up Broad Street around two A.M. when he noticed a dazed, bloodied young girl lying huddled on the sidewalk. He pulled the bus over to the curb and got out.

He knelt next to the girl, her blue eyes staring at him without focusing. She was very young. Her tangled, pale blonde hair and fair skin made the blood and bruises that covered her thin body look livid in the mercury-vapor glare of the streetlights. Ramon took in the bustier top, the short skirt, and torn stockings. He realized she was a prostitute, probably an addict, too, and that she most likely had been beaten by a customer—or her pimp.

Her eyes finally focused on his. She reached up and touched his face. "I want to go home," she murmured through her swollen lips. He picked her up and carried her onto the bus. Rather than call the cops, he decided to take her to his tired-looking twin home in Upper Darby, just outside the city. You're crazy, man, he thought to himself. She'll rob you blind or turn tricks in your bed. But she was so young and fragile that his heart would not let him turn her in.

Her name was Ingrid, and she was a seventeen-year-old runaway from Iowa. When she had arrived at the bus terminal in Philadelphia, frightened and alone, she had been easy prey for the smooth-talking men who used affection, promises, and drugs to enslave naïve young girls. When Ramon found her, she was indeed a crack addict and a hooker, turning tricks for her pimp in return for a supply of crack. That night, a customer had stiffed her after she performed for him, shoving her out of his car and speeding away. Her pimp took out his anger on her, beating her and telling her not to come back until she'd made up the lost money.

He sent her to a rehab and, after she was clean, took her into his home. She responded to his kindness by falling in love with him. Ramon, who was in his forties and never married, became enchanted with her. When she confessed that she was pregnant, he married her, even though he knew he was not the father of the child. As Ingrid healed, both inside and out, he realized that he had found a treasure. She was beautiful, sweet, and devoted to her rescuer. Ramon had never known such complete contentment before, and he thanked God for putting Ingrid in his life.

When Jess was born, he felt a fierce rush of tenderness for the tiny infant who had inherited her mother's beauty. He held the baby close to his heart and crooned, "*Mi querida,* you are going to have a beautiful life. I, Ramon Grasia, promise you that." A tear rolled down his cheek and splashed down on the baby's blonde head. She squalled at the strange sensation, then nestled closer to Ramon and slept.

Jess was perfectly normal, having by some miracle escaped the damage her mother's crack habit could have inflicted during early pregnancy. Ramon could not have loved her more if she was his own blood. For a year, Jess and Ingrid and Ramon were very happy together.

One morning, early, while Ingrid was feeding Jess strained peaches in her high chair, the phone rang. Ingrid answered it, and after a few moments put the receiver back.

She picked up her purse and went to the bottom of the stairs. "Honey, I have to go out for a few. I'll be back. Could you finish feeding Jessie for me?"

"Okay," came the sleepy reply. The floor creaked as Ramon got out of bed.

Ingrid gently closed the front door behind her. She never returned to the snug little home in Upper Darby. After the first grief-filled months passed, Ramon finally accepted that she was gone and dedicated his life to his little daughter. But he never stopped looking for Ingrid as he drove his bus through the city, year after year, always hoping. And Jess was left with an intense dislike of peaches that she could never fully explain.

The fragrance of sesame oil filled the kitchen as Jess scraped her stir-fried vegetables and tofu onto a plate and sat down in the kitchen. She caught a whiff of Heather's cigarette smoke still lingering in the air, under the sesame smell. Suddenly she was no longer hungry. She leaned her elbows on the table and pushed her slender fingers up through her hair. She was alone—forsaken by her mother, her father, and by God Himself, whom she didn't believe in anymore anyway.

Fear clutched at her. She began to talk out loud.

"Daddy, Daddy, I hope I'm doing the right thing. I know I'm only nineteen, but I feel like I'm a hundred. It hurts so much that Heather is dying. God is taking away everyone I've ever loved, and now I'm going to have to be a mom to

Susie. And I don't know if I can do it. I don't know if I can be as good to her as you were to me."

Tears began falling onto the tabletop. "I guess that's why I don't want to date anyone. If we broke up, then that would be another thing to lose. Heather thinks I'm hiding away from everyone. Maybe she's right. I know I should maybe sell the house, go to college like you wanted me to. I know I don't have to work, but then I wouldn't see Dr. Sykes anymore. And he's so kind to me. Just like you were. Oh, Daddy, I'm so lost and scared. Help me, help me please."

It was as close to a prayer as Jess could manage. She closed her eyes and waited for something, some response. A cool breeze blew into the kitchen from the open window, clearing the last traces of smoke from the air. It ruffled Jess's hair like Ramon used to do when she was a child. It also brought the savory aroma of her cooling dinner to her. She felt a little better and began to eat.

Kass threw her head back and laughed. The sound was musical, almost like a waterfall. It echoed off the tall houses along Spruce Street.

"It's true, Mamakass. Seems like old Syl got dumped for a younger woman after her stud muffin got tired of being a kept man. Kept with my money, I might add."

"Oh, Bennett, that's almost as delicious as the dinner." She laughed again and slowed her steps. "Here's my house. Thank you so much for the dinner, and the walk, and the conversation. You made me forget that I'm just a divorced soccer mom."

Bennett walked her up to her door. He looked down into her face, lit up by the outside lamps flanking the big wooden door. "You *are* a soccer mom, Kass. But you're a lot of other things, too. You're smart and charming—and beautiful." Bennett leaned down and kissed her.

Kass's lips parted under his. He kissed her again, deeper this time. Need pulsed through her like lightning. She had never felt so desirable, or desiring, as she did at this moment. Her arms circled around him, and she pressed her body against his.

"Sweet," Bennett murmured. "So sweet."

He kissed her until the sound of footsteps told them someone was approaching. He gently pushed her away.

"I'd like to take this further," he whispered, "but not on the first date. I'm not that kind of boy."

Kass hung onto his arm, trembling even as she giggled. "Well, I'm glad one of us has a cool head. For a minute there, I think I'd have done anything you wanted me to do. Too much of that damn wine, I guess."

Bennett caught her under the chin and looked intently into her shining eyes. "Someday I will ask you to do what I want. But not tonight."

His soft brown eyes bore into hers. She felt her insides melt and puddle somewhere down around her crotch. She smiled, a wide and hungry smile.

"You got it, Dr. B." she murmured. She kissed him once more, on the cheek this time, and unlocked her door. He stepped back as she let herself in and then walked lightly down the steps, waving to her as she stood silhouetted in the front window.

He turned and started back up the street, whistling.

Bennett decided not to go straight home. He was excited from his contact with Kass and the knowledge that she would fulfill his plans for the Society banquet. She's a bit older than she should be, he thought. But she's healthy and clean. Very pretty in her own way. And she's got all the qualities I want—kindness, openness, honesty, intelligence. She'll do nicely for the sacraments.

A wine-and-currant sauce, perhaps. Yes.

He turned and walked toward Thirteenth Street.

A three-block stretch of Thirteenth Street below Chestnut was a favorite place for prostitutes to congregate and solicit business. It was less brightly lit than the main streets of Market and Broad, and there were no homes there, and nothing there of interest to tourists. But it was close enough to be convenient to the Center City bars and nightspots. A man who wasn't quite ready for the night to be over would not have to travel far to find company. Best of all, the cops generally left the ladies alone unless there was trouble, or unless the D.A. wanted more vice convictions. This usually happened only during election years.

After nine P.M., women would line the streets in small groups. There were young, frightened girls who were probably runaways. There were older women whom the years had ridden hard, and it showed in their pale, lined faces. Most of them were addicts. They would stand on the sidewalks, eyeing the passing cars and men, trying to catch an eye and a customer.

On a corner, Bennett saw one of them. A thin woman in a too-short skirt and too-thin coat loitered there, as if waiting for someone. As he approached, he could see that she was one of the older women who plied their trade on the streets. He almost passed her by, but something made him meet her eyes.

"Hey, mister. Looking for a friend?" she asked, in a tired professional voice.

In the ugly cold glare of the streetlights, Bennett looked at her face. It was ravaged by the drugs she craved and the hard life she was living, but she looked like someone he knew. Her eyes were a deep blue, made even bluer by the red-netted whites and pink-rimmed eyelids. He realized with a start that she looked like Jessica. Same long blonde hair, but the color was from a bottle, and the hair was dull and lifeless instead of glossy and wavy like Jess's. Her skin was pale and wan, with high spots of color that came from a compact. None of Jess's fresh rosiness. But the blue eyes were real, as were the full mouth and long, thin limbs.

She opened her coat, showing a low-cut blouse that was none too clean, Bennett noted with distaste. There was a crude tattoo on her left breast. It was a heart, with the letter *J* enclosed within it and adorned with curlicued flowering vines. Her breasts were cantilevered up and outward by a push-up bra, but Bennett knew that once she was naked, the breasts would be small and droopy. She reached into her pocket and pulled out a cigarette.

"Got a light?" she asked.

"Nope. I don't smoke." He looked her up and down again.

"Well, I do," she said. She pulled a lighter from the same pocket and lit her cigarette. She exhaled a cloud of blue smoke and returned his gaze.

"You're a nice-looking dude. Want some company?" Bennett heard something different in her voice.

"Where are you from?" he asked.

"Midwest. Never-Never Land. Wherever you want me to be from." She smiled at him, and Bennett could see her teeth were in bad shape. *Probably hasn't seen a dentist in years,* he thought.

He took her hand without a word and pulled her close, into the full glare of the light. Under the makeup, he could see the gray cast of unhealthy, unwashed skin. The cheap perfume was underlaid with the smell of body reek and foul breath. She was nothing but a street whore. Death was waiting for her, and by the looks of her it wouldn't be waiting much longer.

Death stalked all the women on Thirteenth Street. If the drugs didn't get them, disease would. Or their pimps. Or some crazed customer. You could see death in their flat, empty eyes and hear it in their toneless voices. There was no joy for them in the most life-affirming of human acts. They were simply receptacles for the dark urges of their patrons. Their humanity had been crushed under the weight of their circumstances, and every night death came and waited for them in the shadows.

Bennett was a connoisseur of death in all its forms—he dissected it, analyzed it, determined its causes. He flirted with it, toyed with it, challenged it—even partook of it in a way. After a visit to the whores on Thirteenth Street—their lifeless eyes, their mechanical bodies—he would go home to his clean quiet house and his gleaming brass-and-glass shower. He would stand in the shower for a long time, scrubbing the feeling from his skin. Then he would go to bed and wake refreshed, having faced down death's mysteries again.

But he had never met a whore like this one before. In spite of the heavy makeup and the dirt, in spite of the drugs that coursed through her collapsing veins, her eyes were not empty. A spark of life still flashed in the blue depths. She still clung to something in this world.

He thought about mounting this whore's scrawny, dirty body, probably full of crab lice and other, more sinister diseases. He thought about her dirty fingernails with their chipped red polish, digging into his back. He was excited and revolted at the same time. Did he think this woman looked like Jess? She was a parody of Jess, an evil satire of her. *Like something out of a Hogarth drawing,* he mused.

"Look, mister, are you just going to stare at me? Or are we going to do business?" She pulled away from him. Her eyes narrowed as she returned his curious stare.

He pulled a twenty from his pocket and held it up. "Answer a question, and it's yours."

She smiled. "That's better. Whatever makes you happy. Fire away."

"What keeps you going?"

"What kind of a question is that?"

"Just answer me, or I'll find someone who will." He started to slip the money back into his pocket.

"Wait. I didn't say no, did I?" She held his gaze and exhaled a blue cloud of smoke. Bennett smiled and reached back into his pocket, pulling out a second twenty-dollar bill. He held them out to her.

"Okay. You really want to know? I got a daughter. Haven't seen her since she was a baby. But I know she's out there. That's what keeps me going." She lifted her chin with a mixture of pride and anger. "That's all."

Bennett added a fifty to the bills in his hand. "Go on, please."

She shook her head but took another deep inhalation from her cigarette.

"A man picked me up one night after my pimp beat me up. He was a good man. We married and had a kid. It wasn't even his. But he was happy. We were all happy. But my pimp, may he rot in hell, he tracked me down. Said if I didn't come back, he'd hurt my kid, bad. So I left. And never went back. My daughter probably thinks I'm dead. But I did it for her, so she could have a life, okay? Satisfied now?" She grimaced, as if it had hurt her to say it. But she had said it. After all, she was a whore, and it was her job to please.

He handed her the money. "Satisfied."

"You're a weird guy. Hey, I got other ways to satisfy you. Want to hear about them?" She grinned flirtatiously, showing her stained teeth. Bennett felt a chill run through him.

"Nope. Thanks."

He turned and began walking back. He could feel her eyes watching his back as he walked. He heard a car pull up to where the whore was standing. He heard several male voices dicker with her about her price, then the car door opened. It slammed shut and pulled away.

He turned back and looked. She was gone.

He walked slowly home. Preoccupied as he was with the whore and her story, he did not notice the tiny flick of curtains being pushed aside in the house across the street.

He went upstairs to his bedroom and stripped off his clothes, preparing to take his usual shower. Goose bumps rose on his naked flesh.

Someone's watching me, he thought.

He walked to the windows, with their sheer ivory curtains. The street was empty. The houses across the street were dark. Still, he felt as though someone was in the room with him.

He pulled down the shades and walked away from the window into the bathroom. He turned on the shower. He could not hear the cry of rage and frustration that issued from the house across the street.

Kasidy lay on an exam table in what looked like an operating room. The bright light overhead was blinding. She tried to move but realized her arms and legs were strapped down to the table. She was cold and realized she was naked under the sheet that covered her.

A man leaned over her, gowned and masked in surgeon's green. Kasidy could not see his face for the glare.

"Ready, Mamakass?" Bennett's voice echoed in the empty room.

"Bennett! Help me get off this table!" She struggled a little to show that she was restrained.

"Oh, you're not leaving. We're just starting to have fun." Bennett's voice was husky with desire. He yanked the sheet off her body. His hands cupped her breasts. Kasidy gasped with fright—and desire. He pulled his mask down and began kissing her, working his way down her neck, leaning over the table as he suckled her breast, hard. His hands stroked her smooth belly and traveled down between her splayed legs. His fingers stroked her soft wetness.

Kass forgot her fear. She groaned and arched her hips. Bennett straightened up.

"Are you ready?" he whispered.

"Oh, yes. Yes. Undo me so I can touch you." She moaned.

"Scalpel, please," said Bennett, and Kass heard an instrument being slapped into his hand. She screamed and struggled in earnest now against the bonds that held her wrists and ankles to the cold metal table.

Bennett held up the silvery knife in his left hand, so that she could see it. He grinned at her—his easy, handsome smile—and rammed the scalpel in between her legs, plunging it deep inside her. Blood spouted up in great pulsing arcs, like a fountain. She could feel the drops pattering down on her belly and legs, hot and sticky. Pain tore at her with steel teeth and claws. Bennett pushed the scalpel in deeper, twisting it, and she could feel her insides shredding and ripping under the steel blade.

Kasidy woke up screaming.

A few miles northwest of Kass's bedroom, Susie Troutman also woke up screaming.

"What? What is it, baby?" Heather Troutman stroked Susie's tousled hair as she knelt beside her bed.

"A man with a knife. He was cutting Miss Becky. Right here!!" Susie pointed to the doll's belly, then clutched it close again. "The man wore doctor clothes, and Miss Becky couldn't get away. He was hurting her. There was blood everywhere!" Susie began to sob hysterically.

"Baby, it was only a dream. Miss Becky's okay, see? Look." Heather gently took the doll from Susie's arms and held it up to show her. "Nothing's wrong now. Try to go back to sleep now." She handed the doll back to Susie, who clutched it convulsively.

"But, Mommy, I'm scared. What if the bad doctor man tries to come back and hurt Miss Becky again?"

Heather gazed at her daughter's pale face, pinched with terror. She put her arms around her and patted her back, trying to soothe her. "Honey, he won't come back because it was just a dream. And even if he does, you'll protect Miss Becky. You're a big brave girl, and you're not afraid of any old doctor bogeyman, are you?"

Susie thought a moment. "No, Mommy," she said. She hiccuped and wiped her nose on the sheet. "I'll protect Miss Becky 'cause she's my friend forever."

"Good girl. Now go night-night, and I'll see you in the morning. We'll go up to church, and you can tell St. Jude all about your dream." Heather got up and left the room, leaving the door ajar so that Susie could see the night-light in the bathroom.

"Fucking bogeyman doctors. Where the hell did that come from?" Heather muttered as she went back to her own room.

THREE

Susie knelt in front of the statue of St. Jude. It was tucked into an alcove about halfway down the side of the chapel, near the beautifully painted statue of Mary. She liked St. Jude the best because he helped her find things, and also because he had a gentle face.

She laid the bunch of dandelions she had picked on the way to St. Laurence's at the statue's feet. "Hi, O Blessed St. Jude. It's me, Susie Troutman. Thanks for helping me find stuff this week. Especially Miss Becky. And thanks for taking care of Jessie-ka Grasia for me even though she doesn't believe in you anymore." She could hear Heather fidgeting impatiently behind her. "I had a real bad dream last night, and Mommy said to tell you about it. It was about a bad doctor man who cut Miss Becky." Susie's voice dropped to a whisper. "Mommy said it was only a dream, but I think it was real. It felt real, anyway. Like the things I know sometimes, and then Mommy and Jess look at me funny, like I'm not supposed to know." She looked up at the statue's face. "If it *is* a real thing, let me know 'cause I'm Miss Becky's forever friend, and I have to help her." She raised her voice again. "Mommy wants to sit down, so I have to go. I'll talk to you some more later. Hallelujah and amen." Susie got up and turned to her mother. "It's okay now. We can sit down."

They slipped into a pew near the front. Heather would have preferred the back of the church, but Susie liked to be able to see the priest and the altar boys perform the ancient rituals that were part of the Catholic Mass. She also liked being one of the first in line for Communion.

"What is it with you and St. Jude, Suz?" Heather whispered to her daughter.

"I like him. He's got a nice face. And he helps me find stuff. Did you know he was Jesus's cousin? And he's the patron saint of hospitals and people like Jessie."

Heather had to smile. "Well. I'll have to tell the sisters that you're paying attention in class." She stroked Susie's baby-fine, straight hair.

"I *always* pay attention. I don't want to get in trouble like that bad Ryan Feeney does. Sister Hubert almost hit him with a ruler one time. Did you know in the old days the teachers were allowed to hit you?"

"You get in trouble in school, you'll be in trouble at home, too, young lady," Heather said severely, but her eyes were smiling. She knew Susie would never misbehave in school.

"I know, Mommy." She fixed Heather with her direct gray gaze. "Something bad is going to happen. To Miss Becky. And me and Jess, too. I asked St. Jude to help me figure it out."

Heather sighed irritably. Susie had a way of knowing

things when you didn't want to explain them. She couldn't lie in church, so she said, "What makes you think something bad is going to happen? Where do you get these ideas, anyway?"

Susie did not drop her gaze. "Mommy, I just know." Then she sat back in the pew and looked at the ornate golden crucifix at the altar. Rainbow light from the stained glass windows made colored splotches on her brown hair. Heather just stared at her daughter in the multicolored light as the priest began the Mass.

Bennett had driven up to the northeast early, where the old city of Philadelphia began to meet modern suburbia, with its strip malls and ample free parking. He had a lot of preparation to do before Friday. His first stop was a Kmart, where he loaded two carts with the necessary items.

"Wow, man, you must be planning some camping trip there," said the kid at the register. "You with the Boy Scouts or something?"

Bennett smiled. "Or something."

The pin on the kid's red Kmart vest read SCOTT. "Man, when I was a kid I loved those Scout camping trips. Where're you going?"

"French Creek," replied Bennett. "When did you stop being a kid? Last year?"

It was Scott's turn to smile. "Okay, five Coleman coolers and one bag of Dog Chow comes to $167.38."

Bennett paid cash, and Scott helped him fit them back into the carts.

"Hope it don't rain on you, man."

Bennett loaded up his black Lexus. One of the coolers had to go in the backseat. He spread an old sheet over what was left of the backseat and swung out onto Cottman Avenue.

His next stop was the Humane Society. It was an ugly, prisonlike building on Erie Avenue. When he walked inside, a raucous cacophony of barking, squealing, and growling assaulted his ears.

"I'd like to adopt a dog," he said to the woman behind the counter.

"Through that door and to your left," she replied. She was in her fifties, and her face was set in a permanent frown. Her red lipstick was slowly melting into the lines cut deeply into her upper lip and the corners of her mouth.

Bennett entered the kennel. There he walked up and down the rows of dog pens, with the dogs inside looking like prisoners in a cellblock. They were a pitiful bunch. Some cowered, terrified and uncomprehending, in a corner of their pen. Some snarled angrily as he passed, as if it were his fault they were there. Some just barked endlessly, squeaking and wagging their tails as he passed by the wire mesh that separated them. Finally, he found what he was looking for.

He stopped in front of a pen. The dog inside was a big Labrador/Shepherd mix. She was black and solid, like a Lab, but had the erect ears and graceful muzzle of a Shepherd. An interesting combination, Bennett thought. She sat quietly on her haunches and gazed calmly at him with her soft, intelligent brown eyes. He read the card in the slot on the gate of the kennel.

"So, your name is Lady, eh?" Lady thumped her tail on the concrete in assent. Lady was approximately two years old. Her owner had relocated and was unable to take her. She had been spayed and obedience-trained. Bennett nodded.

Lady walked over to the gate. Bennett extended a finger through the wire mesh, and Lady licked it. Then she stepped back and regarded him with dignity.

"All right, Lady. You'll do fine."

Bennett filled out the adoption papers and paid the fee. He plunked down another five dollars for a leash and snapped it onto Lady's collar. The woman behind the counter smiled at him for the first time.

"She's a love, Lady is. The man who had her before was old, and he hadda move to his daughter's in Jersey. She didn't want no dogs. You shoulda seen him when he left her—crying like a baby." The permanent frown returned to her face. She sighed. Then she said to Bennett, "I hope Lady's found a good home."

"I'll take good care of Lady," Bennett assured her. "I need a dog just like her."

He bundled Lady into the backseat of the car and put the window down. They cruised down I-95 back to Bennett's house, Lady hanging her head out the back window, her tongue flopping idiotically in the wind. He parked the car in the garage he rented around the corner. She walked to his house in a perfect heel position, not stopping to sniff or piddle on the enticing trees that lined Spruce Street. He opened his front door and let her in. She sniffed around the tiny kitchen, ambled into the living room, hopped up onto the cream leather sofa, and fell asleep. Bennett watched her. She was obedient, but not cringing or overly docile. Lady had a mind of her own. He grinned mirthlessly. *That'll make it easy,* he thought. *I've had enough of females with minds of their own.* He walked over to the sofa and patted Lady's silky head.

"Make yourself at home, Lady. You won't be here long enough to get too many dog hairs on my sofa." The dog looked at him but did not wag her tail or respond. She merely tolerated his caress.

He went upstairs to his room and sat down at the computer. He had some e-mails to send.

Susie and Heather walked up to the altar to receive Communion. The priest held the transparent white wafers on a golden plate as the parishoners knelt along the railing, their faces upturned. Each in turn opened their mouth, and the priest placed the wafer on their tongue, where it dissolved.

Susie leaned toward Heather. "Sister Hubert says that Communion actually turns into the body of Jesus in your mouth," she whispered. "Is it true, Mommy?"

Heather looked down into Susie's wide eyes. "Yeah, Suz, it's true. And the wine becomes the blood of Jesus. That way you get to partake of the Holy Spirit, and that helps you to be good. Next year you'll have your First Communion, and then you'll get to do it, too."

Susie looked uncertain. Heather stroked her hair and cast a look at Father Romano, who was drawing nearer to them. "It's okay, honey. Don't get weird on me now, baby."

Susie watched as her mother opened her mouth and accepted the tasteless wafer.

"This is My body you eat," intoned Father Romano.

Heather swallowed.

"Body and blood," Susie whispered to herself and shuddered.

Since she no longer attended Mass, Jess spent her Sunday mornings cleaning. She had just finished vacuuming the threadbare carpets when Susie came in through the back door. She ran over to Jess and hugged her.

"Hey, Pickle. How's St. Jude this morning?" Jess smiled at Susie's fresh, happy face.

"He's fine. I told him to take care of you even though you don't believe in him anymore," replied Susie.

"Well, thanks for that," Jess replied wryly. She had awakened feeling empty and terribly alone. She missed the church—the beautiful hymns, the sense of peace that filled her during Mass, and the chitchat and fellowship with her neighbors afterward. She had thought about going that morning. But she could not pray to a God that would so cruelly take her father from this world. So she stayed home and used her emotional energy on the furniture, polishing it until it gleamed.

"When are you going to stop being mad at God?" asked Susie. Her eyes searched Jess's face with an expression that made her look far older than her six years. "God loves you. He hasn't forgotten you. You should come back to St. Laurence's if you miss it so much."

"Suz, I really don't want to talk about it right now. Stop reading my mind," Jess said irritably.

"I can't help it," Susie said, a little defensively.

"You are definitely psychic," sighed Jess.

"Like those people on TV that cost ninety-five cents a minute? Except you have to be eighteen to call?"

"Better than them," said Jess firmly.

Susie looked up at the photograph of a seven-year-old Jess, dressed in a lacy white First Communion dress, a gold cross around her neck. "Did you eat Jesus's body and drink his blood?"

"What?" Jess followed Susie's gaze. "Oh. Well, yeah, sort of. That's what Communion is. A sacrament so you can share in the Holy Spirit."

"A sac-er-a-ment," Susie repeated slowly. She stood, staring at the picture. Jess shook her head, wondering what was going on in Susie's head.

"Where's your mom?"

"Lying down. She says she's tired. Will you take me to the park and watch me swing?"

"In a little bit. Let me finish here," said Jess.

"Okay," said Susie. She found a dust rag and followed Jess around the house, dusting and chattering about St. Jude and Father Romano and the neighbors she'd seen at church. Jess listened to her prattle, grateful for the sound of another voice. She realized that she was tired of being lonely.

I guess Heather's right, Jess thought. Maybe it is time to get a life.

* * *

Herb brought the kids home. He usually came in, but this time he just dropped them off. *I guess he was afraid I'd freak out on him again,* Kass thought. The kids came in with wary faces and were visibly relieved when Kass swept them into a big bear hug.

"How are you guys? Did you have a good time with Dad and Lou?"

"Sure. Dad and I went to the movies Saturday. *Godzilla, Part Two,*" said Sam.

"Yuck," said Karen. "Lou took me shopping and got me these cool overalls." She spun around with her hand on her hip, like a runway model wearing a ten-thousand-dollar Chanel original.

"That's great, you two. Now go do your homework while I get dinner ready," Kass said.

Karen lingered for a moment. "What did *you* do this weekend, Mom?"

"I had a date Saturday night."

"I knew it!" Karen said gleefully. "I could tell. Who is he, and where did you go?"

"We went to a new restaurant on South Street. He's one of the people in my online support group."

Karen's face changed. "Mom, you have to be careful with these online people. You even said yourself. I know a girl who met a guy online. He said he was a kid her age, and she went to meet him face to face. It turned out he was an older guy—like twenty—and he practically raped her in his car. It was on the news even."

"It's not like that. I met him in a public place and didn't go anywhere with him." *Not that I didn't think about it,* she thought ruefully.

"Mom, check him out. Please? And if he does check out okay, I want to meet him."

"You want to check him out, too, huh?"

"Absolutely." Karen's worried expression softened. "I hope he *is* for real. It'd be so cool to have your mom hanging with someone she met on the Net."

"God forbid you should have an uncool mom," Kass said dryly. "Now go do your homework." Karen gave her mother a quick hug and ran up the stairs to her room.

Kass shook her head in wonder. That was the nicest conversation she'd had with Karen in months. She touched the e-mail note she'd printed out and put in her pocket. Bennett had written:

> Hey Mamakass, thanks for the great evening last night. Haven't had such a good time since Syl broke her leg skiing. <EG>.
> Seriously, you are one terrific lady. Can we do it again on Friday?
> B.

The note had made her day. Of course she had sent back an agreement, and included her phone numbers. Now her kids were in good moods, actually glad to see their old mom. Life is good, thought Kass. Then she shivered.

"Guess someone just walked over my grave," she said, and shivered again.

POUR

MONDAY

Kass looked up and down the row of food carts parked along Chestnut Street. One of the fixtures of Center City Philadelphia was the street vendors, selling everything from hot dogs to falafel. She found the brightly painted converted panel truck that belonged to Konstantin, who made bitter, strong coffee that could revive the comatose. When he saw her approaching he grinned broadly, his teeth shining white and even under his black moustache.

"You are glowing today, Miss Kasidy. You have a lover." It was a statement.

"Maybe," chuckled Kass.

"Ah, why you not wait for me? I needed only the perfect moment to ask."

Kass laughed. She watched him move around the inside of the cramped truck, smelling the aromas of good Greek coffee, garlic, oregano, and cinnamon. He put the coffee on the truck's window ledge and snapped the white plastic lid down on top. She reached into her purse.

"No charge today. A gift. Because you are happy."

"Thanks! Save me some spanakopita for lunch, okay?"

"Anything for you, Miss Kasidy."

When she walked into the office, Mitch looked at her with a grin. "You have an admirer," he said.

Kass stopped in her tracks. Her eyes were wide with amazement.

"How do you know?"

Mitchell gestured grandly at her desk. On it were twenty-four perfect red roses in a crystal vase. A small card was propped against the bottom of the vase.

"Who is it? Do I know him?" Mitch asked.

"Not unless you hang around morgues. Do you mind? I'd like to read the card." Kass picked up the little envelope.

"Our Kass is dating a stiff," Mitch laughed. "Jeez, nobody sends *me* flowers like that. Living or dead." He walked down the hall to his office.

Kass waved her hand to disperse the aroma of Mitch's cologne and then stopped. On a day like this she could even almost like him. She read the card.

Happy Monday, sweet Mamakass! Four more days . . . Bennett.

She grinned. *How did I ever get so lucky?* she wondered. She smelled the faint, hothouse fragrance and looked at the flowers spraying out of the vase in a profusion of red. Suddenly she remembered the dream. Her blood, spurting out from between her legs in dark crimson arcs. Just like these roses.

A warning from the subconscious. Or maybe God.

Now where did that idea come from? *Warnings, my ass,* she thought. *Bennett's a wonderful, sweet, caring man.* She reached out and brushed her fingertips against one of the tightly furled roses, feeling its moist silkiness. Still the image troubled her.

I am not going to let a stupid bad dream ruin this for me, she decided. She began rearranging the roses, bunching them closer together. She smiled, satisfied with her new bouquet. Two of the secretaries approached her desk to admire her flowers, and she laughed as they teased her about her Prince Charming.

Heather was waiting for Jess outside the tall office building on Chestnut Street. She was dressed in the khaki slacks and man-tailored shirt she wore for her job as a technician for a computer-networking consultant. She had become so thin that the clothes just hung on her body. Her long hair was held back with a suede hairband, and she was wearing red lipstick. It looked garish against her gray skin. She dropped her cigarette and stepped on the butt as Jess approached, threading her way through the lunchtime crowds.

"You still want to do this, right?" said Heather by way of greeting.

"Yes, Heather, I do," she replied firmly. She hugged Heather, who briefly returned the hug, and they went up to the lawyer's offices.

Forty-five minutes later, they emerged from the building. Heather was grinning. "Well, girl, when I croak, you'll be a mom."

"Heather, don't talk like that. It gives me the creeps." Jess shuddered.

"Hey, speaking of creeps, I got something to tell you. You sure you never said nothing to Susie about me?"

"Yes, not one word." They walked over to a hot dog vendor's pushcart.

"Saturday night she had the most bizarre dream. She dreamed a doctor was cutting up her Miss Becky doll.

She woke up screaming like hell. I never saw her so scared. I thought for a minute she was going to pee the bed. Then yesterday in church Susie tells me she knows something bad is going to happen. You know how she is sometimes. But this was just too weird."

Jess got two hot dogs with mustard and sauerkraut and a Pepsi. Heather got a Mountain Dew and lit a Marlboro, and they sat down on a sunny bench along the street.

"Susie's never had nightmares before?" asked Jess with her mouth full.

"Not like this one. And it was so bizarre that the bad guy was a doctor. Do you tell her about the stuff you do?"

"No," said Jess. "I'd never tell her anything to scare her."

Heather frowned. "Suz likes her pediatrician okay. And Dr. Shirk always makes a big fuss over her when she goes to my appointments with me. And they're both women. Susie's never seen a male doctor. I don't get it."

Jess said cautiously, "I don't think she likes Dr. Shirk much. Maybe she blames her somehow for you being sick."

"That's possible. Well, she slept okay last night. Practically had to drag her out of the bed this morning. Like she had taken a sleeping pill or something. If that kid's been getting into my pills, I'll fucking kill her."

"Susie wouldn't do that," Jess assured her.

"I know." Heather drained her soda and tossed the can into a nearby trash can. "Still, it worries me. You know how she is with that psychic shit. Kid's never been wrong before."

"Heather, 'bad' to Suz can mean anything. Like that maybe *Miss Becky* will be canceled."

Heather laughed at the feeble joke. "I should be so lucky. Hmm, she did say something bad would happen to Miss Becky. Oh well, back to the salt mines." She turned and looked at Jess. "Thanks. From the bottom of my heart." She reached over and rubbed Jess's chin with her thumb. "Mustard."

Jess smiled. "No problem." Then her smile faded. "Let me know if Susie has any more of these dreams. I'll talk to her."

"Sounds good. See ya tonight." Heather strode down the street. Jess watched her go and saw the little hitch in Heather's stride that meant she was in pain. She frowned a little.

It was true that Susie had yet to be wrong in her predictions. But Susie was only six years old. And everyone knew that psychic stuff wasn't really real . . . didn't they?

Jess's head began to ache. She got up and headed toward the subway station.

Bennett sat down next to Lady, who was curled up in her spot on the sofa. He had almost enjoyed having her for the past twenty-four hours. The lady at the Humane Society had been right—Lady was a love. She had refrained from chewing the furniture or knocking over tables. She had quietly but insistently indicated when she needed a walk. And she had not barked at outside noises, of which there were plenty. It was the price Bennett paid for living in an historic district and a major tourist attraction. She had remained aloof and wary of Bennett, however, and he was beginning to feel a little put off by her detachment.

Now it was time. He had to make sure everything would go smoothly for the Epicurean Society's meeting. He had arranged for china and linens to be delivered to a vacant restaurant on Lombard Street. In the 1970s, it had once been known as Instant Karma, a macrobiotic vegetarian restaurant. At first it had done very well, frequented by college students and health-conscious young singles. Its owners failed to anticipate the coming boom in red meat, fine brandies, and imported cigars now preferred by its former patrons, who had succeeded in business and had different ideas now about the better things in life. It had closed several years ago, and no other restaurateur had taken over the tiny place. The kitchen was well equipped, but the ovens were not large enough for the main course. Bennett would have to prepare that at home.

As a member of the Epicurean Society, he had prepared in advance for the day when he would be called upon. He had built a small, secret room in his basement, fitting it out with an old examination table he "borrowed" from Hahnemann, some medical equipment, a few pharmaceuticals, and a tanning bed. He had replaced the ultraviolet tanning lights with infrared oven elements from a restaurant-supply warehouse. It had been a difficult and tedious job, and he had not yet tested it.

He had selected Lady to be the test subject based on her size. She was only half the size of Kasidy Rhodes, but if Bennett's oven didn't work with Lady, he'd have to think of another method. He badly wanted the main course to be presented effectively. At previous meetings, the main course had been goulashes, casseroles, and seven- to ten-pound roasts. Each dish had been tasty and excellently prepared, but Bennett had always felt that disguising the meat like that diminished the true meaning of the meetings. He was determined to graphically remind everyone exactly what it was they were doing. Which was partaking of death. And the nature of the deceased.

Those selected to grace the Society's altars had to be admirable, possessed of intelligence and grace, of beauty and youth. Females were preferred because of the life-giving essence of woman. They had to be someone you would want to embrace, perhaps to love in life.

Bennett absently stroked Lady, scratching her ears. *Perhaps it comes from the atavistic human desire to touch our gods,* he mused. Long ago, humans created idols from clay and stone, to make manifest the objects of their worship. Today the notion of God as an unseen, pervasive force is a sophisticated one. But the urge to touch, to be physically close still exists. Celebrities who ventured out in public without a bodyguard were apt to be loved to death by their fans, who wanted to touch them, to get a piece of them. Tabloid newspapers and websites did this by proxy, as if knowledge of every detail of the human idols' lives was a form of contact.

He thought about groupies, those camp followers of the rich and famous. The naïve, emotionally intense young women who bedded rock stars and actors, even artists and writers, hoping that a bit of the glitter or genius would rub off on them.

The Society answered that need in a unique way. You selected someone who had goodness and genius, and consumed them in the most literal way, ingesting their essence. Bennett remembered how he savored the sweetbread course served at the banquets. The brain was where it all happened. The knowledge that their last living memory was of a beautiful, blinding white light and soft consoling voices, was an added spice for him.

Perhaps some in the Society might regard these banquets as an extreme gourmet experience, a breaking of the ultimate taboo. For Bennett it was a holy ritual. Literally consuming another human being was just another way of exploring the thin curtain that separated life and death. And there were other forms of consuming people as well. Such as sex.

The raddled whores on Thirteenth Street were walking dead. When Bennett used them he felt like he was challenging death. Thrusting in and out of their hot dark wetness was like a dance with fate. So far, Bennett was the victor.

"Come on, girl," he said pleasantly to Lady. She obediently hopped off the sofa and followed him down to the basement. He opened the door to the little room and ushered Lady in.

He closed the door behind them.

* * *

When Jess ran up the subway steps that evening, she heard a voice calling "Hi, Jessie!"

She groaned inwardly. Then she pasted a smile on her face and turned and waved. "Hi, Dr. Shirk!"

A woman hurried toward her with almost mincing steps. "How are you, Jessie? I haven't seen you in an age. And how is Bennett?"

"He's fine. I'm just on my way down."

"Did he get my card? What did he say?" Meredith's pale blue eyes glittered.

Jess empathized with Susie in her dislike of Dr. Meredith Shirk. Dr. Shirk was thin and wiry, with an intense gaze. She had bright red hair that she wore cut short in an almost masculine style. Her huge, slightly protuberant eyes were practically colorless, and her skin milky and translucent. Her lips were full and pale, and looked a little strange in her thin face. Her face reminded Jess of a fox's—it had a vulpine cast, a sinister craftiness to it. She knew Meredith was kind to her only because she worked with Bennett, and she knew that was the same reason that Meredith was so devoted to Heather's case.

Jess replied carefully, "I saw it on his desk on Friday, but he didn't say anything except that it was from you. A thank-you card."

Meredith looked disappointed. "I spent an hour in the card shop picking out the perfect card, and he doesn't say anything about it?" Her eyes narrowed. *She looks really angry,* Jess realized.

Then Meredith grinned, a shade too brightly. "Oh well, you were probably very busy, and he didn't get a chance to tell you how much he liked it. I miss our little chats, Jessie. We should get together for coffee soon. Your friend Heather is coming in next week, and I have some questions for you."

"I will if I can, Dr. Shirk. We're really busy these days."

"I'm sure Bennett keeps you hopping. Tell him I said hello and that maybe I'll see him later."

Not if he sees you first. "Sure thing, Dr. Shirk." Jess nearly ran for the entrance, barely suppressing a shudder.

When Heather was first diagnosed with non-Hodgkin's, Jess had set up the appointment with Dr. Shirk. She knew Dr. Shirk was one of the best cancer specialists in the city, and she wanted only the best for Heather. Jess had accompanied Heather to her first appointment.

She had waited with Heather in the exam room. Meredith Shirk had opened the door and strode in with her choppy gait.

"Mrs. Troutman," she had said brusquely, not even looking up from the chart. Then she had seen Jess standing next to the table, holding Heather's hand.

"Oh! I know you. You're Bennett Sykes's lab tech, aren't you? Jessica, right? How are you?"

The businesslike demeanor changed instantly to an almost fawning interest. Jess took pains to imply that not only was Heather her friend, but that Bennett Sykes had an interest in Heather's particular case. *Whatever it takes,* Jess had thought at the time. And it had worked. Jess knew that Heather had the best care possible from Dr. Shirk.

But she paid a price for it. Meredith used Heather's case as a pretext to talk to Jess, but she would pump her for gossip and information about Bennett. At first Jess had thought it was funny—it was so hopeless, after all—and had obligingly rehashed the hospital scuttlebutt over coffee with Dr. Shirk. But it gradually became apparent that Dr. Shirk's "crush" was more like an obsession. She began asking Jess to take cards and little presents to Bennett, and questioning her relentlessly about his reaction. *How did he like it? Did she think he really liked it or was he just being polite? What did he say about her?* Jess became increasingly uncomfortable, and tried to get out of her unwanted role as go-between.

"Why don't you just take it to him yourself, Dr. Shirk?"

"Oh, I couldn't do that, Jess," she would reply, giggling. "It would be too forward of me."

"Don't you think this is kind of junior high school stuff?"

"Maybe I'll get him a little something for his office," Meredith said, completely ignoring Jess's question. "A nice amethyst geode for his desk. What do you think?"

One night, after Jess handed Bennett a coffee mug with a stuffed animal in it—another gift from Meredith—he frowned.

"Jess, I have a favor to ask you."

"Sure, Dr. Sykes. What is it?"

"Don't bring me anything more from Dr. Shirk. Don't talk to her about me, don't mention my name to her."

Jess's face flushed. "I'm sorry."

Bennett smiled wryly. "Jess, I know she has a thing for me. I won't be rude to her—not only do I have to work with her, but she's my neighbor, too. She lives in an apartment right across the street from me. You know, sometimes I think she's watching me, like I'm a goldfish in a bowl."

"Really? That's creepy." Jess shivered a little.

"I have my suspicions. But I can't tell her off—and I can't let her think I'm encouraging her in any way, either."

"Umm . . . what should I tell her? I mean, she started being nice to me when Heather went to her for the lymphoma. I don't want to . . ." Jess's voice trailed off.

"Jess, Dr. Shirk is a professional. How she treats a patient should have nothing to do with you. If it does, you tell me, and I'll talk to the administration. In the meantime, don't tell her anything. Just avoid her."

"Okay. No problem." Jess looked at him. "What do you think would happen if you told her what you just told me? I sure wouldn't waste time on someone who didn't want me."

Bennett sighed. "There's something strange about her. I feel like if I told her to hit the road, she'd probably try to carve her initials into me with a dirty scalpel."

Jess tried to laugh, but she knew that there was a spark of truth to what Bennett was saying. Dr. Shirk was getting scarier and scarier.

"I'll stay out of her way from now on," she had said.

"That's my girl," Bennett replied.

Jess walked down the corridor to Bennett's office. The fragrance of Colombian coffee filled the corridor. The scent was not marred by any foul stenches tonight. There was always a faint aroma of formaldehyde and rot down by the morgue, but she was used to that. She poked her head around the door.

Bennett was on the phone. "Well, Mamakass, I've got to get to work. Glad you liked the flowers. See you Friday, pretty lady. Bye."

Jess's mouth widened into a grin. "Wow, you met someone you liked enough to send flowers to? That's great, Dr. Sykes." Bennett returned her grin and wheeled around in his chair to pour them some coffee. He was dressed in a black T-shirt and jeans. As he turned, Jess noticed the bandage wrapped tightly around his upper arm.

"What happened to you?" she asked.

"I adopted a dog from the Humane Society yesterday. They told me she was a good dog, and she was. Until I went to walk her today. Fucking dog—excuse my French—bit me and took off down the street." He grimaced as he replaced the pot on the burner.

"Shouldn't you have someone look at that?" Jess asked, concerned. She could see bloodstains on the bandage. "I bet you could use some sutures." She reached out to touch his arm. He jerked it back.

"No, Jessie, it'll be fine," he said sharply. He stood up and put on his lab coat. Jess was startled. He had never spoken to her that way before.

Bennett saw the expression on her face. He smiled ruefully, as if sorry that he scared her.

"It only hurts when I take out the trash," he said lightly, trying to make her smile.

Jess changed the subject. "So, tell me about your new friend."

The old grin came back. "What makes you think she's a friend? How do you know she's not some stiff I sent flowers to?"

Jess laughed. Bennett was back to normal. "Well, Doctor, it wouldn't surprise me. Nothing like taking your work home with you, I guess."

"You know what they say about necrophilia. They don't kiss and tell." Jess groaned at the joke as he looked over the schedule. "Looks like a quiet night tonight in Forensics Land."

Forensics Land was usually either wildly busy or excruciatingly slow. Jess liked it when it was busy—it kept her from thinking too much. But she had come to enjoy the quiet nights, when she and Bennett would talk over endless cups of good coffee while the rest of the world slept. He was fascinated by his work, and Jess enjoyed listening to him expound on the detective work of forensics and how thin the line was between life and death.

"What do you think happens to someone after they die?" he had asked her one night.

"They go to heaven or hell. Or purgatory."

"That's the Christian idea. But what if there is no afterlife?"

"Then you're just . . . dead, I guess."

"But then what about their essence, their soul, if you will? Don't you agree that there is something about humans that sets them apart from other forms of life?"

"Well, I know that humans are the only beings with self-consciousness. We feel ashamed and guilty when we do a wrong thing. Animals don't have that."

"Spoken like a true Catholic girl. You have that shame and guilt thing practically woven into your DNA. So . . . then what happens when people die? Do you think their souls become part of the world, part of you perhaps?"

"Like the Holy Spirit or something?"

"Or the collective unconscious, or Atman, which is what the Hindus call it."

"Umm . . . yeah. I guess it makes sense, if there's no heaven or hell. I mean, people are energy, right? And that energy has to go somewhere."

"That's what I'm trying to figure out. What happens to this energy, and how can we acquire it."

"You should have been a philosopher instead of a pathologist," Jess had said, her hands curled around her third cup of coffee.

"But then how would I get hands-on experience?" he had asked, grinning.

"I don't get it," she said thoughtfully. "You're the head of the pathology department here. You've had tons of papers published. You're obviously brilliant and everything. Why do you work these crazy night shifts?"

"To be with you, my dear," he had replied lightly.

"Yeah, right," she had snorted.

She never suspected that he was telling the truth. He had been drawn to her ever since he first saw her, dressed in baggy greens, prepping a cadaver for an autopsy. Jess was so unlike his ex-wife—the gorgeous, social-climbing Sylvia. He had married Sylvia for two reasons—she had important connections through her family, and because she was the sexiest woman he had ever met. She came from a Main Line family with more pedigree than money, but she knew everyone worth knowing in Philadelphia. A young, ambitious doctor could use connections, particularly in the city. There were several huge, world-famous hospitals that offered unparalleled research opportunities—if you knew the right people.

He had met Sylvia at a charity party for Hahnemann Hospital. She had been wearing a strapless scarlet velvet gown that showed off her magnificent breasts, and elbow-length kid gloves. Her hair was long and red, and styled in Botticelli waves that rolled over her shoulders. Bennett had been blindsided by lust almost immediately. Apparently she had, too, for she had walked over and introduced herself only minutes after she arrived.

"Are you here by yourself tonight?" she had asked, standing just a little too close. Bennett could smell her perfume, exotic and expensive.

"Yes, I am," he had replied, trying to think of something charming to say and coming up blank.

"Are you married?"

"No."

"How wonderful!" She had tucked her arm into his and pressed against him. He could feel her right breast against his arm. His knees almost buckled.

That night, Bennett had seen nothing but Syl's beautiful face and voluptuous curves. The fact that Sylvia's conversation never went beyond what something cost, or who designed it, completely escaped him at the time.

That night, he tipped the limo driver fifty dollars to take the long way home. His hands were all over her, and hers all over him, before the driver even got the door closed. Just before he entered her, he had leaned back to look at her, sprawled flat on the backseat with her long skirts pushed up around her waist, her breasts freed from the low-cut gown, the huge perfect nipples wet with sweat and his own kisses. But her elbow-length gloves were still immaculate, as was her diamond-and-ruby necklace, which was heavy enough to choke a horse.

The blood roared in his ears.

"I want to marry you," he had said hoarsely.

"Yes, yes, yes," she had sighed deliriously and pulled him back down to her.

The driver really did take his time driving home, because he was able to have her twice before they got there.

So Bennett found himself engaged to be married to someone he had known for approximately six hours. Her family reluctantly approved the match, feeling that Bennett's depleted inheritance and lack of social connections could be amended by his charm and ambition. The wedding had been one of the social events of the season—splashy, ostentatious, but attended by everyone who was anyone in Philadelphia.

Bennett hated his in-laws, whom he perceived as shallow, money-obsessed, and boring. Sylvia's mother was officious and interfering—the mother-in-law from hell.

But Sylvia had enjoyed being a doctor's wife, and her family connections were indeed useful in the insular little world of the Philadelphia hospitals. These connections, coupled with Bennett's own abilities, guaranteed the opportunities he wanted to pursue his pathology studies and culminated in his being appointed head of the pathology department at Hahnemann Hospital. For a time he enjoyed himself immensely, doing the work he loved during the day and exploring Sylvia's rich and exquisite body at night.

For her part, Sylvia adored appearing at charity functions, expensively and provocatively gowned, on the arm of her handsome husband. Having her picture on the Society page in the newspaper the next morning thrilled her. They made a striking couple and were happy for a time.

But as Bennett's obsessions with pathology, with life and death, deepened, he had pulled away from her. He began to find Syl mercurial and dull. She sensed his withdrawal and went on the offensive. She shrilly demanded that he be more involved with her. She wanted a bigger house. She talked of a baby. She accepted more invitations. Finally, Bennett had had enough. One night at dinner, he announced that he would be working nights at the hospital. Seven P.M. to seven A.M., four or five nights a week.

"You'll have to find someone else to go with you to all these stupid, pointless social things. God, Syl, you should ask me before you accept."

Sylvia stared at him. Then she erupted. "It was never a problem before. You were always ready to go. Damn it, Ben, what's wrong with you? You're the head of the department. You don't have to work nights. That stuff is for interns and residents." Her eyes filled with tears—the touching, perfect tears of a professional actress. "You're never home, you never talk to me anymore, you don't want to have a baby. Don't you love me anymore?"

He looked at her sulky, petulant face, the crocodile tears brimming in her brown eyes. Jessica Grasia's pale delicate face rose into his mind. He had just seen Jess in the autopsy room the other day. She had been sobbing into a surgical drape. When he asked her what was wrong, she had blurted out the story of her father's grisly death. Her tears had been genuine, her grief profound. He had put his arms around her to comfort her. She had pressed her face against his chest and trembled like a child. He could feel her slender body against his, smell her freshness. Bennett had made a decision then and there.

He met Sylvia's gaze with a level stare of his own.

"Shut up," he replied coldly.

Sylvia flinched. Then her eyes narrowed.

"What's her name, Ben? What's the little slut's name? Is she one of those floozy nurses down there? I'll fucking kill her!" Sylvia swept her loaded plate onto the floor, where it shattered all over the Mexican ceramic tiles. She looked at Bennett, challenging him to react.

He stood up abruptly, as if to come around the table. Sylvia looked at him smugly. She had gotten a reaction after all. They would fight some more, and maybe he'd even try to hit her. Then they'd go upstairs, and she'd fuck his brains out. In the morning, he'd change his mind. Maybe he'd even buy her an expensive present. That was the way it always worked before.

She met his eyes. Something there made her blood freeze in her veins.

Bennett wasn't thinking about Sylvia at all. He was remembering the Epicurean Society banquet. It had been a wonderful evening, full of mystery. The decrepit old house in the seedy neighborhood that had opened up to reveal such elegance. The Society members, who were introduced to him with what were obviously not their real names. Immediately, he responded with a made-up name of his own. He had recognized one or two from Sylvia's charity parties, but wisely refrained from indicating he did. Israel had warned him not to ask any questions, but to listen and enjoy. And he had.

At the end of the banquet, Israel requested that Bennett go to the kitchen and close the door behind him. Bennett had, taking his brandy and cigar, and stood by the window that looked out over the backyard. It was broken, and a corner of the board had been ripped away. He looked out over the ruin of a formal garden, now full of garbage and truck tires, trash, crack vials, and hypodermic needles. He could hear the rats scurrying, squeaking, and fighting down in the basement. Yet behind him, in the dining room, was a scene of incredible elegance and civility. He had never felt such a sense of *home* since he was two years old. He closed his eyes and saw the ethereal white light and heard the soft whispers of the lovely voices calling to him, calling him home. He opened his eyes. The garbage and the rats replaced the light and the voices.

"You may come back in, Allen," Israel had called to him.

When Bennett sat down, Israel had handed him a leather portfolio. He had opened it. Inside was the missing page to the Poe manuscript.

"Read it," Israel had commanded. Bennett did. In that

last page the source of the meat course had been revealed
to Bennett.

His eyes had widened. He had tasted the sweetbreads,
the liver, and the slices of roast. He had consumed human
flesh. And he had enjoyed it. He was filled with a mixture
of disgust and amazement. He raised his eyes to Israel's
dark ones, deeply shadowed by the candlelight.

"You have partaken in the ultimate," Israel had
replied. "You become what you eat. And what you ate
was good, no?"

Bennett had nodded dumbly. Over brandy and cigars—
as casually as if the main course had been a pig or a
cow—the theology of the Society was discussed. Essences
and spirits. The infusion of the qualities of the deceased
into the living who had consumed them. The conversation
was as delicious as the food. It was as close to the Answer
as he had ever come, among people who enjoyed ponder-
ing the same questions. By the end of the evening he had
pledged himself to the Society. Israel had grinned with
pleasure.

His mind returned to Sylvia. Now, as he looked at his
wife, he had a sudden image of a roasted Sylvia on the
table, eyes sewn shut and an apple in her mouth, like a pig
at a luau. The idea amused and disgusted him at the same
time. She possessed no spiritual essence that he wanted.
Eating her flesh would probably be poisonous. She was
nothing but a grasping social climber who had outlived her
usefulness to him.

He was unaware that his thoughts were plainly visible
on his face, and it was his expression that frightened
Sylvia. The mixture of contempt and disgust, coupled with
a speculative, measuring stare. He took a step toward her,
flexing his hands.

Sylvia began to tremble as she stared back at this
stranger who used to be her husband.

"Oh, my God! You want to kill me!" She shrieked, a

high raucous sound. "Oh, my God!" Her voice notched even higher.

Bennett was jerked back to reality. Hysterics were rapidly approaching, and the last thing he wanted was Sylvia screaming into the phone to her mother that her husband wanted to kill her. His bitch of a mother-in-law would probably believe her daughter. Plus, the reason for her temper tantrum was more accurate than he cared to admit.

He got up and moved swiftly to Sylvia's side. He put his arms around her.

"I'm sorry, Syl. We should have discussed it before. Tell you what."

"What?" Her voice was lower, but she was rigid in his embrace.

He put his lips next to her ear. For a moment he had an impulse to bite her, to feel her blood rush into his mouth, to rip out her throat with his own teeth and watch her silly, self-centered life pour out all over her precious tile floor. With an effort he controlled himself. Perhaps she could still be useful to him, in her way. He could feel her breasts pressed against his chest, her hips against his. Her body still had magic for him.

"Let's take a vacation. To Aspen. Do some skiing, some snowmobiling. Get to know each other again."

Sylvia turned to him and looked into his eyes. "I don't know if I want to know you anymore, Ben. You scare me. There's something different about you now." She shuddered.

He kissed her. Her lips were stiff and cold. He ran his hands over her body, feeling its warm, supple curves. Her flesh and her fear suddenly and powerfully aroused him.

He led her upstairs and sat her down on the bed. She sat passively, looking at him with blank, rabbity eyes. He unbuttoned her blouse and unfastened her bra. He filled his hands with her breasts. He pushed her back onto the bed and began suckling her. She didn't move or make a sound, just stared at the ceiling. Even her nipples refused to harden against his tongue. Bennett found this lack of response, this complete passivity profoundly exciting. Usually, she thrashed and moaned under his hands and lips. But now she was still, simply allowing him to do what he wanted to her. He pulled off her jeans and her lacy thong underwear, using his fingers to stroke her open, make her wet and ready for him. Finally she let out a soft moan, but she did not move. *She's like the living dead,* he thought as he entered her limp, warm body.

Only then did she wrap her legs around him, pulling him deep inside her. He came explosively. It was the best sex he had ever had with her. It was also the last time he ever had sex with Sylvia.

In the morning, she agreed to go to Aspen.

The marriage ended in Colorado, as he had told Kasidy, when Syl ran off with a young ski instructor. She announced her departure by completely trashing their hotel room while he was off skiing. She tore the bedsheets into strips. She broke the television and the mirrors, and ground the glass shards deep into the carpet. She turned the water on in the bathtub and left it to overflow. She poured nail polish on Bennett's sweaters and smeared lipstick in huge red slashes on his shirts. She took his slacks and jeans and literally tore them in half. Then she draped his ruined clothes over the smashed furniture and walked out, leaving him to pay the bill.

Bennett had been amazed—not that she had left, but at the level of rage it took to do what she did. He had not realized how deeply betrayed she felt, as if she finally figured out how he had been using her and her connections—and the contempt he felt for her.

She hired an expensive lawyer and sued him for divorce on grounds of mental cruelty. Bennett knew that on a certain level he had wronged her, and he did not contest the divorce. But she made him pay dearly, over and over, for his use of her luscious body and her family connections.

Now here was Jess, with her impressionable mind and big blue eyes. Not to mention her long slim legs, gently curving hips, and small, high breasts. But Bennett had learned his lesson regarding lust. First, he wanted to mold Jessie's mind, to be certain that his desires were her desires, his opinions were hers. Only then, after she belonged to him mentally, then it would be time to have her physically. The anticipation would make it so much sweeter. The fact that she was a virgin was an added fillip. He could almost hear her soft cries of ecstasy, feel her legs around his waist, her body arching against his own as he initiated her into the realms of physical pleasure.

But for now, for his baser needs, there was always Thirteenth Street.

He looked at Jess and smiled paternally. "You don't look too disappointed at having nothing to do tonight," he said.

"There's always something in Forensics Land. At least, that's what you keep telling me."

As if on cue, they heard heavy footsteps clicking on the linoleum. Two police officers came in.

"Hi, Dr. Sykes. Got one for you."

A wraithlike, black-clad female figure slipped out of one of the houses on Ashland Street. It crossed the narrow cobblestones and stopped in front of the house that belonged to Bennett Sykes. A large, green plastic trash can sat next to the sloping double doors that led to the basement. The figure undid the clamps that held the lid down and lifted out a white garbage bag. She sat down on the basement doors and untied the bag. Using a small high-intensity flashlight, she examined the contents.

Eggshells. Coffee grounds. Junk mail. The figure plunged its hands in deeper, rummaging. A dress shirt with a frayed collar was retrieved and hugged before being placed on the doors. Apparently, she planned to take it with her when she departed. Old magazines. Used Kleenexes and Q-Tips. Scraps of paper with notes on them in Bennett Sykes's handwriting. These were snatched up and avidly read in the small white beam of the flashlight.

Suddenly the figure dropped a scrap of paper as if it burned her fingers. A gasp of anger and pain came from it. Then it snatched up the paper again and wrapped it in the old shirt. It retied the bag of trash and put it back in the can, jamming down the lid. It darted back across the street, back home.

Meredith Shirk ran up the steps and locked her front door behind her. She threw the shirt on her sofa and turned on the light. She reread the note she had plucked from Bennett's garbage.

Send roses 2 Kass—Kasidy Rhodes, Holmes Fein & Co.
1818 Market St 19103 555-8000
Happy Monday sweet Mamakass 4 more days

The paper trembled in Meredith's hands. It was all so clear now what was going on. Her first love, her only love, was in love with someone else. Someone whom Bennett called "Mamakass" in his chat rooms. Meredith had imagined her as fat and homely, not unlike the original Mama Cass. Bennett of course had taken her out for dinner only because he felt sorry for her. Mamakass was such a whiner. And she had bragged to Meredith about her date! Like she was trying to rub her nose in it! Now Meredith decided that Kass must be gorgeous—slim and sexy—in order for Bennett to fall for her so quickly.

She looked at herself in the mirror next to her front door. She saw her thin, pale face, wiry short-cropped red hair, and colorless eyes. Meredith had never had a boyfriend. She had always been too smart and too weird to attract anyone. She remembered the first and last party she had ever attended. It had been a frat party, during her

freshman year at college. Her roommate had practically
dragged her there, telling her she'd have a wonderful time
once she loosened up.

Loosening up was impossible for the tightly wound
Meredith. Music boomed so loudly that conversation was
nearly impossible. Meredith wasn't any good at small talk
anyway. She despised the taste of alcohol, didn't smoke
weed, and finally found herself sitting at the top of the
stairs, forlornly watching her laughing, shouting, dancing,
drinking classmates below. At least it's a little quieter up
here, she thought.

She could hear noises coming from the rooms on the
second floor. Private parties, she thought bitterly. From a
couple of the rooms came the sound of bedsprings creaking and inarticulate moans. She wondered if anyone would
ever want her that way.

A few of the fraternity members were snorting coke in
the front bedroom. She moved a little closer, eavesdrop-
ping on their conversation. Perhaps she would try to say hi
in a minute. She caught her name being spoken through the
half-open door.

"Who's that girl that came with Cheryl? The skinny
redhead?

"Meredith Shirk. She's in my biology class. What, you
wanna jump her bones or something?"

"Her? Man, she's a woofer. Can't even drink her pretty."
Raucous laughter and dog-barking sounds.

"A double bagger. But only if you gag her, too."

"I've seen her around. She's a real ice queen. Your
dick'd probably freeze off in the middle of it." More laughter. Sounds of sniffling as the powdered coke irritated their
sinuses. They came out of the room, still laughing, and
stopped suddenly when they saw her sitting in the shadows, hugging her knees.

Meredith's cheeks flushed an ugly red. She was humili-
ated and hurt, but her pride would not let her shrink away.

She stared at them with her pale eyes. They stared back at her, as if unsure what they should do. Then they dropped their eyes and filed down the stairs past her in silence. She left after that, running all the way back to her cramped dormitory room, tears running down her cheeks.

She threw herself into her studies, majoring in premed, and graduated at the top of her class. She spent her spare time in the company of her books and her computer. She made no real friends. When she graduated from medical school, her socializing was limited to her patients, professional meetings, and symposiums, where her intelligence was more important than her awkwardness. She decided that she would go to the grave a virgin. Hell, she'd never even been kissed.

Hahnemann Hospital recruited her, a rising star in the field of oncology, specializing in cancers of the lymphatic and endocrine systems. On her first day there, while she was being given the tour, she had met a man in the pathology department.

He had turned to her with a grin that left her speechless. His brown eyes had lifted at the corners. He held out his hand to her. She shook it. It was warm and smooth.

"Hi, Meredith. I'm Bennett Sykes, the head necrophile around here. I've heard a lot about you, and I'm glad you are joining us."

A normal person would have smiled, exchanged pleasantries, and moved on, perhaps remembering Bennett as that "nice guy down in the morgue." But Meredith had never seen such a handsome man, much less heard such a warm speech directed at her from a man. She had fallen instantly and hard.

At the age of thirty-seven, it was her first crush. Because of her age, it was deep and profound. It began innocently enough. She asked her colleagues about him. She read all his professional papers. She learned a little about forensic pathology. She made excuses to see him whenever she had a chance. He was always professionally polite when he saw her, but gently refused her invitations to meet outside the hospital. Instead of being discouraged, her obsession deepened and began eating away at her sanity. She decided that she needed to know everything about him, in order to mold herself into the perfect mate for him.

She found out where Bennett lived. She sought out the couple who lived in the upstairs apartment across the street and offered to pay the rent and moving expenses on a new apartment if they would sublease theirs to her. She watched his comings and goings as avidly as if it were a soap opera. She used her considerable computer skills to unearth personal information, like his Social Security number, his unlisted telephone number, and the legal papers pertaining to his divorce. She found out which chat rooms he frequented when online and followed him there. She had even tried to break into his computer, but was unable to get past his security protocols.

She knew his income, his assets, his debts, where he was born, his mother's maiden name, his medical school grades, his real friends, his cyberfriends. But it still wasn't enough.

Finally, still seeking to satisfy her hunger for information, she began rooting through his trash. She collected worn-out items of his clothing. She knew what magazines he subscribed to, what books he read, where he shopped, what he bought, what he ate. The myriad little details she gleaned from Bennett's garbage made her feel connected to him in a deep and mystical way.

Most of all she treasured anything in Bennett's own handwriting. To her they were windows shining into Bennett's mind, the paper something he had actually touched with his long tapered fingers. She saved each stained scrap in a special keepsake box, to be read again and again, brooded over and treasured.

But this note—this was an insult. After all her devoted attention, her efforts to learn everything about him, to be the perfect woman for him—this was how he repaid her! Sending flowers to some Barbie doll he had met on the Internet. Calling her "sweet." Meredith began to breathe hard, her narrow chest rising and falling, her lips pulled back from her teeth in a horrible grimace. She dropped the note as she seized the mirror with both hands, throwing it on the floor with terrible force. Broken glass shot everywhere. The wooden frame splintered. Meredith snatched up the note again and crumpled the paper in her hand, her nails digging deeply into her palm.

But wait. Undoubtedly this little slut had beguiled him with sex. He had been too blinded by his hormones to see the clear purity of Meredith's devotion, the depth of her love for him. It wasn't his fault. He couldn't help himself, could he? Boys will be boys, after all. The grimace was replaced by a sweet, forgiving smile. If she could send Mamakass packing, wishing she'd never laid eyes on Bennett Sykes, then of course Bennett would turn to her.

He would look at her, finally, with those brown eyes. He would open his arms and say "Meredith, how could I have been so foolish? You're the only one who understands me." He would sweep her into his embrace and never let her go.

She unfolded the hand that clutched the paper scrap. It was bloodstained from the cuts Meredith's nails had opened in her palms. She smoothed it out.

"So, you're Mamakass. Well, let me see what else I can find out about you, you bitch." She went upstairs to the computer—and her new keyboard—and began to piece together a dossier on Kasidy Rhodes.

"Your basic homeless drunk. Found him dead in Suburban Station an hour or so ago. No sign of foul play. Just another poor bastard who drank himself to death."

Jess shuddered. She had heard about where the homeless lived, under the tracks of the train station, in black and forbidding warrens full of rats. The noise from the commuter trains and the stench of excrement and vomit had made her think that hell could not be much worse than that. But it was dry and warm down there, and to the homeless that was all that mattered.

One of the police officers was watching her closely. He was young, with green eyes and curly red hair. She'd never seen him before, and she thought every cop in the precinct had been down to the Hahnemann morgue at least once or twice. He caught her eye and smiled sympathetically.

"I know what you're thinking. Guess you've been there, down in the catacombs, huh? You know what's weird? We take these guys to shelters, where it's light and clean and they get two squares and a shower. But they always go back. It's like, that's their home, even if it's a cardboard box. They want their independence."

"Guess they figure that's all they have left." She smiled ruefully. *He's cute,* she thought. Then, *Stop it. I don't want a boyfriend.*

"My name's Mike. Mike O'Keefe. What's yours?"

"Jessica Grasia," she answered.

Mike was silent for a few moments. But his eyes never left hers.

"Um . . . I'm off duty at seven. Would you want to go out to breakfast or something?" His cheeks reddened.

Jess was about to say no, but the blush was endearing. Her blue eyes met his green ones. She remembered Heather's tobacco-roughened voice telling her to go live her life.

She heard herself saying, "Okay, sure. Breakfast sounds good."

"Pick you up at seven, then." He grinned. She noticed he had a dimple in his cheek.

"See you then." She turned down the corridor and went to prepare the autopsy room. *Hope I didn't sound too dumb,* she thought.

Bennett and the other police officer, a strongly built African-American woman, had observed the exchange. Bennett saw the appreciative gaze on the cop's face as he watched Jess walk gracefully down the hall.

Bennett was seized by a burst of rage, which he barely controlled. How dare this boy look at his Jess that way? His innocent, untouched Jessie? He had an urge to punch Mike O'Keefe right in the face. Blow that leering smile to hell, along with a few teeth. With an effort, Bennett regained his self-control.

"You be nice to her, young man, or I'll come after you with a scalpel," Bennett said with a wolfish grin. "She's a special girl, you know." He followed Jess down to the autopsy room. As he passed another of the pathology technicians in the hall, he called, "If Dr. Shirk comes down, tell her I'm busy and can't be disturbed."

Mike stared after Jess until she was gone. "LaVyrle, that's the prettiest girl I've ever seen. I can't believe she said yes," Mike said.

His partner rolled her eyes. "Rookies."

Bennett rubbed his throbbing arm absently as he read over the police notes regarding the John Doe they were about to autopsy. It was not his first autopsy of the day. Lady had been a good dog, all right. She had lain quietly on the exam table in the basement of Bennett's house as he had prepared the dissection tray and the lethal injection. Her soulful brown eyes had watched calmly as he pulled on his gloves and a lab coat.

"Well, Lady, I'm sorry it has to end like this. You know, they use dogs for research all the time. But it's generally drug research, not cooking experiments." He pushed her onto her side and picked up her foreleg, probing for a vein.

As if she had understood what he said, she clamped her jaws down on his bicep. Bennett howled in pain and jumped back. Lady released his arm and stared at him, blood dripping from her lower jaw. She did not snarl or growl, but in the depths of her eyes Bennett saw something that chilled him. It was the focused, dispassionate look of a wolf just before it dispatches its prey.

His fear and the burning pain in his arm almost overwhelmed him for a moment. He grabbed her foreleg again and jabbed the injection roughly into the upper leg. No searching for a painless vein for her. She did not even flinch. She closed her eyes. Moments later she was dead.

Bennett had washed out the bite. It was deep in places, but he didn't have time to have it treated by anyone else.

He got back to work.

He skinned Lady and gutted her. The tanning-bed oven worked just fine, maintaining the correct temperature, roasting her evenly on all sides, crisping the meat nicely on the outside and leaving it juicy and tender within. Bennett's house had been fragrant with the aroma of roasting meat. When Lady was thoroughly cooked, he had carved her into small pieces, wincing at the pain in his left arm. He had sampled his efforts. The meat was tasty and sweet, with an interesting texture. A Dijon hollandaise would have complemented it well. He had wrapped the remaining bits of dog meat up in foil and tossed it into a Dumpster frequented by the street people, along with the bag of Dog Chow.

Still, the look in her eyes as she had stared at him, his own blood dripping from her jaws, had unnerved him. That look had stayed with him for the rest of the day, taking much of the pleasure out of knowing that his tanning-bed oven worked perfectly. He caught himself wondering if the dog had cursed him somehow, then brushed the thought away. It was crazy to think like that.

Later, as he and Jess examined the stomach contents of the John Doe, he saw chunks of half-masticated golden-brown meat, swimming in a broth of hydrochloric acid laced with large amounts of Thunderbird wine.

"Looks like his last meal was a pretty good one," Jess said as she made her notes.

Bennett smiled. "Very good indeed, Jessie."

Jess looked up. "Think your dog will come back?"

"I don't think so. It's just as well. Guess I'm not a dog person after all."

"That's too bad," Jess replied.

FIVE

Mike O'Keefe and Jessica Grasia walked down Broad Street toward City Hall. There was an espresso bar on Seventeenth Street that would still be fairly quiet at seven A.M. Even though she had been on her feet most of the night, it felt good to walk in the fresh air, thought Jess.

In the rosy early morning light, she stole glances at Mike. He was tall, broad-shouldered, and solidly built, with an open, boyish face. A light dusting of golden freckles across his nose. Curly, copper-red hair. Not handsome in the way Dr. Sykes was, but easy on the eyes. She found herself wishing she had put on some lipstick and changed out of the shapeless smock and pants that identified her as a health-care worker.

I don't want a boyfriend. I really, really don't want a boyfriend.

You can't hide forever just because life bit you in the ass, Heather's voice replied.

They found a table next to the window. Mike brought over two steaming cups of cappuccino and sat down.

"Mmm, that smells good," said Jess. "Dr. Sykes is a real coffee freak, but I think even he would approve."

"Dr. Sykes is your boss, right?"

"Yes."

"How did a nice girl like you end up working in forensics? That must be so gross."

Jess smiled. "You get used to it after a while. I wanted to work nights, and it really is interesting work. Always something different in Forensics Land, as Dr. Sykes would say." She raised her eyes to his. "Now it's my turn. How'd you get to be a cop?"

"My dad was a cop. From the time I was a kid, I wanted to be just like him. He was the best friend I ever had. Five years ago, he was killed. Some twelve-year-old pusher in the projects had an AK-47 and just mowed him down." Mike shrugged.

Jess looked at him somberly. "My father was killed last year. He was a SEPTA bus driver. Some crackhead didn't want to pay his fare and just blew him away."

Mike reached over and took Jess's hand. "Wow, I didn't mean to bum us out. I'm sorry about your dad."

"Me, too." Jess was a little surprised to feel how nicely her hand fit into Mike's. It felt right, somehow.

"Let's change the subject," she said, calling up a smile. "Where do you live?"

The conversation took on more of a first-date quality. Jess discovered that Mike lived in South Philly with his mother, that he liked the Phillies baseball team even when they stunk, that he thought Adam Sandler was the funniest man on earth, and that his partner, LaVyrle Jackson, was the bravest, toughest cop he had ever met. Except for his father, of course.

"I love being a cop. Even though most of the time you deal with assholes—excuse my language. But there's always something cool happening, too. Like when the kids come up to you and ask questions, like you're a cop on TV. Or like the time when LaVyrle and I got to check out a ghost ship down at the waterfront."

Jess's eyes widened. "A ghost ship?"

"Yeah, a real ghost ship. It came in a few months ago. Coast Guard towed it in from off the Jersey coast. It was a freighter from Honduras. LaVyrle and I went with Jay Stanley from Homicide to see if there was evidence of foul play. All we found were these little piles of gray ash, and nobody on board. Man, that was weird. Detective Stanley said he'd never seen anything like it. They even had an article on it in the paper."

"Creepy," Jess agreed.

Jess explained to Mike that she lived alone, that she took care of Susie in the afternoons, and that she liked the Flyers hockey team better than the Phillies. She told him how her dream of becoming a doctor had been postponed, probably forever. And she told him about Bennett.

"He's not all full of himself like some of the other doctors," she said. "He's really good to me. He's kind of taken over as a father figure, I guess."

Mike grinned. "I don't think he likes me. He got this really weird expression on his face when he told me to be nice to you or else."

"Well, you are." Jess smiled shyly. "Nice, I mean. Umm . . . I don't get out much."

Mike looked at her with astonishment. "No kidding. I figured you must have an incredible social life."

Jess laughed. "Yeah, right. I work nights. I take care of Susie. On the weekends, I run errands, clean house, and do laundry and help Heather out." She dropped her eyes.

"Heather—Susie's mom—has cancer. Terminal. When she's gone, I'll be Susie's mom." She looked up again and met Mike's eyes. "So, you see, I'm pretty busy. No time for partying."

Now he'll make an excuse to go, and I'll never see him again, she thought.

To her surprise, she found that the idea bothered her a little.

But Mike did not drop his gaze. His hand tightened a little on Jess's. "Sounds good to me. I work nights, too, you know. I don't like to go out drinking. I like kids. Mostly I hang out at home, work on my car, and go to ball games. Jeez, we're so boring, aren't we?"

"Are we pathetic or what?" Jess said with a giggle.

There was a pause.

"So . . . um . . . wanna be boring together? Like maybe Thursday? Before work?"

Jess grinned. "Sure."

"Cool," said Mike.

When Susie came home from school, Jess hugged her warmly. Her cheeks were pink, and she hummed to herself as she sat with Susie as Susie did her homework.

Susie looked at Jess. "You had a date," she said. It was a statement, not a question.

Jess was taken aback. "Yes, I did. How did you know?"

"Jessie's got a boyfriend, Jessie's got a boyfriend," Susie sang. "Oooh, can I meet him? When's he coming over? What's his name?"

"Knock it off, Suz," Jess said with a smile. "Of course you can. His name is Mike, and he's a policeman." Jess helped Susie put her homework into her book bag. "Okay, time for a rest. Your mom says you've been dragging these past couple of mornings."

"Jessie-ka, I'm too big for naps!"

"Yeah, but it seems to me that you always fall asleep. I'll wake you up in time for *Miss Becky.*"

"I can't help it if I can't wake up in the morning," Susie muttered.

Jess looked at Susie. "Your mom wants to know if you've been into her medicine. It's not like you to be slow in the mornings."

Susie's face took on a look of righteous indignation. "I do *not* take Mommy's medicine. Miss Becky said never to take other people's medicine. Only the medicine you're supposed to. From the doctor."

"Well, Miss Becky is right. You're a good girl, Susie. I knew you wouldn't do it."

"How come Mommy's medicine doesn't make her better? Will she have to go back to the hospital? I don't like the hospital. Mommy comes home sicker from that chemical stuff every time. And I don't like that Dr. Meredith. She's weird."

Jess silently agreed with Susie's assessment of Meredith Shirk. She decided not to lie, but not to tell the truth, either. She said, carefully, "Susie, you know your mom is sick. She might have to go to the hospital again. We don't know."

"Yuck," Susie said. "I always get better from my medicine. Maybe Mommy should go to my doctor. Dr. Mest is a real nice lady." She stopped and looked at Jess. That odd, direct stare again. "Mommy's going to die."

Jess groaned inwardly. She could think of nothing to say to Susie.

Susie got up and put her arms around Jess's neck as she sat at the table. "You'll take care of me when Mommy dies." Again, it was a statement.

Jess turned and put her arms around the little girl. "Of course I will. I love you, my little dill Pickle."

"That's 'cause you're my forever friend."

Jess kissed Susie's thin cheek. "Right. Forever friend, friend forever."

They held each other tightly for a few moments. Then Susie wiggled out of Jess's arms and began to question Jess excitedly.

"You didn't tell me when Mike is coming. Did you know that St. Sebastian is the patron saint of policemen? Will he come in his police car? Can I wear his hat? Will he have a gun? Guns are dangerous, you know. Miss Becky says . . ."

Jess smiled and stroked Susie's hair as she half-listened to the barrage of questions. Susie had always been a sensitive child. She seemed to know when Jess needed to hold her and would cuddle with Jess for hours. Other times, she would insist on being taken to the playground or the store, and Jess would discover that she had really needed to get out of the house for a while. When Jess wanted to be alone with her own thoughts, Susie would make fairy castles with Legos and play happily by herself.

Susie's uncanny perceptiveness could be unnerving at times, but then she would turn around and do something very childlike and typical. Such as becoming obsessed with a television show. Or the saints in the chapel of St. Laurence's. Or losing her favorite toy. Or asking endless questions.

"Slow down, Suz! One question at a time," Jess said.

Dr. Meredith Shirk took the elevator down to the basement of Hahnemann Hospital. She had an envelope under one arm. The autopsy rooms were bustling with activity. In addition to the usual crop of murder victims and the homeless, the bodies of five children, burn victims, had come in that morning. Dr. Singh Pandit and his forensics staff were extremely busy.

"Can I help you, Doctor?" asked a lab technician at the front desk. He was paging through a folder and looking very distracted.

"I have some lab reports here for Dr. Sykes. You go on. I'll just deliver them myself." Meredith smiled sweetly.

The tech hurried off down the corridor, grateful to be spared conversation. Meredith walked down the hallway to Bennett's office and put the envelope in the bin on Bennett's door. Surreptitiously she tried the doorknob, but the office was locked.

"Plan B, then," she said softly.

She walked back down the hallway. Looking both ways to make sure no one noticed her, she quickly slipped into the morgue.

It was cold in there. The scent of disinfectant and decay hung in the air. She pulled open one of the big drawers that held the cadavers. Her eyes fell on the tiny body. It was a child, no more than four years old. A boy. One side of the body was badly burned. The undamaged side of the face showed that he had been a handsome child. Long black eyelashes curled over his ashy, pale cheek. The lips were parted, as if he were dreaming.

Meredith reached into her pocket and pulled out a scalpel. She'd had an idea last night. And this was absolutely perfect. This would scare the shit out of that little bitch. She picked up one of the boy's plump little hands. The fingers were gently curved in toward the palm. Yellow finger paint was caked under the delicate oval nails.

A voice inside Meredith's head said, *If you get caught, it will be the end of everything. Don't do it.*

Meredith looked down at the tiny, cold hand in her own. In her other hand, the scalpel shone under the glare of the fluorescent lights. For a moment she stood there, frozen by indecision.

She thought of Bennett in the arms of Mamakass, seduced away from her, lost to her forever. He would never know how much she loved him unless she did something to prove it to him.

She set her mouth in a thin line and began cutting.

* * *

Kass parked her minivan in front of the house.

"Okay, guys. Upstairs and get started on your homework while I get dinner going," Kass said.

"Get off my book bag, you little creep," Karen snarled at Sam as they gathered up their things and piled out of the minivan.

"Girls go to Jupiter to get more stupider," replied Sam, sticking his tongue out at his sister.

"Knock it off *now*. Get going!" Kass sighed in irritation as her children had a brief shoving match at the door and then went in the house. She went around behind the van and took out the groceries. Fortunately Sam and Karen had left the door open. As she walked back to the kitchen, staggering under the weight of four bags of groceries, her briefcase and her purse, she noticed the cardboard box next to the door, tucked away behind the planter.

"Jeez, couldn't one of you kids have picked up this box and brought it in?" she called upstairs.

"Sorry, Mom."

Sorry doesn't cut it, thought Kass. *I'm tired and cranky, and I want nothing more than a hot bath, a good book, and some peace and quiet.* She went back out, picked up the box, and set it down on the kitchen table. It was a good-sized box. No return address, delivered by Speedy Courier Service. She wondered for a moment if it was from Bennett. She decided to wait until she had taken care of the bags to open the box.

She turned her attention to the grocery bags, unloading them and putting away the contents in the refrigerator, cupboards, and cabinets. Her eyes fell on the Chinese takeout menu by the telephone.

Screw cooking, thought Kass. *I'm just beat. Well, let's see what's in the box.*

She picked up a paring knife and cut through the tape

sealing the box. The box was full of Styrofoam popcorn and shredded newspaper. She dug down into it with her hands. *I feel like a kid looking for the prize in a box of Cracker Jack,* she thought, a smile touching her lips. A faint smell of burned, slightly rotten meat came to her. Her nose wrinkled.

Her fingers finally touched plastic. She pulled a large plastic bag from the box, spilling some of the shipping popcorn on the floor as she did so. The rotted smell got worse.

A neatly typed freezer label attached to the bag read KEEP YOUR HANDS OFF HIM YOU BITCH OR YOU WILL FRY. Kass stared at the label. *What the hell is going on?* she thought. Fear began to creep into her. Slowly, she pulled off the tape securing the bag and looked inside.

A small hand—a child's hand—was inside. It was blackened and blistered. The delicate fingers curled into the palm. Kass could see crescents of yellow under the nails. The hand had been apparently torn off just above the wrist. She stared at it for a few moments, unbelieving. Then she quickly closed the bag and bit back a scream. Her knees turned to jelly. She wanted to vomit.

"Mom? What's that smell?" Karen called.

Oh, my God, the kids! They can't see this! Kass thought frantically. She stuffed the bag deep into the box. *What can I do with this thing? Where can I put it?* Her mind whirled.

"Mom?" Karen's voice came again. Kass could hear footsteps coming down the stairs. Almost panicking, she picked up the box and opened the French doors that led out to the little courtyard in the back. Herb was always good with home improvement, but here he had outdone himself. He had turned the tiny backyard into a miniature Eden, with brick pathways along raised flowerbeds. Pink dogwoods and arborvitae grew along the high brick walls that enclosed it. In the center of the garden was a huge old sycamore tree that shaded the entire yard in the summer.

He had built a large brick patio just off the kitchen, with French doors opening out onto it and wisteria twining on the latticework that enclosed it. Kass shoved the box behind one of the arborvitae along the fence.

"Mom? What's going on? What's that gross smell?" Karen stepped outside, looking at her mother.

"The pork chops were bad, sweetie. The pork chops I was going to make for dinner. I . . . threw them over the fence and into the alley." Kass was shaking badly. She took a deep breath. *I can't let Karen see how shook up I am,* she thought. *I can't scare her.*

"Jeez, Mom, you want to poison the rats?" Karen began to grin, then looked at her mother's pale face in the dim light from the kitchen. "Wow, are you going to throw up or something? You look sick."

"I'm okay, sweetie. You want Chinese tonight?"

"Okay. Sweet and sour chicken and an eggroll."

"All right. Now go upstairs and finish your homework."

Karen took another look at Kass. "You sure you're okay? Want me to call Dad?"

"There's no need to call your father just because I'm . . ." *Scared out of my mind,* she thought. "A little sick to my stomach. You would be, too, if you'd smelled those pork chops."

"I guess," said Karen. "Maybe we'd better not go to that store anymore." She turned and went back upstairs, saying "Eeeeew" as she passed through the kitchen, where the stench still hung in the air. Karen turned on the ceiling fan. Then she stopped and turned to face Kass. "Hey, Mom, what was in that box?"

Kass flinched. "Nothing, hon. Go on upstairs now, okay?"

Karen frowned. "A box of nothing?" Then she grinned wickedly. "A nothing from Victoria's Secret, right? For your new boyfriend? Can I see?"

"You are too smart for your own good, Missy. Now get!" Something in Kass's face took all the devilment out of Karen's face. "Okay, okay, I'm going," she said. "Want me to ask Sam what he wants for dinner?"

"That would be helpful," replied Kass.

After Sam shouted down his order, Kass poured herself a large glass of wine and picked up the phone. She dialed Hahnemann Hospital.

"Dr. Bennett Sykes, please."

It had been a busy day in Forensics Land. Dr. Singh Pandit passed a hand over his bleary eyes. He had finished the autopsies of the five children that had been brought into the morgue. They had perished in a fire that had consumed a suspected crack house in North Philadelphia. They had died of smoke inhalation and second- and third-degree burns over their small bodies. Now Dr. Pandit was overseeing their transfer to the funeral home. He stood at the front desk, signing off on the mountain of paperwork, and grieving a little over the wasted promise of the five little lives gone in the fire. Kids always affected him that way, mostly because he deeply loved his own little daughters.

Bennett Sykes walked into the pathology department. "Good evening, Singh. How's it going?"

"Hello, Bennett. It was busy as hell today. We are just finishing here. Five kids. Another fucking fire in another slum crack house. No smoke detectors, and even if there were, the adults were probably too high to get the kids out." He sighed. "Some days I do hate this job."

"Yeah, it's hard when it's kids." Bennett wondered briefly if the children had been awake before they died. Death probably would have been a welcome rescuer from the smoke-fouled, searing air filling their lungs and the dull orange flames licking at their tender skin.

"I am so tired," Dr. Pandit continued. "And you are right, it is terribly hard with kids. It's hard to concentrate and not think of your own children. Oh well, it was pretty obvious. Burns and smoke inhalation. A couple of the bodies were charred." He sighed deeply. "Another one came in just a few minutes ago. A homicide, female. Allegedly beaten to death. They are prepping her now." Singh sighed again. His dark brown eyes were netted with red. Bennett couldn't decide if it was fatigue or tears.

"Go home," Bennett said. "A drink and a good night's sleep will make you feel all better."

Singh smiled faintly. "A nice prescription, Dr. Bennett Sykes. But I think this night it will be difficult. I have kids of my own, you know."

"I know. Go home," Bennett repeated.

The phone rang. Singh picked it up.

"Pathology, Pandit," he said in his soft, accented voice. A pause.

"It's for you, Bennett. A lady."

"I'll take it in my office," he said and began walking down the hall.

"Oh. Thomas said Dr. Shirk was here earlier. She had something for you. It's on your door."

"Thanks, Singh." *Hope it isn't another stupid card,* he thought irritably. He opened his office, pulled out the envelope and threw it on his desk, and then closed the door. He picked up the phone.

"This is Dr. Sykes."

"Bennett, its Kass."

"Hello, Mamakass," he said, feigning warmth. He didn't feel like cooing sweet nothings at the moment, but . . . *oh well,* he thought, *just two more days and this charade will be over.* "What's up?"

"Bennett, I . . ." She faltered, then took a deep breath. "I got a package today. It was a hand. A human hand. And a note. It says 'Keep your hands off him you bitch or you will fry.' Bennett, I'm scared." Her voice trembled.

Bennett was stunned. "A hand? Kass, are you sure?"

"Yes, I'm sure. It stunk. It had burn marks on it. It was a kid's. Christ, Bennett, it even had paint under the nails. I wouldn't be calling you if it weren't real." Her voice had steadied. Bennett had to admire her strength. Most people would have been in hysterics if they'd received such a grisly package. *She's a worthy one, all right,* he thought.

"I'll have to call the police, of course. But I just thought you'd like to know that someone . . . someone doesn't like what we're doing. Would Sylvia do something like this?"

"No, Sylvia's still in Colorado. She doesn't even know you exist." He paused. "Don't call the cops, Kassie. Maybe I can find out what's going on. Body parts aren't easy to come by, so that narrows down the suspects considerably." He paused, looking for the right tone of tender concern. "If I wasn't so busy here, I'd come over. You know that, don't you, Mamakass?"

"Yes, Dr.B. I do. You're so sweet to me." There was a pause, then a quick intake of breath. "But do you think maybe we ought to cool it for a while? I mean, some nut is stalking us. I really should call the police." The fear had crept back into her voice.

"No, Kass. I want to see you Friday, and I am not going to let some ghoul scare me away from you. But I tell you what. Meet me at my place. We won't go out. We'll just stay safe and sound at home. Okay?" He tried to sound commanding and reassuring at the same time. It was imperative that Kass come to him on Friday. He had to begin the process.

"Okay. I guess if you're not scared, I'm not, either. Besides, I want to see you. More than ever, now."

"Me, too," he said softly. "Just one thing. Don't tell anyone about our date. Not even your kids. The fewer people that know anything the better. For their own safety. Trust me on this."

"But shouldn't someone know where I am? Where you are?"

"Kass, I have to go. Don't call the cops. Let me see what I can find out here first. I have connections."

"Okay, Bennett." She sounded much better. He gave her his address, and after a few more assurances and endearments, he hung up. His brow darkened.

I wonder who the fuck would be trying to scare her off? I can't lose her now. It's too late to find someone else. And I can't have the cops involved with her, either. Too risky.

There was a soft knock at the door. "May I come in?" Jess asked.

Bennett quickly rearranged his features into a welcoming smile. "Yeah, Jess, come on in. Coffee's on."

Meredith stared out her window at Bennett's darkened house across the street. She was smiling to herself. *By now Mamakass has gotten my little warning,* she thought. *She's probably terrified. I hope she opened it in front of her kids.*

Meredith had worn a thick scarf, sunglasses, and a shapeless trench coat when she dropped the package off at the courier's. She had paid cash and used a fake name and address for the return. She was not concerned about the police at all, especially since there would be no fingerprints to lead them to her. She had not taken off her gloves until just before she walked into the courier service's office. The few smudgy prints on the box would mean nothing.

She was more concerned about the pathology staff discovering the missing hand, but she had cut the hand off raggedly at the wrist. And they had not autopsied the boy yet when she took the hand. It was safe to think that they would assume the hand was either burned off, or came off when the bodies were being loaded into the ambulance.

Her eyes fell lovingly on the two symphony tickets on the desk. Dress Circle seats, second row. She would go over to Bennett's on Friday and ask him to join her for dinner and the concert. She had made reservations at that hot new restaurant, Chiennes Noir. He would be unhappy about losing Kass, and she was just the one to cheer him up. A good meal and good music would do wonders for him. So would she.

By the time the evening was over, he would forget all about old Mamakass. Meredith was sure of it.

Her smile widened.

"Something's bugging you," Jess said to Bennett as they scrubbed up.

"Yeah. Something weird happened to Kass today," he replied.

"What happened? Is she okay?"

"Yeah. Real okay, considering." He thought of telling Jess about the hand, and then decided not to. Jess waited, expecting him to tell her what it was all about. When he didn't, she shrugged.

"Guess it's none of my business, huh? But I'm glad she's okay. Bet you are, too," she said with a grin.

"That's my girl," said Bennett. "Speaking of none of your business, how was breakfast with your new admirer?"

Jess's cheeks grew pink. "I'm seeing Michael on Thursday. My day off."

Bennett felt a sharp stab of jealousy. The thought of having to share Jess's wide-eyed devotion with someone else angered him. An image of Mike bedding Jess flashed through his mind. She would no longer be his innocent acolyte. He pushed it aside with an effort.

"Well, you must have liked him," he replied.

"I did. He's nice." After a moment, Jess looked at Bennett. "What did you think of him, Dr. Sykes?"

"Well, he did seem like a nice guy. But you have to be careful, Jessie. These young guys are usually after just one thing. I know, because I was young once. And with your looks . . ." He paused meaningfully. Jess dropped her eyes and blushed again. "I think you're still a little vulnerable yet, after what happened to your father. You don't need to be dating boys. I'd like to see you with an older man, eventually. Someone who has patience. Who would take the time to get to know you, and want to take care of you." Now it was his turn to look at her expectantly.

Jess looked a little confused. "He didn't seem like that at all. He said he liked kids, and liked just hanging out at home. Not a party animal at all."

"Jessie, guys will say anything if they think you want to hear it," Bennett replied dismissively. He did not want to talk about Jess's love life right now. He had better things to think about. He'd turn his full attention to Jess after the Epicurean Society meeting on Monday. He'd find a way to get the cop out of her life. Then he'd step in and take control of Jess's heart and mind—and body. In the meantime, he hoped he'd said enough to bring her back down to earth.

They walked down the hall in silence and entered the autopsy room. A sheeted figure was on the autopsy table.

"What do we have here?" asked Bennett. "Singh said it was a homicide victim. Female." He looked around the room. "Where's the damned chart?"

"Isn't it in here?" Jess asked.

"No, goddamn it, " Bennett said irritably. "Be a good girl and see if you can find the chart on Jane Doe here. Someone must have forgotten to bring it in."

"Okay, Dr. Sykes." She pushed her way through the doors and went to find the paperwork. He pulled the sheet down, exposing the corpse's face and torso.

He stared intently at the woman's face. It was battered and swollen, with purple bruises on the pasty flesh. The lips were pulled back, revealing broken, blood-crusted teeth. Blue eyes, now obscured by a milky film, stared sightlessly at the ceiling. Dirty, bottle-blonde hair tangled around her shoulders. Recognition hit him like an electrical shock.

It was the whore. The one who had a daughter. The one whose small spark of life had mystified him. The curlicued *J* was visible on her chest.

Death had finally come to this woman, this whore. He could tell by the marks on her body that she had struggled mightily with her attackers. This bitch had had nothing to live for. She should have thrown herself into the bright, lovely light and welcoming arms of what lay beyond. But she had fought to stay in this bitter world, to the very end of her strength.

An image of Lady, sinking her teeth into his arm as she realized what he was planning to do to her, flashed into his mind. He stared down at the cadaver.

Jess found the missing page of the police report half-hidden in an untidy stack of papers at the pathology department's main desk. She pulled it out and slipped the top of the sheet into the paper punch. As she did, she scanned the report.

"They found her under the Walt Whitman Bridge, beaten and mutilated," she read softly, and sighed. *Probably a prostitute,* she thought. *I just don't get why anyone would live that way.*

She returned to the autopsy room with the chart and saw Bennett staring down at the corpse. She walked over and stood beside him. She saw the gray skin, the blank eyes, and the bleached hair. She took a breath. The usual pungent smell of death, mingled with faint traces of cheap perfume and whiskey, filled her lungs.

The corpse stared back at Jess. A shock of recognition made Jess's stomach turn over. The face was some kind of bizarrely gruesome fun-house reflection of her own face. She touched her gloved hand to the woman's battered cheek.

"What is it?" asked Bennett.

"Nothing," Jess replied. They began the autopsy, but Jess was silent, her mind whirling.

I know this woman, she thought. *But from where? I don't know any prostitutes. Maybe from church?*

The picture at home rose up before her eyes. The woman in the picture, with beautiful, shiny blonde hair and a full-lipped smile. She was holding baby Jess in her arms. This woman looked as if nothing had ever existed behind those filmed, fly-specked eyes.

But the women were one and the same.

"I thought you were dead," she said. "You were supposed to be dead."

"What are you taking about?" asked Bennett.

She looked up at him, meeting his eyes with a level stare. In a controlled, toneless voice, she said, "This is my mother."

Bennett was silent for a few moments. This diseased, addicted street whore had been Jess's mother. Jessie had been what this dead bitch had clung to life for. The *J* on her chest was for Jessie.

He walked over to Jess, who was standing pale and tense beside the table, staring down at the corpse. He put his hand on her shoulder. She stepped away and shook her head.

"I'm okay, Dr. Sykes," she said in that same toneless voice. "I cried all my tears for her a long time ago. I'm just glad I don't have to go home and tell Daddy about this. He never stopped loving her, you know." She reached out and traced the *J* tattoo with her gloved finger, and her shoulders slumped. "I don't remember her at all. Except—there's something about her and peaches. That's all." She straightened up and turned away.

"Guess we need some blood for toxicology tests. I'll get vaginal smears and fingernail scrapings, too. For the DNA tests." She reached for the Vacu-Tainers.

"Jess, if there's anything . . ."

"Yes. Please, Doctor, just be quiet, okay?"

They worked for the rest of the night in almost total silence, each engrossed in their own thoughts.

"Thanks for coming. I must ask you to keep your voices down. My kids are sleeping, and I'd rather they not know about this."

"No problem, ma'am. Now, the dispatch says someone sent you a body part? A hand?" LaVyrle Jackson's face was impassive.

"Yes." Kass indicated the box on the living room floor. Mike O'Keefe knelt down beside it. He put on rubber gloves before he opened it. He stared down into the plastic bag and paled visibly. His freckles stood out on his cheeks like brown paint on a white wall. "It's a hand, all right. A kid's, like Mrs. Rhodes said."

Officer Jackson took a look. Her face did not change.

"Ma'am, do you have any idea who would send this to you?"

Kass answered their questions in a steady voice. She said nothing about Bennett. He had told her not to involve the police, and she was sure that he would be furious with her if he knew she had. She didn't want to lose him, but she couldn't just sit with a hand in a box outside under the shrubbery, either. Besides, she had Sam and Karen to think of.

"I have no idea who the 'him' in this note is. My husband and I are divorced, and I'm not seeing anyone."

"Who is your ex?"

"Herbert Rhodes. He's a lawyer. He's not capable of doing this. If he found a spider, he'd catch it and put it outside."

"Do you get along? Any custody problems?"

"Herb and I get along okay. We have no problems, at least no major ones. And I said he'd never do anything like this. He's not the jealous type. He's getting remarried this weekend." Kass sighed.

"Does that bother you?"

"A little," Kass admitted. Then she looked up, and her eyes flashed. "But not enough to stage something terrible in order to disrupt his plans, if that's what you're thinking. Besides, where would I get a body?"

"Just asking, Mrs. Rhodes. It's my job, okay?" La Vyrle Jackson looked at Kasidy Rhodes. No, you don't look like the type, her instincts told her. She was rarely wrong about people. She had seen enough feigned emotion in her time on the force to know the real thing. And this lady was genuinely frightened. But she had enough spit in her to get angry when she thought she was a suspect. Even so, La Vyrle knew she was hiding something. Protecting the "him" in the note, no doubt. Probably a married man who had promised her everything, but this woman'd be lucky to get a bottle of perfume out of the deal. But, since she wasn't a suspect—yet—LaVyrle decided to let it go for now.

La Vyrle and Mike made her go through her story one more time. She answered their questions with a steady control that obviously cost her an effort to maintain. Then Mike picked up the box with his gloved hands.

"We'll take this back to the crime lab and try to figure out who it belonged to and who sent it to you. We'll keep you posted. In the meantime, be careful. And don't open any more suspicious packages. Call nine-one-one if you receive any. Who knows, next time it could be a bomb."

Kass shuddered.

"You should tell your kids," Mike added. "This creep may know about them. They'll have to be on guard for themselves."

"But wouldn't it be better if they didn't know? I don't want to scare them," said Kass. Her eyes filled with tears. "Plus, the fewer that know . . ."

"Tell them. Don't worry, ma'am. Just take it easy and keep your eyes open. We'll do our best."

They left, and Kass sighed again. She turned off the downstairs light and went upstairs. She opened Karen's bedroom door and looked in at her daughter, who lay sleeping in her ruffled pink bed. She was snoring gently. Posters of Johnny Depp and Brad Pitt looked down on her as she slept, her brown hair scattered on the pillow.

"Watch over my girl," Kass whispered to the poster boys. She closed the door.

Next she checked on Sam. He was sprawled out on his narrow bed, covers kicked off. His thin, pajama-clad body stirred. He opened his eyes partway.

"Was someone here, Mom? Thought I heard something," he murmured sleepily.

"No, just the TV." She went over to him and smoothed his hair back from his face. He smiled, and his eyes turned up at the corners. Just like his father's, thought Kass.

"Good night, little man," she whispered and kissed him. His wiry arm slid out from under him, and he circled her neck, squeezing her tightly. It hurt Kass a little, but she leaned down closer to him.

"G'night Mom. I love you." He unwrapped his arm from around her neck and closed his eyes. He was immediately asleep again.

Kass quietly closed his bedroom door. She went into her own room and fell down on the bed. She sobbed quietly in the silence.

SIX

"O Blessed St. Jude, it's me, Susie Troutman. I have to talk to you."

A shaft of light, broken into many colors as it streamed through the stained glass windows, illuminated the little girl in the plaid jumper kneeling in front of the statue. Susie looked up at the blank, painted face of the statue.

"I can't stay too long 'cause I told Sister Hubert I was going to the library. But I feel all scared and mixed up inside. Somebody is trying to kill Miss Becky. I had a bad dream about a bad doctor man hurting Miss Becky. And then last night I had a dream where somebody sent Miss Becky a hand. A cutted-off hand. From a little boy who died. Yuck! I didn't tell Mommy 'cause she doesn't believe my dreams. I think Jessie does a little but not really. And in

the dream there was a nasty letter with bad words in it. I
don't know if the bad doctor man sent it to Miss Becky or
not. But what I do know is that the bad doctor man is going
to kill Miss Becky, and I don't want him to. Please tell me
how I can help. Maybe you can ask God what I should do."
Tears began to roll down Susie's cheeks, through the rainbow patterns of colored light on her thin face.

Suddenly she felt irresistibly sleepy, kneeling in the
pool of warm light. She rubbed her eyes and yawned.
"Help me, Blessed St. Jude, in this my hour of need," she
murmured. She tried to get up but couldn't. Her legs were
too heavy to move. She closed her eyes.

She opened them again.

"Hello, Susie Troutman," said a kind voice. A hand was
extended to her. Susie grabbed it and pulled herself up to
her feet.

"I'm sorry, Father. I'll get back . . ." Her voice trailed
off as she met the eyes of the man who helped her up. "St.
Jude?" she breathed. Her gray eyes were wide with wonder.

The statue—if it was still a statue—had taken on the colors of life and stepped down from its pedestal. Susie saw
that St. Jude had soft brown eyes and olive skin. His dark
hair brushed his shoulders, and he had a thick full beard. He
was dressed in simple linen robes. He smiled down at her.

"Yes, Susie." He picked her up as if she were a feather,
seating her in the crook of his arm.

"I'm dreaming, aren't I?" She touched his beard and
hair. It felt soft and silky. She put her arms around his neck
and kissed him. His cheek felt warm and smooth.

"You're all warm. You have to be really for real! Wait
till I tell Jessie-ka. She doesn't believe in you anymore, but
now she will."

"You tell Jessie that she may not believe in me, but I believe in her." St. Jude chuckled.

Susie grinned for a moment, then grew serious. "How
come you're being real for me?"

St. Jude's eyes met Susie's. They were full of warmth and compassion. "You asked me to show you how you can help Miss Becky."

Susie's face lit up. She hugged St. Jude's neck in her excitement. "Oh, how? Tell me!"

"I have things to tell you, and things to show you. The rest will be up to you."

"Okay," said Susie. She nestled closer to St. Jude. He made her feel safe.

The light from the stained glass windows suddenly blazed into thousands of glowing colors. Susie closed her eyes against the brightness. When she opened them again, she was standing in a cobblestone street. Colonial-era town houses lined the street on either side. The sun shone down through the trees that grew tall behind the rows of homes. St. Jude put her down and took her hand.

"Where are we?" whispered Susie. "Did we go back in time?"

"No," answered St. Jude. "If you want to help, you will have to find this place. An evil thing is going to happen here."

"To Miss Becky," said Susie.

"And to other people as well. My child, you have a lot to face in the coming months . . ."

Susie looked down at the gray stones. "I know. Mommy's going to die. I wish she and Jessie would talk to me about it but they won't." She stamped her foot angrily on the cobblestones. "I know lots of things about people and stuff. Sometimes I wish I didn't. Nobody believes me anyway."

St. Jude reached under her chin with his free hand and turned her face up to his. "Susie, you have a gift of knowing, of seeing into things and people. This gift is from God. Now you have a chance to use this precious gift, to save a life and the lives that will come after. You have a purpose to fulfill, and only you and Jessica can do it. I will always be here for you to help you, but you must remember that God helps those who help themselves.

"I know that, too. Sister Hubert told us in class."

"Remember this place. You will have to come here to fight the evil. Your gift will help you."

"What evil?"

"It goes back more than a hundred years. Misguided, soulless men committing murder and other unspeakable acts in the name of a devilish theology." St. Jude's voice was full of righteous anger. "They take unholy communion in the blood of innocents and feed on their desecrated bodies."

"What does 'unspeakable' mean?"

"It means terrible beyond description."

She looked back up into St. Jude's face. "Does that mean you won't tell me 'cause I might be scared?"

St. Jude laughed. "Yes, little Susie." Then he grew serious again. "You will be having more dreams. I will send you signs when Miss Becky is in trouble. But you will have to find your own way here. You will have to make them see and believe."

"I don't understand. How come you can't just tell me what to do? And how come you can't stop it your own self?"

St. Jude reached down and grabbed her shoulders. He began shaking her, gently at first and then harder.

"Wait! What did I do? Why are you shaking me? St. Jude, wait!"

St. Jude and the street were melting away. But the shaking was still going on.

"Is she feverish?" Susie heard someone ask.

A hand stroked her forehead and then pinched her earlobe. "No, I don't think so."

Susie blinked. St. Jude had become Father Romano. Sister Hubert was crouching down next to him. Father Romano was holding her shoulders.

"Where am I?" asked Susie, confused.

"In the chapel. Do you remember coming here?" Father Romano asked.

"Yes. I came to talk to St. Jude about my bad dreams. And then . . ." Susie looked up at the statue of St. Jude. It stood in its alcove, a lifeless piece of carved wood.

"And then I don't know. I must have fallen asleep. I'm sorry, Father. I'm sorry, Sister Hubert."

"There is a time and a place for everything, Susie. Now it's time for you to go to class."

Father helped her up. Susie saw his kind, dark Italian eyes smiling at her. Sister Hubert took her hand. Sister Hubert's thin mouth was drawn up in an angry frown. Susie figured she was in big trouble now. *Maybe Sister will hit me with a ruler.*

Father Romano saw the frown, too. "Sister, do not punish the child. Praise God she seeks the consolation of prayer with the saints at such a young age. But Susie, if you need to come and pray, see if it can be done before or after school. Not during. Do you understand?"

"Yes, Father. Thank you, Father," whispered Susie.

Sister Hubert pulled a little too hard on Susie's arm and dragged her back to the classroom, muttering under her breath. She gave Susie extra catechism to learn in the afternoon and glared at her all day, but Susie was grateful for Father Romano's injunction.

She walked slowly home after school. She didn't understand what St. Jude meant by a purpose or unspeaking evil. And he had said there would be more of those terrible dreams. How could she make Jessie believe her and help her find this place he had showed her?

She sat down on the curb near the corner, hugging her book bag in her lap. She remembered Jessie crying to her mother one night in the kitchen, after Uncle Ramon died. Jessie had said she would never set foot in a church again. Uncle Ramon was wandering around in purgatory for no

good reason, just because he died before he got the Last
Rites. How could God be so cruel—to take her daddy away
and leave her all alone? Then Jess had cried so hard that
Mommy had made her drink a glass of yucky wine to set-
tle her down.

Jess probably wouldn't want to help her or St. Jude. Or
Miss Becky.

"Blessed St. Jude, help me now in this my hour of need.
Hallelujah and amen," Susie whispered.

She got up and went home.

Jess yawned and stretched her arms out in front of her,
linking her fingers.

"Tired, Jessie?" Bennett asked.

"A little," she admitted. "It's been a really long night. It's
past nine." She was cleaning up the autopsy room. They had
had several more bodies come in that night after Ingrid's,
and had just finished working on a young man who probably died as the result of a drug deal gone bad. His body had
been riddled with bullets fired from a semiautomatic, high-
caliber gun—most likely an illegally modified Uzi.

"Dr. Pandit will take over from here," Bennett said. He
took down the X rays from the light cabinet and switched
them off.

Jess sighed, and Bennett turned to look at her. Jess's
face was pale, her eyes dull with fatigue. She wiped her
arm across her forehead and continued sorting surgical
instruments.

"Is it about your mother?" Jess turned and looked over
at him. He was leaning against the wall in his green scrubs
and lab coat.

"Not really, Dr. Sykes. I never knew her, so it's not like
I have anything to miss." Jess shrugged.

"I know she's in a better place than she was here," Bennett said.

Jess stared at him. Then she grimaced. "How do you know?" she said bitterly. She turned away from Bennett and put a tray of instruments into the autoclave. Suddenly her cheeks blazed with angry color, and frustration poured out of her in a torrent of words. "I don't care. I don't think there really is a heaven or hell. There is no God. It's just one big lie. My mother was a junkie prostitute, and another junkie blew my father away. What a wonderful world we live in, huh, Doctor? This is hell, right here and now. Afterward, there's just . . . nothing." She slammed the door on the autoclave with more force than necessary.

Bennett came over and stood next to her. She kept her head bowed, her cheeks flaming, not looking at him. He decided it was time for a little test.

"Jess, when I was young I nearly died."

She lifted her head and met his eyes. "You did?"

"Car accident. My father was killed. I was thrown from the car and broke nearly every bone in my body. Had a concussion. Ruptured spleen and lots of internal bleeding."

"Wow," Jess said. Her eyes were wide and exquisitely blue.

"I remember watching myself in the ER. I floated over myself. Then I looked up. I remember seeing a white light and hearing voices before I came back down into my body. So I know that consciousness—the soul, if you will—goes somewhere after death."

"So you think we really do have an immortal soul, then? Is there a life after death for sure?"

"There's more to it than that. I believe that the essence of a person remains in the body for a time after death. A kind of a cellular memory. Properly used, these essences can become part of someone else. To enhance the living who partake of this essence."

"Cellular memory? It sounds cool," she said. "But kind of New Agey. Why do you think this essence stuff would enhance the living?"

"Think about it. If a person led a good life, wouldn't that mean that their very cells would have some of that good stuff, that karma, if you will?"

Jess nodded.

"So, then, if there was a way for you to ingest it, then those qualities would become part of you, enhancing your own."

She stared at him for a moment. Then she dropped her eyes. "It makes sense, kind of, but I don't see how you could ingest it. I guess you could eat the dead person, but that's way gross." She turned away from him and lowered her head, busying herself with another tray of surgical instruments.

"Someday you'll understand," he said. He looked down at the nape of her neck, gilded with tendrils of her wavy hair that had escaped the claw clip she used to keep her hair up while she was working. He moved behind her and put his hands on her neck and shoulders. He began rubbing them, with a touch as tender as a father's—or a lover's.

Jess brought her head up against his hands. She was a little startled, but then she relaxed. It was only Dr. Sykes, after all. His hands were warm. He brought his fingertips up and drew them gently down the sides of her neck, stroking all the tension away.

"Mmmm," she said. She was lost in the sensation.

Bennett felt the pulse of her strong young life under his fingers. Her skin was silky and surprisingly warm for its fairness. He was delighted at how easily she yielded to his touch, how completely she trusted him. He placed his thumbs at the nape of her neck and brought his hands down slowly onto her shoulders, feeling the muscles relax under his hands.

Jess swayed on her feet a little, bringing her closer to him. He felt the warmth of her body through his clothes.

He kept rubbing and stroking her shoulders, and she arched back toward him like a cat. She was potter's clay in his hands. He smiled.

After a minute or two, he deliberately tightened his grip on her, his fingers slipping over her shoulders and down toward the smooth rise of her breasts. For a second, she brought her body against his as if seeking his touch on her breasts.

Then the spell was broken. Jess came back to reality, suddenly realizing the change in his touch. She reached up and put her hands on his wrists.

"Thanks, Dr. Sykes. I'm okay now." She lifted his hands off her shoulders and stepped away. She turned back to him and flashed a bright smile to prove that she really was all right.

He deftly wrapped an arm around her shoulders and hugged her in a friendly, asexual way. She leaned into him, allowing him to pull her body against his own.

"Anytime, Jessie. I can't have my girl all tired and tense. You never know what's next in Forensics Land."

Jess chuckled. "I'll go put on a fresh pot of coffee for you," she said and left the room.

Bennett smiled to himself as she went through the doors. He was immensely pleased with the results of his experiment. It was plain that she trusted him. She was willing to accept what he had told her about essences. All that was left was just the small step over her own squeamishness, her own unsophisticated attitudes. And he had managed to subtly signal her that his interests lay beyond friendship. And for a moment, she was ready to yield to him.

But she had stopped him. So it was also plain that she was not quite ready yet. *I can't rush this, or I'll lose her,* he thought. He had to be patient. It was imperative that Jess should believe that she came to him of her own free will.

There was still the cop to deal with. Competition for the fair lady's hand. He hoped he had shown Jess enough to divert her from falling into Mike's arms before Mike could be dealt with.

The rich fragrance of brewing coffee seeped into the autopsy room. He threw the door open and left the room.

SEVEN

Jess's doorbell chimed.

"I'll get it!" Susie sang. She had dressed for the occasion in the same outfit she wore to watch *Miss Becky and Friends*—the feathered satin mules and the string of plastic pearls. Jess was aware of the honor Susie was bestowing on Mike by dressing up for him.

Susie yanked the door open. A young man with curly red hair and golden freckles dusted across his nose grinned at her. He was wearing jeans and a white, Oxford-cloth shirt under a denim jacket.

Susie's face fell. "Where's your hat? And your gun?"

"You must be Susie," Mike said. His grin widened as he took in Susie's costume. "I'm Mike O'Keefe. It's a pleasure to meet you." He extended his hand.

Susie took it gravely and shook it.

"You may come in," she said in a dignified tone. "Jessie-ka's upstairs. Sit down, and I'll go and get her."

Susie's bizarre outfit contrasted wildly with her grown-up demeanor. Mike bit back a laugh and sat down on the sofa. Susie started up the stairs, keeping her eyes on Mike. She stopped and smiled at him.

"If you think she was pretty before, just wait," she said.

"How'd you know I thought she was pretty?" Mike asked.

"I just knew," replied the little girl. She turned and shouted up the stairs. "*Jessie!* Mikey's here! He forgot his hat and his gun, but I like him anyway."

A few moments later, Jess came down the stairs, Susie following behind her as if she were Jess's lady-in-waiting. Mike's eyes widened. Jess's wavy fair hair was loose and flowed down her back. She wore a pink sweater and jeans that hugged her slender hips and long legs. She was not just pretty, she was beautiful. Susie caught his eye and smirked. *Told you,* she seemed to be saying.

Jess smiled. "Hi, Mike."

"Hi, Jess." They stared at each other and blushed. Neither could think of anything intelligent to say. Susie decided to take matters into her own hands.

"Mikey, can I get you a Coke or something?" She was being formal again.

"That would be great," said Mike. "Can I help you in the kitchen, Susie-Q?"

"Please do," she replied. Jess could not suppress a giggle, and so the ice was broken.

Mike took Jess to dinner at a Thai restaurant in University City. It had once been a diner, but now the chrome-and-glass Art Deco lines were accented by paper lanterns and brightly colored Oriental paintings. Over the lemongrass soup, Jess asked, "So, how did it go last night?"

"I don't know if you want to hear about it while you're eating," Mike replied. "It was pretty disgusting."

"Hey, I work in Forensics Land. Gross is my middle name," she said, smiling.

"Someone sent a lady a hand. A little kid's hand. Trying to warn her away from her boyfriend. It was totally bizarre. I almost threw up," he admitted.

Jess's eyes grew round. "That *is* bizarre!" she exclaimed. "Do you guys have any idea who did it?"

"Not yet. The guy at the courier service who sent the package gave us a description, and we're working on it. LaVyrle says the lady is hiding something, trying to protect the boyfriend. LaVyrle thinks maybe the boyfriend is married or something, and this lady doesn't want him involved."

"Wow," Jess said again. She thought for a moment of Meredith Shirk, and then decided not even Meredith was that weird. Still, hadn't Bennett said something strange happened to Kass last night? *Quit it,* she thought. *Who do you think you are, Sherlock Holmes?*

"So, how was your night?" Mike asked.

Jess's face grew still. "I think I can top you," she said. "I autopsied my mother."

Mike stared at her, speechless.

"Remember how I told you she left when I was just a baby? Well, it looks like she went back out on the streets. She was a junkie and a prostitute, who finally got beaten to death by a customer, or customers. We're still not sure." Her voice quivered a little. "She had my initial tattooed on her chest, so I guess she never forgot me." She paused. Then her voice hardened a little with anger. "For all I know, *J* could have been a boyfriend. I'll never know, now."

Mike stared at her for a moment. "Wow. I thought we were supposed to be boring together. No such luck, eh? Jessie, I'm really sorry." He reached over the table and took her hand.

Jess shook her head. "It's okay. Really. Mike, I am sick of grief and loss and death in my life. Which is weird, because that's what I do, you know?" She squeezed Mike's hand, and he returned the squeeze. She was silent for a few moments. "It just hurts because I know my dad never stopped looking for her. Never stopped loving her. So if I have any grief, it's for him. He would have been crushed to know how she ended up." She sighed. She looked into Mike's open, concerned face and smiled. "Now that we got all the work stuff out of the way, let's just forget it and have a good time, okay?"

"Okay," agreed Mike. "But Jess, I want to be your friend, and friends listen. So if you want to talk . . ."

"I'd rather eat," said Jess, eyeing the plate of steaming, spicy vegetables and cellophane noodles the waitress placed before her.

"Your middle name really is Gross," Mike groaned.

EIGHT

Jess was awakened at seven A.M. by an insistent pounding on her door. She stumbled downstairs, pulling her pink terry-cloth bathrobe around her. She opened the door.

Susie stood there, dressed in her plaid school jumper.

"I want to hear about your date with Mikey," she said pertly. "I was asleep when you got home."

"And I was asleep until a minute ago, Suz," Jess said irritably. She looked at Susie's crestfallen face. "Oh, okay. Let me put on some coffee first." She padded into the kitchen on her bare feet. Susie followed.

"Where did you go? What did you do? Did you have a good time? What . . ."

"Slow down, Pickle. Jeez, I'm not even awake yet!" She filled the coffeemaker with water and coffee, and set it to brew. Susie sat down at the kitchen table and waited expectantly.

Jess sat down and took a deep breath. "Let's see. We went to the Golden Palace for Thai food—it's like Chinese only better—and then we went for a walk through University City, and then we came back here and had coffee, and then he had to go to work. Yes, I had a good time. Mike's a very nice boy." She rose and took a cup of coffee from the half-filled pot, even though she knew it would be too strong and very bitter.

"Mike's not a boy," said Susie. "He's a grown-up man."

"Yes, I guess he is," Jess replied a little vaguely.

"Dr. Sykes doesn't like him," Susie said suddenly.

Jess started. "How do you . . . What gives you . . . Dr. Sykes doesn't even know him," she stammered.

"Dr. Sykes doesn't like him, and he's trying to make you not like him," Susie said flatly.

Jess thought of the way Bennett had touched her. No matter how hard she tried to convince herself that it was only a neck rub, even she knew it had been more than just that. And his patronizing remarks about Mike, and his suggestion she date an older man . . . *like him,* were the words he had left unspoken. Could it be true? Could he be trying to sabotage her friendship with Mike? She pushed the thought out of her mind. He was her friend, and that was all.

"Suz, Dr. Sykes is just worried about me. Like Uncle Ramon used to be, when I went out on dates." She pushed her hair out of her face. Doubt still nagged at her.

"No, he's not," said Susie. "I like Mikey a lot. Don't listen to Dr. Sykes."

Jess looked at the clock. "You're going to be late for school, Pickle. Better run."

"You don't believe me, do you?" Tears filled Susie's eyes.

"I don't know. I just don't know!" She pushed her coffee mug away from her. Coffee slopped onto the plastic tablecloth. She bit her lower lip.

Susie leaped up from the table, put her arms around Jess, and kissed her. Then she stepped back, put her hands on Jess's face, and pulled it up until Jess's eyes met her own. Jess looked into Susie's depthless gray eyes, too old and knowing for a six-year-old. A sense of peace filled her. Suddenly her anger and confusion were gone. Everything fell into place with a nearly audible click.

Weird, Jess thought. *But right.*

She placed her hands on Susie's cheeks. "I like Mike a lot, too, Suz. He's a nice *man.*" She folded Susie into her arms. "Thanks," she whispered.

"I know more than that old Dr. Sykes does," Susie said, tossing her head and making her ponytail swish.

"I'm beginning to think you do," Jess said, smiling.

Bennett put the box down on the kitchen counter. It contained the supplies he needed for Kass. He had pilfered them from the hospital. He wasn't worried about the catheters and such, but he did have some drugs in there. Controlled substances, subject to careful FDA scrutiny. Part of his mind was worried, but he shrugged it off. Hahnemann was a city hospital, after all, with all kinds of people there at all hours. Even the best security couldn't keep drugs away from someone who really wanted them. Someone might get in trouble eventually, but it wouldn't be him.

A knock sounded on the front door. Quickly he seized the box and ran down into the basement. He had a special place down there to store his supplies. While he put them away, the knocking continued. "Coming!" he shouted, irritated. He wondered who it could be. Some tourist, no doubt, hoping to get a peek inside his certified historic home while pleading that she was lost. Christ, it was almost impossible to get lost in Old City Philadelphia unless you were a moron. *Which most tourists were,* he thought.

He yanked the door open with a frown. Meredith stood there, smiling.

"Hello, Bennett. May I come in?" Her pale eyes looked almost avid in her narrow face. Her cheeks were red, and she seemed nervous. *Weirder than ever,* he thought, groaning inwardly.

"Sure, Meredith," he said. "What can I do for you?"

"I have two tickets for the orchestra tonight. I'd like you to come with me to the concert and dinner. My treat," she added, trying to look arch but succeeding only in looking pathetic.

Bennett felt himself beginning to lose patience. "I'm sorry, Meredith. I have a date this evening. It was kind of you to think of me, though," he said. He could not keep the coldness out of his voice.

"You do?" Meredith asked in amazement. "Are you sure about that?"

"Very sure. Sorry. Now would you excuse me? I have . . ."

Meredith's eyes glittered oddly. "Bennett, maybe you should double-check. Mamakass may have had second thoughts by now."

Bennett turned on her. "How do you know about Mama . . . Kasidy? What fucking business is it of yours?" His brown eyes, which Meredith had imagined melting at her tender devotion, blazed with anger. Too late, she realized she had made a terrible mistake, admitting that she knew so much about him so soon. But blindly, she blundered on.

"You *are* my business, Bennett. I know everything there is to know about you. I . . . I love you, Bennett." Her eyes filled with tears. One rolled down and dripped off the end of her nose. This was not turning out the way it was supposed to. Not at all.

"Everything? Did you say everything?" Anger was tinged with a stab of fear.

"Yes, my darling, everything. What you eat. What you wear. What you read. What you like. I know about your awful ex-wife and how she left you. Left you! And wanted so much money! As if I would ever leave you!" Her voice rose, almost hysterical. "I found the note you wrote to send flowers to that Kasidy slut. I sent her a warning to leave you alone. She can't love you the way I do. Bennett, please, I love you so much. Let me love you. Love me back. Love me, please."

"I threw that note away," he said. His eyes narrowed. "So you're the dog who's been digging in my trash," he said.

"I had to, Bennett. I had to learn everything about you so I could love you," she sobbed.

Bennett was relieved. She knew nothing about the Epicurean Society, because he had taken great care never to write anything down about it. And the e-mails were always encrypted. He doubted Meredith could crack the code, no matter how brilliant she thought she was.

Relief gave way to shock. Meredith must have been the one who sent the hand and the note to Kasidy. How else would she know that Kass had been scared? How had she done it, and how could she do something like that? Did she know how close she had come to ruining everything? Rage filled him. Meredith's obsession had obviously gone past the point of the schoolgirl crush he had assumed it to be. This had to stop. Now. Before it was too late.

He reached out and grabbed Meredith's heaving shoulders painfully. "Listen to me! Meredith, I don't love you. I have never loved you, and I will never love you." He let go of her shoulder and grabbed her chin, pulling her face up to his, boring into her eyes with his own. His voice was cold and menacing. "You're a deluded, incredibly stupid woman, and I don't have time for this teenage bullshit." Her face was contorted with grief and humiliation. She tried to shake her head, to take her eyes from his, but he only tightened his grip on her face. She winced with pain.

"If I ever see you in my house again, or in my garbage, or my office, I will make you sorry you ever laid eyes on me. I think the administration at Hahnemann might be very interested in your little message to Kass." She gasped incoherently, and he pulled her face closer to his. "Oh, yes, Meredith, I know all about your message. You disgusting bitch." He released her and pushed her away, hard. She stumbled and leaned against the wall, sobbing. She lifted her eyes to his face in one last desperate plea for pity. He looked her up and down, contemptuously. "I don't even hate you, Meredith. I just don't give a flying fuck about you. So stay the hell out of my life."

He opened the door and indicated that she should leave. "Will you go now? Or do I have to kick you out of my house?"

She stared at him. Her pale eyes were wild in her blotchy face. The marks of his fingers were like red weals on her livid skin. With a low, wordless cry, she ran out the door. Bennett slammed and locked it behind her.

That's over with, he thought.

But he knew it wasn't.

Kass rechecked the house numbers and knocked at the door of 315 Ashland Street. She glanced up and down the street as she waited for the door to open. The row of red-brick homes, deceptively small from the outside, looked cozy and safe.

It's so pretty here, she thought. Then she heard footsteps inside the house, and her pulse quickened.

"Hey, Mamakass." Bennett grinned at her as he opened the door.

Kass's breath came in a quick, sharp gasp. She'd forgotten just how attractive he was. Bennett was wearing a gray sweatshirt and jeans, and his feet were bare. Kass thought he looked like a pagan god. He ushered her in and took her coat. Then he turned to her, cupped her face in his hands, and kissed her.

"I have champagne in the fridge. May I get you some, fair lady?" he asked.

Kass smiled, her lips reddened from Bennett's kiss. "Sounds great."

"Make yourself at home," he said and left the room. Kass could hear the sound of crystal tinkling in the kitchen and then a soft pop as he opened the bottle.

The living room was immaculate and elegant. An Oriental rug covered the hardwood floor. A curvy Italian sofa, upholstered in cream leather, was placed before the fireplace. The fireplace was flanked by floor-to-ceiling bookshelves, which were full of every kind of book. A fire blazed brightly in the brass grate. Kass browsed briefly through the beautiful, expensive leather-bound books. In a glass cabinet off to one side was the latest acquisition. Her eyed widened at the Manet illustrations. They were lovely. She was amazed at his exquisite taste.

"I should have known you loved books," she called.

"How so?" Bennett replied.

"Because you know so much about everything," she said, a little lamely.

He reentered the room with two champagne flutes. In each one was a ripe, red, out-of-season strawberry. Kass smiled as he handed one to her and sipped.

"Wow! This is the best champagne I've ever tasted," she said.

"Only the best for you, Kass. Only Dom will do."

"I'm impressed," she replied. "With everything. The house. The books. You most of all." He sat down on the sofa and patted the place next to him. She sat down, and he put his arm around her shoulders. She leaned into his warmth.

"A friend of mine is a rare-book dealer. He found me the Poe you were looking at."

"It's beautiful," Kass said admiringly.

"He's also a member of a society I belong to. The Epicurean Society. As a matter of fact, we're meeting this Monday. Would you like to go?"

"What's it all about? Gourmet food, I suppose?"

"Among other things, Mamakass."

"I'd do anything for a meal I don't have to cook. I hate cooking," she said, making a face.

"Anything?" Bennett asked, lifting his eyebrows. Kass looked up into his face and giggled. He looked at her champagne glass, which was still full.

"Drink up, there's lots more," he said. He drained his glass.

Kass pouted. "And I was going to propose a toast."

"To what?"

"To my favorite doctor. Here's to you," she said impishly and swallowed her champagne. She settled back into the warmth of Bennett's arm. It was so comfortable and nice here. They had all evening, the entire weekend to look forward to. And he had just made another date with her. Kass sighed contentedly.

"No more nasty messages from the stalker?"

"None," replied Kass. "But still, I took your advice and didn't tell the kids about our date this weekend. The less they know about all this, the better, even if they are in the Caribbean for a week."

"Good girl. I don't think you'll have any more trouble."

"Did you take care of it? Did you find out who it was?"

In reply, Bennett lifted her face to his and kissed her, hard. She put her arms around him and returned his kiss with ardor. He pulled her closer and ran his free hand up her leg, pulling up her skirt with it. He saw the stockings and the garters Kass had selected with such anticipation.

She moaned at the touch of his hand on her bare thigh. "Is this where I get to do what you want?" she murmured into his ear.

"Yes, Kass," he replied and kissed her again. Then Kass shuddered.

"Bennett." She tried to pull away. "Bennett, I'm so dizzy all of a sudden."

Bennett grinned when he felt her go limp in his arms.

Bennett carried Kass down the cellar stairs and into the secret room. He laid her limp body down on the exam table and removed her clothing. He smiled when he saw the lacy lingerie Kass had donned for him. Very sexy. He would burn it later or perhaps toss it into the Delaware River. He pulled the extensions out from the edges of the table and strapped her wrists and ankles down.

Kass groaned. She lifted her arms and legs feebly against the restraints. Her eyelids fluttered as she strained to open them.

Bennett realized that Kass was starting to come to and worked quickly. He hung a bag of glucose solution on one of the IV poles, picked up Kass's left hand and probed swiftly for a vein. He got the drip going and injected the line with pentobarbital. Enough to keep her asleep for at least six hours. He knew he risked putting her into a coma, perhaps killing her, but he would have to spend the next three days preparing her for the Epicurean Society's meeting. Better she should sleep through it, rather than be awake and terrified. If she were awake, there was also the risk of escape or rescue.

Kass tried to scream, then she was motionless. Completely unconscious.

Bennett stood over Kass's nude body and rechecked the straps on her wrists and ankles. Satisfied that she was secure, he slowed the IV drip into her left arm. She was spreadeagled on the table, arms extended out and legs slightly spread. She really did have a pretty body, thought

Bennett. His fingers traced down over her apple-shaped breasts and her smooth, round belly. She lay passive and still under the strange caress. Bennett moved up to the head of the table and ran his fingers through her heavy, silky hair.

"Such beautiful hair," he whispered. "So beautiful." He picked up a pair of scissors from the small metal table next to the IV pole. He took a handful of her hair and cut it off close to the roots. He moved her head, making certain he cut every hair on her head. Then, when there was nothing but chopped stubble, he took a can of shaving cream and a straight razor. He lathered her scalp tenderly and shaved her head, gently removing every trace of foam with a warm wet washcloth. He planted a lover's kiss on her shiny damp head, and then repeated the procedure between her legs.

From her dark room across the street, Meredith Shirk shook with rage. That stupid slut had come brazen as brass to Bennett's door, and he had let her in. Smiling. She had just been able to glimpse the kiss. Obviously, the slut had a bigger hold over Bennett than Meredith had thought. Otherwise her Bennett would never have treated her like that, talked to her that way. She had forgiven him once she calmed down. He couldn't help it. He was the deluded one, not her.

I should have sent the fucking head to the bitch. A hand obviously wasn't enough.

She looked down at the papers in her lap. It was too dark to read them, but Meredith had them memorized. Kasidy Rhodes. Her address. Where she worked. Names and ages of her children, and their school records. Legal records. Credit ratings.

"It's not fair! He's mine! Mine, do you hear?" Meredith's voice crescendoed to a shriek. Then she settled down and trained her binoculars onto the bedroom.

For several hours there was no sign of any activity in the house. Meredith sat and waited, with the patience of a spider. Finally, she saw Bennett enter his bedroom. Alone.

She breathed a sigh of relief. *How did Kasidy get out?* she wondered briefly. Then Kass was forgotten in the rapture of watching Bennett undress for bed. The files on Kass fell to the floor as she fingered herself to a climax. She sighed as Bennett sat down naked at his computer and turned it on.

It didn't matter how that slut got out. What mattered was what Meredith would do to her next. Breathing heavily, she gathered the papers off the floor.

Maybe I'll fuck up her credit to hell and back unless she leaves him alone. Or maybe her kids. Something with her kids. Got to be careful though. Can't let Bennett find out.

Maybe I should just kill her and be done with it. Then she'll never come back.

Meredith's lips curled in a vicious smile. She looked like a fox that had just discovered a well-stocked henhouse.

The cheerful, obnoxious theme song blared into the room. Jess came downstairs and sat next to Susie. It was time for *Miss Becky and Friends.* Again.

"I'm glad you like to watch this with me," Susie said. "Mommy hates Miss Becky."

"She does not," replied Jess. "She's just . . . a little old for Miss Becky, I guess."

Susie looked over at Jess. "Can me and Miss Becky have a snack, please? Milk and cookies? I'll be careful."

"Raisins and juice, okay? I don't want to spoil your dinner."

"Is that okay, Miss Becky?" Susie paused a moment. "Miss Becky says okay. Thank you."

Jess went into the kitchen and got a box of raisins. She was reaching for the bottle of apple juice in the refrigerator when a piercing scream came from the living room. The juice bottle hit the floor and bounced. Juice splashed everywhere.

She sprinted toward the living room. Susie had stopped screaming and was staring blankly at the television set, trembling. Her face was ashen and tears rolled down her cheeks.

"Susie! What's the matter, honey?" Jess knelt and clutched her shoulders.

Susie was unable to take her eyes off the TV screen. "Make him stop! Make that bad man stop!" she moaned.

Jess turned around and looked at the TV. Miss Becky and Chucky were singing a bouncy little duet about how friends do nice things for each other.

"Sweetie, there's nothing wrong." Jess planted a kiss on Susie's clammy forehead. "It's your favorite show. You sit tight, and I'll be right back after I clean up the mess in the kitchen. You scared the daylights out of me."

Susie whimpered but said nothing. She stared wide-eyed at the TV screen. Jess looked at Susie and shook her head, and went to take care of the spilled juice.

Susie did not see Miss Becky dancing and singing with Chucky. She saw Miss Becky strapped down naked to a table. A man was standing over her. It was the bad doctor man from her dream. She watched, frozen with horror, as the bad man poked needles in Miss Becky's arms. He picked up a pair of sharp, pointed scissors. He cut all Miss Becky's hair off. Then he kissed her.

Susie reached down and grabbed for her doll. She cuddled it close to her. Something felt wrong. When she looked down, Miss Becky's hair was gone. Clumps of curly brown acrylic hair were scattered all over the sofa. Susie ran up the stairs to her room and slammed the door. Jess found her there, huddled under the bed and crying over her mutilated Miss Becky doll.

"What happened, Suz? What happened to Miss Becky?"

Susie came out and crawled into Jess's lap. "The bad doctor man is hurting Miss Becky. Right now! St. Jude told me this would happen! Jessie-ka, I'm so scared!" Susie was shaking with fear.

Jess hugged Susie close and rocked her in her arms.

"I don't *know* what happened, Heather. All I know is that she's scared to death."

Heather Troutman shook her head. "She loves that stupid TV show. That Miss Becky doll is her favorite toy. I wonder what possessed her to cut off its hair?"

Jess shifted uncomfortably on the sofa. "She says she didn't do it, that the bad doctor man did it to Miss Becky. She says the bad man is keeping Miss Becky locked up somewhere and is doing terrible things to her."

"Did she eat anything strange? Anything happen at school today?"

"Not that I know of."

Heather pulled the elastic band out of her hair and rubbed her temples. "She's getting too weird with this bad-doctor-man shit. First the dreams, and now this. If that son of a bitch father of hers would pay his goddamn child support, I wouldn't have to have a fucking job, and I could be here for her." Her face contracted but only for a moment. "Thank God for you, Jess. You're like a sister to her."

"Heather, do you keep, like, sewing scissors in your room or something? The only scissors I know of in this house are the ones in the kitchen. Susie's play scissors and the big shears."

Heather looked surprised. "I don't have scissors anyplace else in this house. Who has time to sew?" She stubbed out her half-smoked cigarette.

Jess looked thoughtful. "You know, I was in the kitchen the whole time that this was happening. When Susie screamed the first time, I came out to see what was wrong.

Then I went right back into the kitchen. I *know* both pairs of scissors were in the kitchen while I was there, because I looked in the drawer. Unless she has a pair of scissors hidden somewhere, I don't know how she could have cut off Miss Becky's hair."

Heather called up the stairs. "Susie, come down here please."

Susie came downstairs, clutching the doll with its chopped hair. Her face was still pale, but she seemed composed. She went to the sofa and sat down between Heather and Jess.

Heather turned to her daughter. "Look, honey, I know you're scared about something, and I'm not going to get mad at you. Just tell Mommy why you cut Miss Becky's hair off."

"I didn't! I told Jessie-ka I didn't! It was the bad doctor man on TV! He's hurting Miss Becky." Susie's lips trembled.

Jess put an arm around Susie. "Susie, I really don't understand all this about the bad doctor man. And I'm sure the scissors were in the kitchen. C'mon, Pickle, tell us what happened. I really want to know."

Susie flew off the sofa and turned to face her mother and Jess. Her face, pale a moment ago, flushed red with anger. "I told you what happened! There's a bad, bad man who wants to hurt her! He was the bad man in my dream, remember, Mommy? The boogie doctor? He tied her up and cutted all her hair off! I didn't do it!" She stamped her foot. "Why doesn't anyone ever believe me?" Her eyes filled with tears.

Suddenly Susie stood still. She looked past them, as if remembering something. The flush of anger left her face and was replaced by an eerie calm.

"St. Jude said he would send me a sign. And this was it. Now I have to go fight the evil and save Miss Becky," she announced. "And I'll do it myself, since nobody believes me."

"Like hell you will," said Heather, her patience gone. "I have to work Saturday. They're installing a big network at an accounting firm. I don't have time to play these games with you. Go on up to bed. Now." Heather went into the kitchen and began preparing herself a late supper.

Susie looked at Jess with the same deep calm. "Tuck me in?" she asked.

"Sure, Pickle," replied Jess. They went upstairs hand in hand. Susie climbed into her canopy bed and snuggled under the sheet. The shorn Miss Becky never left the crook of her arm. She looked up into Jess's face, a plea in her eyes.

"Jessie-ka, I need your help. Please can you help me find Miss Becky? 'Cause if you don't, I'll have to go myself. St. Jude showed me where she is. He said he would send me signs when Miss Becky was in trouble. And this is the first one."

Jess smoothed a lock of Susie's hair out of her face. "Pickle, I know you're upset. Why don't you say a prayer to St. Jude, and things will be better in the morning."

Susie sat up in the bed and looked at Jess. Her gray eyes were suddenly hard and cold in the dim light. Jess flinched at the expression on Susie's face.

"You don't believe me. Mommy doesn't believe me. You think I'm just a little girl and I don't know anything. Well, you're wrong. Wrong! And it's not fair. St. Jude said an unspeaking evil was happening and that Miss Becky was going to be killed."

"St. Jude told you this? Did you actually hear him?"

"Yes. He came alive in the chapel. He picked me up and took me to a funny old street. That's where the evil lives. He said Miss Becky and other people would die unless I found her and fought the evil. Father Romano woke me up before I could find out more stuff." Susie's face was pinched with anger. "Well, I don't care if you believe me or not. I'm going to find the bad evil doctor man and fight him and save Miss Becky." She flung herself back down on the pillows and turned away from Jess.

Jess stared at Susie's thin form under the blanket. Could it be true? Of course not. Evil was a thing in scary books. Evil was drug addicts who shot fathers. But did St. Jude really speak to her? Was this a part of Susie's psychic gift? Which, Jess had to admit, was the real thing. She sighed.

"Okay, Suz. Tomorrow we'll go up to the chapel and see St. Jude. Together. Maybe he'll talk to us and help us understand better."

Susie turned and faced Jess. A relieved expression shone on her little face. "I knew *you'd* believe me. St. Jude said he believed in you even if you didn't believe in him. We'll save Miss Becky. You and me. 'Cause you're really a princess." Susie's eyes got that heavy-lidded look. She sighed sleepily.

St. Jude believes in me even though I don't believe in him. A chill went down Jess's spine. But she leaned over and kissed Susie gently on the forehead.

"Goodnight, Pickle. Sleep tight."

Then she rose, closed Susie's door halfway, and walked slowly downstairs.

NINE

"Now here's a little beauty," the beefy man behind the counter said, as he handed Meredith a pistol. She held it awkwardly in her hands. It was black and cold, with a sinister sculpted elegance. She turned it over, feeling its weight. Suddenly she was afraid of it. She laid it quickly back down on the counter and stared at it.

"Hey, it won't bite you. It's a nine-millimeter Glock Twenty-six. It'll fit real nice in your purse or pocket. It's small and light, feels like part of your hand. So you don't need to be no Annie Oakley to hit your target." He chuckled at his own joke.

Meredith glanced up at him warily, hating him for laughing at her. She had never touched a gun before in her life. How was she supposed to know what to do with it? He smiled easily at her and picked up the gun. "And it ain't no cheap shit Saturday Night Special, neither. Lookit. You load the magazine here," he said, ejecting it to show her. "Holds nine rounds. Then just pop it back in and bingo! You're ready to rock and roll."

He slid the magazine back into the butt and laid it down on the counter. It shone dully in the ugly overhead fluorescent lamps of the little gun shop. Meredith stared at it for a few moments.

"I'll take it," she said, and laid her Visa card on the counter.

"Need your driver's license, too. Background check." He pushed a form toward her. "And you need to fill this out. Twenty-two-dollar fee for the check, pass or fail. And if you plan on carrying it with you, you're gonna need a concealed-weapons permit."

Meredith quickly wrote down the information and wordlessly pushed the completed forms and her driver's license back over the counter. While the gun shop clerk entered Meredith's information into the computer, he kept up a babble of small talk.

"Meredith, huh? I like that name. You live here in the city? Little thing like you, guess you feel you need some protection, huh? Don't blame you one bit. I tell you, there are animals out there. Animals. Kill you for two lousy bucks nowadays. Used to love this city after dark, but now I fucking hate it—pardon my French. Shouldn't complain though. It's good for business."

A tiny voice inside Meredith's head kept asking her what she was doing inside this gun shop, buying this expensive pistol. What was she doing, thinking about killing someone? She was a doctor, for God's sake, sworn to do no harm. What had Kasidy Rhodes ever done to her, really?

Tried to steal Bennett away from me, that's what.

Give it up, give it up. She's innocent.

"Innocent—I don't think so," muttered Meredith.

"What'd you say, lady?"

"I said right, there are animals out there. I need this for self-defense. You never know. Self-defense," she repeated.

"No shit, lady. Okay, you're clean."

"Clean?" she asked, confused.

"No criminal record." He smiled. "You are kinda new to this, aren't you?" He slid her Visa card through the authorization machine.

"Very new," she replied. She watched him pack the gun back into its box. Suddenly she began to tremble, afraid of what she was doing. She thrust her hands into her pockets to hide their tremors, but it was too late.

"Now, don't you be scared of this. This little baby here may just be the best friend you ever had someday." His face took on a look of professional concern. Meredith had seen this look many times in the hospital—had even used it herself. It did not make her like him any better. "I'm including a box of cartridges, and I'm gonna give you a business card. Friend of mine, runs an indoor range. He'll show you how to handle it. Just remember, you got every right to this gun. You got every right to protect yourself and your loved ones."

"Protect my loved one," she repeated.

"Damn straight," the gun dealer agreed.

Meredith smiled. It was going to be all right.

Meredith drove the rented, dark blue Lumina sedan around and around Kasidy's block until a parking space finally opened up across the street from the house. The dashboard clock read 9:30 A.M. For a moment Meredith worried that she might be too late to catch Kasidy at home, but the *Inquirer* was still on the front steps. Mamakass must be a late sleeper, she decided. She parked the car and began her stakeout. She loaded the pistol and slipped it into her coat pocket.

She mentally ran through the scenario she had devised during the sleepless hours of the night. She would wait until Kasidy came out to get the paper, and then she would approach her. She would be very friendly. She'd say she was a friend and coworker of Bennett's, and he had sent her by with a message. She looked down at the bouquet of flowers she had bought from a street vendor, to lend her story credibility. When Kasidy was done oohing and ahhing over the pretty flowers, Meredith would suggest brightly that perhaps they might take a ride over to visit him. What a delightful surprise that would be! Kasidy could thank him in person for the flowers. How charming! Meredith would wait so patiently while Kasidy put on her lipstick and perfume for Bennett. She would compliment Kasidy on her lovely taste in home décor.

Once Kasidy was in the car, seat belt buckled, her little heart pounding with eagerness to go and see her sweet Bennett, Meredith would shoot her. Once in the heart and again in the throat for good measure. Then she would drive out to the Tinicum swamps near the airport and burn the car with Kasidy in it. She would report the rental car stolen. The fire would destroy any link between Meredith and Kasidy.

If Kasidy hesitated, Meredith would show her the gun. That would get her to cooperate quickly. If worse came to worst, she could shoot Kasidy inside her own home and then burn it, but that was much riskier. There was more of a chance of being seen fleeing the house on a busy city street than in the empty marshes.

Either way, Kasidy would be dead, and Bennett would have to turn to her. She smiled at the thought and settled back to wait.

The chapel at St. Laurence's was empty on this late Saturday morning when Jess and Susie entered. They exchanged glances but did not speak. The peaceful hush settled on them like a benediction.

Jess looked around. It had been nearly a year since she had set foot in the chapel. Light streamed through the stained glass windows, making rainbow patterns on the floor. She looked up past the rows of mahogany pews with their red velvet cushions and kneeling pads, up to the huge crucifix over the altar, with the suffering Jesus nailed to it. Bright red rivulets of painted blood flowed down His pale cheeks from the crown of thorns. Jess remembered how that blood had upset her as a child, so much that she would sit through the entire Mass hiding her face against her father's shirt.

The brass chalice and wafer dishes rested on the altar, flanked by tall brass candlesticks. Huge sprays of pink, red, and white flowers adorned the steps leading up to it. Jess decided that there must be a wedding scheduled for the afternoon.

The walls were flanked by the statues of the saints, each in its own niche. The Virgin Mary of course had the place of honor nearest the altar. At her feet was another floral spray. Susie tugged her hand, leading her toward the tiered stand of votive candles burning brightly for the souls departed but not forgotten.

"Light one for Uncle Ramon, Jessie-ka," she whispered.

Jess's first instinct was to say no, but she allowed herself to be led to the candles. She picked up a box of matches and held it in her hand for a moment. *What can I say?* she thought. *That I hate God for taking Daddy away from me? That I miss Daddy so much it still hurts, after all this time? Should I tell him that Mother died a pathetic and ugly death? That this perfect world that God made really and truly sucks?*

She struck the match and lit a fresh candle in one of the amber votive glasses. She watched it catch and flicker, sending gold and brown lights over her hand. Suddenly she knew what to say.

"Daddy, I love you," she whispered. She felt a presence behind her. She looked up. Susie was on her knees in front of the statue of St. Jude.

"Hello, Jessica," came a voice.

Jess started and whirled around to face Father Romano. "I didn't mean to frighten you, child," he said. He touched her arm to steady her.

"I'm all right, Father. Hello, Father." She could not help but return the warm smile on Father Romano's face.

"It's nice to see you again. It's been some time since you've been here," he said.

"Yes, it has. I'm here with Susie," she replied, a little defensively.

Father Romano looked over at the kneeling girl, her lips moving in earnest conversation with her personal patron saint. He smiled again.

"In this age of television and video games, it's wonderful to see such a spiritual quality in such a young girl," he said.

"It's not just spiritual, Father. It's more like mysticism," said Jess. "She seems to have connected with St. Jude." Jess wondered if she should tell Father Romano that Susie claimed to have had a vision. She knew he was a kind man, compassionate and open-minded, but she thought even he would have trouble believing Susie's story. She was having trouble believing it herself. Jess sighed.

He looked at Jess's worried face. He asked, "Have you noticed that Susie seems to have . . . very keen perception? Almost as if she could read your mind?"

"Yes. She's, well, psychic. Sometimes."

They began walking toward Susie and St. Jude. "Wednesday morning I found her lying on the floor in here. She was in a trance," Father said.

"Oh?" Jess kept her voice neutral. Susie's comments about bad doctor men and unspeaking evil came to mind. She decided not to say anything until she knew what Father Romano knew.

"I don't know what happened, exactly," he continued. "When I roused her, she claimed to have fallen asleep. But it was more than sleep. Her eyes were open, as if she was seeing something. Has she said anything to you?"

Jess cringed inwardly. She might be a newly converted atheist, but her early religious training made it impossible for her to lie in God's house. "Yes, a little. She said St. Jude came to her and talked to her."

They stopped a few feet away from Susie, who was still rapt in prayer. Father Romano shook his head, which was covered with thick salt-and-pepper hair. "I don't know what to make of it," he whispered. "I think she may have a gift."

"I think so, too," Jess replied.

"I'd like to speak with her," he said. "I'd like to know more about this . . . connection you spoke of."

Susie turned her head toward them. Her eyes were wide and unfocused, as if she were sleepwalking. She reached out a hand. "Come here, Jessie-ka," she murmured.

Jess knelt down beside the little girl and took her hand. She was suddenly filled with a sense of peace and strength. She heard her father's voice, soft and strong and clear, as if he were kneeling by her side.

Believe her, mi corazón. *Believe her, and all will be well.*

Jess clutched Susie's hand so hard that Susie winced. "Daddy?" Jess cried. "Oh, Daddy, where are you?"

Father Romano knelt beside the two girls. "What? What is it?" he asked anxiously.

"I . . . I heard my father," Jess said. She began to tremble.

"St. Jude said you would," said Susie. She had the grave, old expression she usually wore when she made one of her astonishing observations.

Father Romano looked at them and crossed himself.

"St. Jude said to tell you that Uncle Ramon isn't in purgatory, Jessie-ka. He's in heaven."

Jess and Susie were seated in Father Romano's office. He sat behind his desk, his hands folded in front of him.

"So St. Jude talks to you, Susie," he said thoughtfully.

"Yes, and he shows me stuff, too. I was afraid to tell you last time 'cause I knew Sister Hubert was mad at me. She would think I was fibbing. But I'm not," Susie assured him.

"What does he show you?"

"He showed me a funny old street where unspeaking evil lives. He said I had to fight the evil to save Miss Becky. He said the evil takes unholy communion in blood. Then last night he sent me a sign. He showed me on TV a bad doctor man cutting off all of Miss Becky's hair. And then I looked at my Miss Becky and all her hair was gone! Cutted off just like on the TV!"

Jess nodded, confirming Susie's story.

"Did you see this, too?" Father Romano asked her.

"Not the TV part. But I was right there. The hair was cut off the doll. I . . . I'm pretty sure Susie didn't do it herself. I was in the kitchen when it happened."

"Why do you have to fight this evil, Susie?"

"'Cause of Jess. The evil wants Jessie-ka."

Jess turned to Susie. "What do you mean, it wants me?" Her face was pale.

"I asked St. Jude how come he couldn't fight the evil. This morning he told me that it was you. You have to fight it, too. I can't remember exactly. He said you would know what to do when the time comes. He said you are strong. I told him I knew that already." She grinned at Jess.

Father Romano matched his fingertips and leaned his chin on his thumbs. "Did St. Jude tell you what exactly the evil was?"

Susie shook her head. "Only that it was unspeaking, and that it had been going on for a long time, and that it lived on this street that he showed me. What's unholy communion? Is it like regular communion? Like the blood and body of Jesus?"

He looked at Susie for a long time. Then he said, "Can you go back to the chapel and sit quietly for a few minutes? I'd like to talk to Jessica for a few minutes."

"Okay, Father," she replied. She slipped out of the office, closing the door behind her.

Jess met his eyes. "Look, I know what you're going to say," she said defensively. "She's a little girl with a vivid imagination." *But I know what I heard when I touched her,* Jess silently added.

"That wasn't what I was going to say at all," Father Romano replied mildly. "I'm not sure what to think. It's very possible that she is seeing St. Jude. It's not unheard of, you know," he said dryly. "Remember St. Bernadette? She had conversations with the Blessed Virgin when she was not much older than Susie." He got up from behind his desk and came around in front of Jess. He took her hands and folded them into his. "Keep watch over her," he said. "I am troubled by the evil Susie speaks of. Unholy communions in blood sound very dangerous to me, and I don't want anything to happen to Susie—or to you." Jess shuddered in her chair.

Father Romano paused. "It may be very true that you have been given a purpose, a mission, as it were. But be careful. Let things unfold as they will. Have faith, Jessica. I know faith does not come easily to you now, but try. A willingness to believe is often all you need." He squeezed Jess's hands comfortingly. "I will pray for her, and for you, my child. Let me know if anything else . . . unusual happens. Call me if you need to."

"I will, Father. Thank you, Father. For . . . for not disbelieving her."

"As I told you, I think she has the gift of second sight. Whether she is using it to communicate with the Divine . . . well, that will be revealed to us in God's time. Bless you, Jessica."

"You, too, Father."

* * *

Jess and Susie went over to the park to play after they left the chapel. Susie went into the sandbox and began digging with a shovel that a forgetful child had left behind.

"What did Uncle Ramon say to you?" asked Susie.

"He told me to believe," Jess replied with a sigh.

"Do you?" Susie lifted her chin and stared into Jess's eyes.

"I guess I do, kind of," Jess said slowly. "But I'm scared, Pickle. I don't understand what any of this is about."

"Me, neither," Susie admitted.

"Why does this evil want me? And what for? And if it's such a big deal then why do *we* have to fight it alone? It doesn't make any sense, Suz."

"I don't know. But I know St. Jude will show us what to do." Jess stared at the little girl. Susie's confidence was comforting and unnerving at the same time.

"Where's Miss Becky now? Do you know that?"

"At home, silly."

"No, no. The Miss Becky in your dreams." *She may be having divine visions, but she's still only six,* thought Jess. *I have to remember that.*

"Um . . . I don't know, Jessie-ka. All I could see was the little room, with all the needles and stuff. And the bad doctor man."

"Do you know where it was that St. Jude took you?"

"Not exactly. But it looked like Philadelphia. The part with all the fancy, little old houses. Remember last winter when Mommy took us skating by the river? We droved through it."

"Society Hill," said Jess.

"Oh, I remember something else. The evil's house is number 315. Do you think the dream Miss Becky is in that house?"

"I don't know, Suz." *Well, Sherlock,* she thought, *we have a house in Society Hill numbered 315. That should leave us with only about two zillion houses to look at.*

Suddenly a thought occurred to her. She remembered that Bennett's address was 315 Ashland Street, in Society Hill. She had never been there, but he had told her about it many times in the long midnight conversations they had had on slow nights in Forensics Land. She knew it was old—an historical landmark, in fact—and that Ashland Street still boasted the original cobblestone paving laid down over two hundred years ago. Meredith lived across the street at 316, a fact that made Bennett uncomfortable.

Could Meredith be the bad doctor? She did look kind of mannish, with her short hair and angular face. But Susie knew Meredith well, from her visits with Heather. She would recognize her, even in a dream. Wouldn't she?

Maybe Susie was just acting out her fear and anger over Heather's illness.

Jess felt a sudden sense of relief. Of course! That was it. Just some overheated childish fantasy, generated by her anxiety about her mother. And Susie did have a tremendous imagination. Such a simple explanation. Why didn't she think of it before?

She opened her mouth to begin scolding Susie about scaring everyone with her wild tales when a familiar, much-loved voice sounded behind her.

Believe her, mi corazón, and all will be well.

Jess jumped and looked around. Nobody was near her but Susie, who was staring very hard at her.

"Do you really truly believe me, Jessie-ka?"

Jess looked at Susie and smiled tremulously. "Your Uncle Ramon says I have to."

"That's good," Susie replied.

Meredith awoke with a start. The car, which had been nicely shaded when she parked it that morning, was stifling hot from sitting in the sun. How long had she been sleeping?

She rolled down the window and breathed the cooler air from the street.

The newspaper was still untouched on Kasidy's doorstep, and apparently the mail had been delivered while she was napping. Meredith could see a piece of mail poking out of the brass-trimmed slot in the door. It had gotten caught on the way in. Nobody had been in or out of the house all day. The shades were still drawn.

Meredith shifted uncomfortably in her seat. Her muscles were cramped from sitting still so long. She was hungry and thirsty, and her bladder was full. The bouquet of flowers was wilting. Could she have been wrong? Could Kasidy have stayed at Bennett's last night? But if she did, why did Bennett go to bed alone? And wouldn't she have come home, if only to change her clothes? And what about Kasidy's brats? Where were they?

Give it up, spoke the voice of reason. *Go home. Get a life.*

"No!" Meredith shouted. People on the sidewalk turned to look at her. She rolled the window back up. She had to do this for Bennett. To prove how much she loved him, even though he had hurt her so. For a moment, she remembered his contorted face, his fingers bruising her arms and face, the hateful words issuing from his mouth. But she forgave him. After all, that awful Mamakass had deceived him. Maybe the two of them were laughing at her right now. Well, she'd show them. Kasidy would be gone soon enough, and Bennett would see how wrong he had been about her.

But she had been spotted. She would have to come back later, when everyone who had seen her shouting was long gone. When it was dark, she might not even have to wait for Kasidy to come out. She could just knock at the door, and when Kass answered it, then she could play out her little scene. Under cover of darkness, she might not even bother taking her to the swamps. She could just shoot Kass right there in the living room, and then burn the house down. She might not even have to burn it if she were careful about not touching anything in the house. She would wear the gloves she used when she sorted through Bennett's trash.

She decided to go home and wait until night. She could use the bathroom and get something to drink. She started the car and pulled out into traffic.

Kasidy's house stood silent and empty.

From the Journal of the Epicurean Society
August 1857

I am visiting the home of my dear childhood friend, Bob Smedley, in Uwchland, Chester County. Back home in Philadelphia it is oppressively hot and the air loaded with contagion, but here the breezes are balmy and scented with late summer roses.

We sit in the parlor of evenings and smoke cigars and talk. Bob has a thriving medical practice here among the farm families. I am dean of the Female Medical College of Pennsylvania, with all the annoyances of administration and public relations on my hands. Though it is a goodly endeavor, teaching women to practice sound midwifery and "doctoring," I miss the slow pace and friendly intimacies of the family practice.

We hear horses' hooves coming up the driveway. A courier from Philadelphia has a message for me. I am curious—what urgent matter needs my attention so much so that a courier is sent? It is from the Epicurean Society. The annual banquet will be held in three weeks' time. Would I do them the honor of hosting? I am suddenly overcome with anxiety when I consider the scope of the project and the work entailed; however, I feel it is an honor I cannot refuse.

The courier waits as I quickly write my assent. The banquet will take place at the College on the appointed day. He leaves, and Bob is intrigued.

"What kind of society is this, Fussy?"

"We study philosophical issues and dine on magnificent food, in the manner of the Greeks," I reply. What manner of philosophy and food, Bob asks, when there is another knock at the door. It is soft, yet we are both startled.

Bob opens the door. "How many?" he asks into the darkness.

"Six," comes a whispered reply.

"Come round to the kitchen."

The kitchen is an old building behind the house, a relic from the days when the kitchen was kept separate from the house for fear of fire. Bob picks up his "doctoring bag" and we slip out the back door without a candle or even a cigar stub to light the way. In the darkness I can barely discern shadows moving silently toward the kitchen from the other side, supporting each other in their exhaustion.

Bob pulls the door open and steps inside. He moves confidently, even without benefit of light. He has done this many times before. I catch my head up against something hard and sharp, but stifle my oaths.

A creaking noise is heard. A board is being pulled up from the floor. Our shadowy guests disappear under the floor, and Bob and I follow. Once safely concealed, Bob strikes a match and lights a lantern.

Six—no, seven, there is a babe in arms—fugitive slaves crouch before us. Bob's home is a station on the Underground Railroad, as was my father's. I truly believe that the only thing nobler than ministering to one's fellow human beings is guiding these poor earnest souls out of Egypt and into the Promised Land. One old man hunkers down in pain, his face creased with agony.

"What is it?" I ask. Silently the man removes his shirt. His back is gridironed with welts from a recent whipping. Bob brings the lantern closer. As I gently touch the wounds to examine them, pus flows in streams. This is not the only flaying this man has ever received—his back is etched with

craters and scars from years of beatings. A life of suffering detailed in flesh.

"Why?"

"I went off to visit my wife. Master sold her to another plantation 'cross the county. Boss man caught me comin' back, and I got whupped."

I pull back to allow Bob to poultice and bandage the man's back, when I catch sight of a young lady seated slightly away from the others. Her shoulders are slumped with fatigue. I cannot help noticing her black almond eyes and her fine skin, tan and velvety. She smiles shyly, and I can see her fine white teeth. Then she drops her gaze and moves closer to the safety of her traveling companions. I immediately name her Cleopatra, after the beautiful Queen of the Egyptians.

Bob points out the bucket of fresh water in a corner along with a basket of bread and cheese. He promises that we will bring food in the morning, and we leave them safely concealed. We go to bed, and I feel as if a great weight has been lifted from me.

The next day, we examine all our guests for health problems. Our poor whipped man still has the cuff from leg irons around his ankle, and it is a job of work to get it off. His gratitude when freed of the noxious ornament is dignified and touching. His wife, who had escaped with him, cries tears of joy. Everyone else is reasonably healthy, even the infant who has not known bed or shelter in his short life. But Cleopatra is feverish and complains of pains in her belly. By gentle questioning, I determine that she is about fourteen years old, had been employed as a maid in a fine plantation home, and has been repeatedly ill used by the five grown sons of her master's family in the past few months. She has an infection and internal damage, but will recover. If she had been white, I would have recommended two weeks bed rest and a healthy strengthening diet, but she *is unlikely to get such care on the Underground Railroad. I offer to take her back to Philadelphia and restore her health, but she shakes her head violently and refuses to leave her companions. I will not force her to come with me—that is not what the Society recommends, and besides, my dear Bob will think I have taken leave of my senses. So, regretfully, I pack my bags and make preparations to return to the city on the following day. I will continue my search there, but I long for the exotic Cleopatra.*

Late that evening, we hear hoofbeats again pounding up the driveway, followed by frantic cudgeling of the door. Bob opens it, and Simon Bernard, the young son of a neighboring family, fairly falls into the room.

"Slave catchers! Less than two miles down the road. They know you've got some hidden, and they're coming for 'em!"

We hurry out to the kitchen and hastily advise our guests of this unwelcome development. They immediately bundle up their meager belongings to leave. Bob gives them some ham and potatoes in a sack. However, Cleopatra has taken a turn for the worse, and can barely walk, much less run. I take her hand and look into her pain-and-fear-filled eyes.

"Come with me now, to Philadelphia. You will be safe there, and I will make sure you get to Canada, if you wish, when you are recovered. If you leave with your friends, you will likely be caught, or worse, cause them to be caught as well."

She nods dumbly, and her eyes fill with tears. Her companions take several precious minutes bidding her a fond farewell, then cross the yard and melt into the woods beyond. Fortunately, the night is clouded and the darkness deep. Bob and I offer a prayer for their safe escape. I throw my bags onto my horse, and Bob boosts Cleopatra up in front of me.

"Bless you, Fussy, and Godspeed. Take care, young lady."

We ride off through the fields, staying off the roads. I feel guilty about leaving Bob to deal with those scoundrels alone, but now he has nothing to hide, and I'm certain that young Simon has also taken care to alert the county sheriff, who will forestall the slave catchers from releasing their frustration onto Bob's property and person. Now my only concern is getting my precious cargo to the city.

We arrive home without incident, and I find to my relief that the weather has moderated somewhat, so that the city climate is no longer as oppressive. Cleopatra thrives under a regime of rest and all the milk, fruit, and meat she can consume. With prodding, she tells me a little about herself— her name is Addie, she comes from Georgia, her parents were sold off long ago, whence she does not know. She tells me nothing about her owners and the wretched men who treated her so badly. She is passive and quiet. I watch her eat a plum, her white teeth cutting avidly into the ripe dusky skin of the fruit, the juices flowing down her chin and arm, and I feel awed by her perfect beauty. She is Cleopatra personified, and I will not call her by her slave name.

As the days pass and she comes to believe that she is truly safe with me, she loses some of her reticence and begins to ask questions. She is naturally intelligent and curious about her new surroundings. She stares at books for hours, looking at the pictures and puzzling over the words. I find myself growing a bit fond of her, teaching her the alphabet and numbers, and telling her stories of this great city. She listens raptly and is a perfect pupil. However, when I tell her of the Women's Medical College and its noble purpose, she is unsurprised. She tells me about a woman slave called Mazie that she knew who could cure anything with herbs and poultices, and a bit of voo-doo magic. It seems perfectly normal to her that a woman should practice medicine. I admire her open-mindedness and offer to take her to visit the College.

"Yas'sir," she says in her soft voice. In a day or two I will take her.

I have brought Cleopatra here after hours, and I light the gas jets on the walls as we go, so we can see our way. She walks behind me as we tour through the school, silent, but her eyes take it all in. We come to the anatomy classroom. She is fascinated by the life-sized posters of musculature and the various organs preserved in jars, but most of all she is attracted to the articulated skeleton that hangs in the corner of the room. She touches her hand, and then the skeletal hand, comparing the two with a keen interest. She peppers me suddenly with questions—what is it, how many, how much, why? Again I am impressed by her quick mind.

For a moment, I consider keeping her with me and educating her properly. She could do great service, working as a physician to the Negroes of Philadelphia. But, no, she will be of great service in another way. A quick blow to her unsuspecting head, and she crumples limply to the floor. I carry her over to the zinc basin by the specimens and pick up a scalpel. Yet still I hesitate—the desire to keep her is strong. I suddenly have a memory from my boyhood come to mind, my father in butcher's apron and boots, splattered with hog's blood, busy amid the carcasses newly slaughtered and hanging on hooks in the barn. I am clutching a baby rabbit, feeling its warmth and softness, while my father's voice warns me not to make pets of the calves and piglets, the bunnies and chickens, because they would only grow up and become food for our table.

I cut the throat and then lift the body high by the legs, keeping the head down in the basin as it bleeds out.

Once the body is bled, I take it to the surgery theatre. Then it all becomes a matter of dissection. The body is thin and muscular, with not much fat on it—an effect of hard work and poor nourishment. I cut the haunches and thighs away, putting them into buckets of cold water. The organs are preserved in specimen jars. I spend the rest of the evening cutting away skin, hair, cartilage, and ligaments from the bones, which will be prepared and assembled for the College's use. I make it plain that no questions are to be asked, and none will be.

A few days later I make a stew from the meat, cutting it fine and simmering it for hours until it is tender, adding potatoes, carrots and peas, and herbs fresh from the late-summer garden. At the last I put in some red, ripe tomatoes. Again I return to the College after hours, this time to the meeting room next to my office. The stew is much enjoyed by all the Society, and we stay up until the wee hours discussing the potential of the human spirit, the fire of intelligence that burns bright even in the most downtrodden of us, and our instinctive, imperious desire for freedom.

Dr. Edwin Fussell

Bennett entered the secret room in his basement. He crossed to the locker and took out an IV bag, an enema bag, and a small pink item. He turned on the overhead light. Kass was still sleeping on the exam table, her bald head turned toward him. The down comforter he had tucked around her last night was still snugly wrapped around her body. A half-smile played around her mouth, as though she were having a pleasant dream.

He gently pulled Kass's arm out from beneath the comforter and changed her IV bag. When he was sure it was dripping properly, he picked up a hypodermic needle. He filled it with another dose of pentobarbital and injected it into the IV line. He wanted to be sure she slept through the cleansing process, as it was not very comfortable.

He undid the straps from around her ankles and tucked her legs up close to her as he slid in the table extension and pulled out the stirrups. He placed her feet in the stirrups and removed the comforter from her body, letting it slide to the floor. He went over to the sink and filled the enema bag with warm soapy water, and the small pink douche with a mixture of vinegar and water.

When he returned to the table, he hung the enema bag from the other side of the IV pole and looked down at Kass. The chilliness in the room had caused her nipples to harden. Her lips were still slightly parted. Her legs were spread wide apart with her feet in the stirrups. She was as sweet and clean as a baby.

Bennett gazed almost reverently at Kass's naked perfection. Soon this caring mother, full of life and laughter and a healthy sex drive, would be part of him. And others. Locked together in an intimacy beyond Kass's imagination.

He ran his hand over her apple-shaped breasts, her smooth round belly, down to her pubis. Pink and perfect, like a hidden flower. Less reverent thoughts began crowding into his mind. Kass lay resistless in front of him, in an anesthetic-induced coma. As close to death as a healthy person could get. His erection pushed painfully against his jeans.

"No, this will never do," he muttered to himself. She was destined for a holy rite, and he could not defile her. Still, he could not resist running his hand over her body once more. Kass moaned softly under his touch but did not move.

He chuckled softly and straightened up. He turned her on her side, lubricated the tip of the enema bag, and inserted it. After the enema was administered, he used the douche to finish cleaning her internally. He used his best bedside manner, speaking to her subconscious softly and reassuringly.

"There, what a good girl you are, Kasidy. I'm sorry, but we'll have to do this at least two more times before Monday. And then on Monday, my dear, you become the sacrament at the Epicurean Society Ball. You'll be part of me then, and part of many others, too." He turned her onto her belly and washed her backside, admiring her fair skin, then dried her with a fluffy white towel and wrapped her again in the warm blanket. He placed a pillow under her head and wrapped her head in a soft wool scarf. When he had attended to her comfort, he stepped back and looked at her.

He was very proud of himself. By keeping her deeply anesthetized rather than simply locked away, fully conscious, the meat would not be flooded with adrenaline and the other hormonal by-products of terror. That would have contaminated the fine essences that had led him to choose Kass in the first place. Also, she would be at her freshest when she went into the oven.

He would keep her warm and comfortable until it was time.

He adjusted the comforter once more and smiled at Kass's still face on the pillow.

"Well, I'm off to visit some friends now. Sleep well, Kass."

He turned out the lights and left her in darkness.

Jess gladly went home when Heather arrived. She was exhausted from the day's revelations and wanted to be alone. She and Suz had decided not to tell Heather about the morning's visit to St. Laurence's chapel, feeling that it would only upset her needlessly. The lines of fatigue and pain had been deeply cut into Heather's face, and Jess knew that Heather could not go on much longer. Better to wait until they had something real to tell Heather.

She curled up on the sofa to watch the Flyers' home opener and eat popcorn, trying not to think. She wanted to forget that saints and dolls and evil bad doctors even existed. She wished Mike wasn't working tonight. A few hours spent in his stable, sane presence would have been so soothingly normal. Like what nineteen-year-olds were

supposed to do. Not chasing off after enigmatic pro-
nouncements by a saint via a six-year-old girl.

She cheered when the Flyers finally beat the Pittsburgh
Penguins, 3-2, winning their home opener.

She made some more popcorn and watched the late
news. She was grieved a little by a story covering the funeral of five children who had perished in a crack-house
fire. The pictures of five tiny coffins being carried out of a
storefront church in North Philly were heartbreaking. The
reporter had broken the solemn tone of the report to mention in a righteous voice that the mother was unable to attend her children's funeral, as she was in police custody.
But by the time *Saturday Night Live* came on, Jess finally
was able to laugh again. When it was over, she took a long
hot bubble bath and went to bed.

A noise woke her up just an hour later. Jess opened her
eyes to see Susie gazing at her solemnly, holding her Miss
Becky doll. She sat up with a start.

"My God, Suz, what time is it?"

"The clock said three-fifteen. I couldn't sleep so I got
the key and came over. Can I sleep with you?"

Jess moved over and made room in the narrow bed.
"Sure, Pickle." Susie climbed in and nestled closer to
Jess's warmth. They lay in silence for a time. Jess was
drifting back to sleep when Susie began speaking.

"He gave Miss Becky a bath. After you left. I saw it in
my sleep. He washed her on a big metal table. He leaned
over her and did stuff to her. Then he wrapped her up and
left her in the dark."

Jess was suddenly wide awake. She pulled Susie close
to her. She desperately wanted to ask just exactly what
"stuff " it was that the bad man did. She wondered if the
dream had been of a rape. But what did Susie know about
rape? *Better to not say anything,* she decided, *or you'll end
up explaining things little girls are better off not knowing
at six years of age.*

"See? I wrapped Miss Becky up just like he did." She held Miss Becky up so that Jess could see the doll. Susie had swaddled the doll in an old baby blanket and wrapped her head up in a turban made from an old sock. Then she looked at Jess, her eyes wide in the dim light.

"What's rape? Is that what the bad doctor man did to Miss Becky?"

Jess sighed deeply. *You and your damn mind-reading gift,* she thought. "Rape is when someone touches you in a private place, and you don't want them to. It's very bad, Susie."

"Well, I guess that's what he did to Miss Becky, except I think she slept through it. She just lay still, and her eyes were closed. It was really weird. Kind of icky, too." Susie lay back down and snuggled up to Jess's warmth, clutching her doll close to her.

Jess lay her cheek against the top of Susie's head, breathing in her sweet, clean little-girl fragrance. "Oh, Pickle, I don't understand these dreams. I wish I could find a way to make them stop."

"Jessie-ka, I told you it's not dreams," said Susie in a re-proving tone. "It's for real. I see it. Just like TV, except it's in my mind." She snuggled the doll in her arms. "St. Jude told me he would send me signs, so I'm not scared any-more. Now that you believe me." Jess put her arm around Susie's shoulders. She pulled the little girl close to her. *I'd give anything to wake up and find out that this is all a bad dream,* she thought. *No bad doctors or Miss Beckys or evils or rapes or communions. Maybe if I close my eyes and go to sleep, it will all go away.*

Susie spoke again in the darkness. "Know what else that bad doctor man said? He said Miss Becky would be the sac-er-a-ment at the Curer's Ball. That means they're go-ing to eat of her body and drink of her blood, right? Like Communion."

"Communion is only symbolic," Jess answered. "You

don't really eat of the body." *Curer.* Why did that sound familiar?

"Well, Mommy and Sister Hubert said it was real. So we have to find her. Soon. Tomorrow, maybe." Susie sounded sleepy now. Jess held her tightly while she drifted off.

It was a long time before sleep found Jess again.

Bennett drove slowly along Thirteenth Street, eyeing all the whores waiting along the curb. Some of them recognized him and called and waved, but he ignored them. He was looking for a particular type tonight. Someone who could be Kass and Jess and Ingrid all rolled into one. Someone who was ready for a little "edge play."

He spotted a woman he'd never seen before and pulled over. She was tall, with long legs that looked longer in the high heels and short leather skirt she was wearing. Her long, cornrowed hair was thickly beaded. She looked almost too fine for Thirteenth Street. He motioned her over to the car.

"I'm looking for someone. Maybe you, Long Tall Sally. What do you think?"

"Maybe you is, and maybe you ain't. What you got in mind, honey?"

"I want to party all night, lady. Live life on the edge. Who's your friend there?" Bennett could see a younger girl, who seemed a little less sure of herself than Long Tall Sally. She was big-breasted and thin-hipped, and wore a red satin jumpsuit and big, gold hoop earrings, but her hair was pulled back with a smudgy office-type rubber band. He was intrigued by that slightly sleazy detail.

Sally grinned. She had a gold cap on one of her front teeth. "Looking for a black cow, maybe? Little chocolate and vanilla? Hey, Tanya, c'mere. Mr. Man here is looking for a couple of party girls." Tanya walked over to the car and bent down. She looked about eighteen years old, and Bennett could see traces of white powder on her upper lip.

"Sure, I like to party," Tanya said, and wiped her nose on the back of her hand. Sally rolled her eyes.

"How much?" asked Bennett.

"Two hundred. Each." Sally looked down at Bennett, daring him to argue with her. "Plus, you better treat us good, you want us hangin' with you all night."

"Get in, Sally. I like your attitude," said Bennett.

"That's not your name," Tanya said as Sally opened the door and slid into the front seat next to Bennett.

"No, it ain't, but it will do. Get in the car."

Tanya slipped into the back. "Ooh, leather," she said. "Nice car, Mr. Man."

"That's Doctor Man to you," said Bennett. They drove off.

"Here," said Bennett, handing the car keys to the valet and pocketing the claim ticket. "Shall we go, ladies?" With one on each arm he escorted them into the Fairmont Hotel, walking through the opulent, chandeliered lobby as though he owned the place, nodding and smiling at the hotel's employees. Sally followed his lead, and walked right beside him with her head high. But Tanya lagged behind a little, as if she expected the cops to chase them off.

"Come on, Tanya. What are you afraid of?" asked Bennett as they stepped into the elevator.

"Don't mind her. She's from Arkansas or something. Came to the big city looking for fun, din'cha? And all you got was a head full of shit." Sally snorted.

Tanya looked down. "Shut up, bitch," she muttered.

Bennett unlocked the door of his suite. It was richly furnished, with heavy damask draperies at the window and leather upholstered chairs. In the next room was a king-sized bed, folded down, and a box of four Godiva chocolates on the pillow.

"Check this out!" called Tanya. "There's a phone in the bathroom!"

Sally looked at Bennett. "Nice. You want to make small talk first or fuck, Doctor Man?"

"What's your hurry, Sally? I think I'd like some dinner first," Bennett replied coolly. A knock came at the door, and he opened it. Two waiters came in with a room service cart each, covered with crystal and silver salvers. Two bottles of Dom Perignon were chilling in the large ice bucket, and the suite quickly filled with delicious odors. Tanya stared wide-eyed at all the opulence. The waiters busied themselves setting up dinner for the three of them.

"That will be all for now," said Bennett. He tipped the waiters with a twenty each and turned to the whores. "Shall we eat, ladies? I've ordered us some filet mignon with asparagus and new potatoes. I hope you'll like it."

Even Sally was impressed. "Well, Doctor Man, I do like your style," she said.

"What's for dessert?" asked Tanya eagerly.

"You," replied Bennett. She giggled.

Bennett actually ate very little. He watched the whores as they ate. Sally wolfed her meal down with a minimum of manners and a great deal of gusto. Tanya began eating heartily, and then she suddenly stopped. She looked pale and a sheen of sweat broke out on her forehead.

"Gotta go to the bathroom," she muttered, and abruptly left the table. Sally began eating the other girl's food. "She ain't gonna want it when she gets back, if you know what I mean. Not after she powders her nose."

"Did you know a woman named Ingrid?" Bennett asked.

"Met her one or two times. Skanky old bitch. Haven't seen her around lately."

"She's dead," he replied.

"Shit happens," Sally said. She pointed to his plate with her fork. "You gonna eat that?"

Later on, Tanya was lying underneath Bennett, wearing nothing but a necktie, as he pushed ever deeper into her. Sally was behind him, tossing his salad with a long, nearly prehensile tongue.

"Oooh, baby! Fuck me good!" Tanya moaned, grinding her thin hips against Bennett's.

"Ready?" asked Bennett.

"Ooh, yeah. Ooh, yeah, baby. Do it now!"

"Good," said Bennett. He reached down and grabbed the tie. He pulled it tight with a jerk. "Here's one you'll never forget." Tanya's eyes bulged, and her tongue thrust from her mouth. Her face turned purple, and her eyes rolled back in her head. Her body flailed crazily for about fifteen seconds.

"What the fuck?" asked Sally. She stopped licking and came up to see what was going on. "Shit, man, you gonna kill her."

"I'm a doctor, remember?" He waited until Tanya stopped thrashing and lay still beneath him. He rolled off her and pulled the tie loose from her neck. She did not move. He turned to Sally and grinned.

"Think she's had enough? Ready for your turn, Long Tall Sally?"

"I told you, I don't play no breath games."

"Yeah? Maybe you should." Bennett pushed her back onto the bed and began fondling her breasts.

She tried to move away. "Seriously, Doctor Man, see if the girl's all right."

"Don't try to get away from me," he said, shaking her left breast. But he turned back to Tanya's still form. Tanya's face was mottled, and her eyes were closed.

"Hey, wake up."

Tanya did not respond. Bennett shook her and tapped his fingers against her cheek. Nothing. Then he reached for her wrist and felt for a pulse.

"Is she dead? She ain't dead, is she?" Sally's eyes were wide. Bennett did not answer her. He rolled off the bed and pulled Tanya's body down onto the floor next to him. He pushed her onto her back and tilted her chin and nose up. Then he straddled her.

"What are you doing? Oh, Jesus, you're gonna kill her." Sally's voice notched up toward hysteria. Bennett leaned forward and pressed his mouth down over Tanya's, blowing until he saw her chest rise. Then he straightened up and gave two short thumps to her chest with the heel of his hand, and repeated the process.

"Oh God, don't let her die. Sweet Jesus, don't let her die." Sally moaned and clutched a pillow to her breasts, rocking back and forth. "Please don't let her die."

Bennett ignored her as he worked on Tanya. A fine sheen of sweat broke out on his back and face. A minute passed, and then another. The only sounds in the room were Bennett's breaths and the hollow sound Tanya's chest made when he thumped it. Sally began to whimper like an animal.

"Shut up," Bennett said shortly. Suddenly Tanya's body spasmed, and she gasped, a deep ragged breath. Then she began to cough. Bennett yanked her into a sitting position.

"Thank God, Doctor Man, you saved her life!" Sally scrambled off the bed and crouched down next to Tanya, patting her on her back. Tanya was alternately gasping and coughing. Bennett got a glass of water from the table and handed it to her.

"Sip this, it will help with the coughing," he said. She did and slowly stopped coughing. "Thanks, Doctor Man, I guess," she said feebly.

Bennett took her hands. "Look at me, Tanya." She raised her eyes. "I need you to tell me what happened while you were out cold. I need to know what you saw."

"I don't know what I saw. All I know is that you choked me, and it hurt, and the next thing I know you're beating on me," she replied petulantly.

"No, no. You must have seen something, heard something."

"Like what?"

"Honey, you was dead there," said Sally. "I think Doctor Man wants to know if you saw angels or something."

A light slowly dawned in Tanya's eyes. "You mean when you choked me, I died?"

"You weren't breathing, and I couldn't find a pulse," replied Bennett.

Tanya was silent. Sally got up and filled a glass with champagne and handed it to her. She looked at it, and then tossed it back like whiskey. She coughed reflexively, and then looked at Bennett again.

"I died, and you brought me back," she said tonelessly.

Bennett nodded.

"Well, all I remember is that it was just black and . . . nothing. No angels or anything were looking for me. Just nothing."

"Are you sure? Think, Tanya. I need to know."

Tanya raised her hand and touched the rapidly purpling bruises on her neck and chest. Her eyes filled with tears. "I told you, there was nothing. Not a goddamned thing. And you know what else? You should have left me there, you son of a bitch. What'd you bring me back for?" She clenched her fist and punched Bennett on the chin. He fell back, more from surprise than the force of the punch. He got to his feet and looked down on the two naked whores. Tanya was sobbing uncontrollably, and Sally was trying to soothe her. She looked up warily at Bennett.

"Look, I'm going to take a shower." He walked over to his pants and pulled out a roll of bills. "There's five hundred here," he said and put it on the dresser. He went into the bathroom and turned on the shower, knowing full well that they would search his pockets while he was in there. There was no more money to be found—but there was a bag of pharmaceutical-grade cocaine and a set of works. He felt angry and cheated. Tanya had been dead. How could she not have something to tell him? How could it just be "nothing" for her? It didn't fit in with what he knew, and with the theories he was developing from the Society, and hoping to test on Kass. Now it was just an ugly incident with a whore who probably should be dead. And likely would be by morning—that coke was probably 100 percent purer than anything else she'd ever snorted or popped.

When he emerged from the bathroom, both Tanya and Sally were lying on the bed watching TV. Tanya had the last bottle of champagne, and both of them had sniffles.

"Sally? You, too?" said Bennett, chuckling.

"Well, I was upset. I needed something to calm me down, and Tanya had some extra," she said defensively, her eyes glued to the car chase on the TV screen.

Bennett said nothing and finished dressing. As he expected, a surreptitious patting of his pockets revealed that they were empty.

"Well, ladies, it was fun. I suggest you think about leaving fairly soon, before security comes to make sure you do."

Tanya looked at him, her eyes glazed with coke and champagne. "Bye. And thanks. For nothing, you asshole."

Sally jabbed her in the ribs. "Never mind her, Doctor Man. Me, I wouldn't mind seeing you again. But you best be on your way before this stupid bitch pisses you off."

And so you can shoot up that coke, Bennett thought. He left without another word and went to get his car. The image of Tanya's body trembling, then coming to life again, kept replaying in his mind.

TEN

"I can smell the ocean, Mommy!" Susie started to put her head out the window.

"Sit down this instant, Susie. You're not a damn dog!" Heather tugged on Susie's arm.

Heather had suddenly decided early that morning to take Susie down the shore to Townsend's Inlet. It was Susie's "most favoritest place on earth," and the rolling ocean and sandy, pale-gray beaches always had a restorative effect on Heather. They had rented a cottage on Pleasure Avenue every summer since Susie was an infant. She could think of no better place to tell Susie that she was going to die. From what Jess had told her, it was past time Susie knew.

Even though it was a warm October Sunday, most of the cottages were empty, closed up tightly against the winter storms. The patches of gravel that served as front lawns had leaves scattered among the stones. Heather parked the car in front of the house they rented in the summer. She and Susie got out. Heather opened the hatchback, taking out an old blanket.

Susie stood on the sidewalk, looking at the cottage. "Mommy, it looks so lonesome now. Do you think it misses us?"

"Sure, Suz. Come on, let's go." Hand in hand, they walked toward the beach.

Susie pulled off her shoes and went barefoot, carefully walking over the small grassy dune. She kept Miss Becky, still in her turban and blanket, tucked firmly under her arm.

"Mommy, look! There's hardly anybody here! We have the whole beach to ourselves!" Susie saw a forgotten lifeguard's chair pulled back near the dunes and climbed up. "Mommy, I can see Avalon from up here!" She pointed south, to another island. Huge dunes sheltered the tall glass-and-cedar-sided homes.

"Susie, get down! You're not allowed up there!" Heather called as she fumbled with a cigarette and her lighter.

"Oh, Mommy. Nobody's using it," she complained. But she scrambled down and ran to the edge of the water. She gently placed Miss Becky on dry sand and began picking up shells. Heather spread the blanket and sat down. As she exhaled the smoke from her cigarette, she closed her eyes and felt the sun's healing touch on her pale face. The ocean rolled and roared, as it had done for untold eons, and would continue to do long after Heather and Susie were gone from this earth. Knowing that somehow brought peace to Heather.

She opened her eyes and watched her daughter rinsing shells in the water, darting back as the waves ran up onto the sand. Heather's brow furrowed. *It's bad enough that I have to tell her she's gonna lose me, but now she's getting weird on me,* thought Heather. She made a mental note to call Sister Hubert on Monday. *Freakin' St. Jude and his freakin' signs.* Heather buried her cigarette butt in the sand.

Susie came up, her hands full of gray-and-lavender shells and Miss Becky under her arm. She dropped them on the blanket and stared hard at her mother.

"Mommy! It's blasphem . . . blasp . . . bad to think of St. Jude that way! You could go to eternal damnation for that!"

Heather flinched. "Okay. I'm sorry. Damn it, Suz, how do you do that?"

"I just knew. Like I always do." She sat down. "How come you don't believe me about St. Jude? Jessie-ka does?"

"Honey, it's hard to believe in something you can't see. And I didn't see St. Jude talking to you. I don't think you fibbed about cutting Miss Becky's hair anymore, if that helps."

Susie began sorting her shells by size and type. She made a neat nested stack of clamshells and then looked up at Heather. "I know you're going to die, okay? I know you and Jessie-ka don't want to talk to me about it, but it's all right." She met Heather's eyes with her own level gaze, as gray as the ocean in front of them. The breeze blew her hair over her cheeks. "You brought me here to talk to me about it."

Heather's eyes blurred with tears. "Suz, you scare me."

Susie's shoulders suddenly hitched up, and she wiped her eyes with the backs of her hands. Her mother opened her arms and folded Susie's thin little body into them. They sobbed and held tightly to each other.

"Mommy, I'm scared, too, a little. I mean, you'll be safe with Uncle Ramon in Heaven, but it will be just Jess and Miss Becky and me left."

Heather stroked Susie's hair. "Baby, I'm scared, too. It's not going to be easy to leave you. I'm gonna be real sick for a while before I go. It'll be hard for all of us. Oh, Suz, you're all I got, and I worry about you." She hugged Susie tighter. "But Jess'll take real good care of you. Or I'll come back every Halloween and scare the sh—crap out of you guys." Heather tried to smile. "St. Jude will watch out for you, too, I guess. Seems like you're kinda special to him." It cost Heather an effort to say that, but it was worth it when Susie turned a tear-streaked face up to hers. She smiled up into her mother's drawn and tired face.

"He will, Mommy. I know it."

They were silent for a minute. Susie wrapped her arms around her mother's bone-weary and wasted body protectively. Then Heather sighed, as if coming to a decision. "Suz, I don't know how you know stuff. It must be a gift from God."

"St. Jude told me it was a gift. Jess said it's called side-kick or something."

"Psychic, baby. It means you can see things that other people can't. In a special way. You know what I mean." Heather put her finger under Susie's chin and tipped her face up to hers. She looked intently into Susie's wide hazel eyes. "Listen up now. I just want to tell you . . . no matter what, no matter who doesn't believe you, you listen to your own self."

Susie held her mother's gaze for a second, then she nodded and blinked. "Okay." She shrugged out of Heather's arms, picked up her doll, and said, "I'm going to go and play tag with the waves. Wanna come?"

"In a minute, Suz."

Heather watched her daughter run away from her, down to the gray water and foam-flecked surf.

Mike was waiting for Jess under the black, wrought iron arch that spelled out PHILADELPHIA ZOOLOGICAL GARDEN. She ran up to him, grinning.

"Michael, I am so glad you called. This is such a cool idea. I haven't been to the zoo since I was a kid," said Jess.

"You still are a kid," said Mike, grinning back at her.

"Yeah, and you're a wise old man of twenty-two," retorted Jess.

Mike began singing, " 'You are sixteen, going on seventeen . . .' " until Jess poked him with her elbow. "Who's paying for our tickets?"

"I am. I'm old-fashioned that way." He reached for his wallet in the back pocket of his jeans.

Jess smiled. "You have a nice voice, even if you do sing stupid songs."

Mike bought the tickets and began singing "Do Re Mi." Jess groaned and dragged him through the turnstile.

"What are your neighbors up to today?" Mike asked, after Jess let go of his arm.

"They went to Townsend's Inlet for the day. Left early this morning," she replied.

"Man, they got a great day to go down the shore today," Mike said, taking off his jacket and slinging it over his shoulder.

"Yeah, they did. I think Heather wants to have a talk with Suz about what's going to happen." Jess shrugged.

"You want to talk about it?" Mike asked.

"Not right now," she replied. "I want to see the zoo." She walked over to a map of the zoo. "So, Michael, where do you want to go first?"

Mike wanted to see the reptiles first, so they entered the warm, musty smelling Reptile House. They watched in horrified fascination as a beautifully patterned boa constrictor slowly swallowed a large white rat. The recently suffocated rat was disappearing headfirst by centimeters through the grotesquely unhinged jaws of the boa. Jess felt a chill pass through her.

"Eeeew, how can you watch this?" She hid her head on Mike's shoulder.

"It's really cool. Just think, he won't have to eat again for a month."

"Blech," Jess replied. "Let's go look at something else."

The lizards were much more pleasant to watch. Jess liked the quick little geckos with their jewel-like eyes, and the lazy gray iguanas that looked like leftovers from the Jurassic Period.

They toured the newly rebuilt Primate Park, where Mike made Jess laugh by making faces at the bored monkeys. One young orangutan came down to the front of the glass that separated them and imitated every face Mike made until Jess could barely stand up, she was laughing so hard. Mike put his arm around her to steady her.

"Stop it, Mike, or I'll—" The orangutan rolled his lips back and pressed them against the glass. Jess was again overcome with laughter.

Exhausted from laughing, she led Mike to a bench in front of the elephant yard. The two of them watched the elephants eat from the huge piles of hay in the yard, using their trunks to stuff their mouths. Jess bought a soft pretzel and fed it to the wandering peacocks and a few pigeons. Mike kept his arm around her shoulders. It felt warm and secure and right to Jess. She leaned into him and smiled up into Mike's green eyes.

"I haven't laughed so hard in ages," Jess said. "I think I really needed to."

"I haven't seen anyone laugh so hard in ages," he replied.

Jess suddenly realized why the boa and the rat had disturbed her so much. When Mike wasn't around, she felt exactly like that unfortunate rat. Like she was being swallowed headfirst by something huge and relentless that she didn't understand. Her face became grave.

"Mike, I have to talk to you," she said.

She told him what had happened yesterday at St. Laurence's. "I know you'll think I'm nuts, but I heard my father's voice telling me to believe Suz. Twice. Once in the chapel, and then again outside, right when I had made up my mind it was all in Susie's head. So now I need to figure out what this evil is and what we're supposed to do about it."

Mike looked thoughtful. "Read any good books about Joan of Arc lately?"

"Mike! I'm telling you the truth, at least as much as I understand it."

"Look, Jess. I know Susie's a little psychic. She sure read my mind when I came to pick you up the other night. It was kind of weird. And I'm a good Irish Catholic. I believe in God and the Virgin and the saints. But all this stuff about talking statues and walking evil and bloody communions—man, that's like way out there." He shook his head.

"Well, what about this ghost ship you were telling me about? You believed in that, didn't you?"

"That was different. I saw it. I was there. Nobody had any kind of explanation."

"I know what I heard," Jess said quietly. "I'm not asking for your help. You said you wanted to listen and to be my friend, okay?"

"I did say that," Mike replied. "All right then. Let's say it's all true. There's an evil stalking you, and you and Susie have to do battle with it. What have you done about it?"

"Nothing, yet. Susie thinks it's down in Society Hill. She's got a house number but no street name. It's the same number as Dr. Sykes's house, and there's this slightly psycho doctor that lives across the street—Meredith Shirk. She's Heather's oncologist. It's occurred to me that Meredith might be the evil. She's sure weird enough."

"But then why wouldn't Suz have her house number instead of Bennett Sykes's? Could he be this evil thing?"

Jess was shocked. "No way! Dr. Sykes is the nicest man I know, except for you. He's been so kind to me. He was wonderful to me after Daddy died, and he's always trying to help me, teaching me stuff and talking to me like a person and not a stupid little tech. There's no way he could be evil."

Mike looked at Jess. "Maybe he's not, but he sure looked at me funny when I asked you out to breakfast. Jess, has it ever occurred to you that he might be in love with you? I mean, he's a department head, right? So he probably doesn't have to work nights. Maybe he wants to be with you."

Jess shook her head, sending her hair flying around her face. "No, Mike. He's . . ." Her voice trailed off. It *was* strange that Dr. Sykes worked the night shift. No other hospital department chief did that. And he did single her out for special attention. In a world where the techs were the lowest of the low, he acted as though she was his peer. It was all very professional and aboveboard of course. But she had overheard gossip about "Bennett's little protégée," and the speculation about the nature of their relationship. She'd dismissed it. Hospitals were always full of gossip.

With a twinge of discomfort, she again remembered how he had rubbed her neck and shoulders the other night. What bothered her was that she had enjoyed it. His hands had felt so good on her body. In a different place and time she might have allowed him to continue. No, not allowed— *wanted* him to. Thank God Susie had come to her the next morning and helped her to see things clearly. She wasn't sure just how Susie had done it, but she knew with unshakable certainty that she didn't want to be anything more than a friend to Dr. Sykes. And that perhaps there was some truth to what Susie and Mike were saying.

Her cheeks flushed. "Well . . . I guess it could be true, kind of. But would that make him evil? If he likes me?"

"I don't know. It would depend on his motives, I guess. But if you're going to take this seriously, Jessie, you have to look at all the options. Your Forensics Land may be a crazier place than you think."

"Now I'm totally confused," wailed Jess. "Susie doesn't know Dr. Sykes. She's never even met him."

"That explains why she didn't recognize him. Duh."

Jess smiled in spite of herself. "So, Mr. Detective, what do you think?"

"I think you need more evidence. I think you need to keep your eyes and ears open and watch your back. I think you need a bodyguard, and I volunteer for the job." He grinned down at her.

"You're sweet," Jess said. Then she paused. "Do you believe me?"

Mike became thoughtful again. After a moment, he said, "I don't not believe you. Is that good enough?"

"I guess it will have to be," she said.

"Well, your bodyguard wants to go and see the bears, so you have to come. C'mon, I'll buy you a soda."

As they stood up, he pulled her into a hug. "Jessie, you are such a liar."

"What!" She stared up at him, eyes wide.

"You had me thinking you led such a dull life. You are the most unboring person I've ever met."

"Same to you. Duh," she replied with a grin.

Mike bent down and kissed Jess. She put her arms around him and returned his kiss. They stood there for a long time. The peacocks and pigeons discreetly wandered away.

Meredith groaned in frustration and tapped her forehead against the steering wheel. She was sick of sitting in her rented car. The Sunday newspaper lay on top of the uncollected Saturday paper. It was obvious that nobody was home and hadn't been since Friday. She had seen no sign of Kass at Bennett's house. Bennett slept alone last night, as he had on Friday night. But she hadn't seen Kass leave Bennett's house, either. Apparently she had missed something. She had wasted a perfectly good weekend stalking someone who refused to cooperate.

She had returned to Kass's house late last night. First, she had spent an hour at the shooting range the gun dealer had recommended. She learned how to load and unload the gun. Then she was given a pair of ear mufflers and led into the range, where she actually shot the gun for the first time. The recoil had hurt her wrists at first, but after a while she found she enjoyed it. The laser sighting made it so easy to hit the target. Just follow the dot, she thought. Easy as pie.

After she had loaded and fired just three rounds, she slipped off her ear protection. She stared at the gun in her hands. The range owner was watching her, another big, beefy man. This guy had the added attraction of heavily muscled and tattooed arms. He looked like he could break her in two with one hand.

"That's pretty good for a first time," he had said, grinning with approval. Meredith noticed that one of his front teeth was capped in gold.

Meredith looked at the target, a silhouette of a head and torso. She had hit the target each time, and some of the shots were fatal. She looked back at the gun in her hand. The tiny voice had returned. It whispered that she was a doctor, sworn to do no harm. Now here she was, thinking of murder. Meredith shook her head, angrily. She was beginning to hate that voice.

"Hey, lady, don't feel bad. That's an excellent piece you have there. Only a few more sessions, and you'll be dead on every time."

Meredith flinched and looked at the man. "I hope so," she had replied.

Then, she had gone home and waited until Bennett came home—alone—around eleven P.M. She waited until she was sure that no one was sharing Bennett's bed, then got into her car and parked in front of Kass's dark house.

Where could Kass have gone? She was such a blabbermouth in the chat room, where Meredith masqueraded as a childless divorcée in order to monitor Bennett's online activities. If Kass had been planning a vacation, she certainly would have announced it to all her cyberfriends.

Maybe Meredith's little warning had worked after all. Perhaps she had gone to tell Bennett in person that she couldn't see him anymore. Then she had left town to get away from him. She smiled to herself. That must be it. A perfectly logical explanation.

It was getting late. Meredith decided to return the car, go home, and write a letter of tender apology to Bennett. Maybe if he saw how sorry she was, he would forgive her and begin to see that she really was the one for him. Her heart ached for Bennett, who must have been so hurt when Kass told him she didn't want him anymore, and was going away so he couldn't find her.

Still, Meredith wished that she knew for sure that Kass was gone for good. It would be even better if Kass were dead.

ELEVEN

MONDAY

Kass slowly came to, fighting her way up from the endless darkness. The last thing she remembered was Bennett embracing her in his living room . . . Then nothing. Not even dreams.

A bright light shone in her eyes. She was lying on something. She was cold. She realized that she was naked. She tried to move but she was strapped down. She tried to speak, to scream, but only a rusty croak issued from her throat. Her lips were parched.

A form blocked the light. A thumb pulled back her upper eyelid.

"So, you're awake now, Mamakass. Good. Very good. It means the pentobarb is leaving your system. You have a great metabolism, my dear."

"Bennett?" A hoarse whisper.

"Yes, ma'am." Something wet hit her eyes. "A little saline will help keep them nice and moist." Through the blur of the saline solution, she saw him reach up to an IV bag and inject something into it. The IV line ran down . . . and into her arm.

"Bennett . . . please . . ."

"I know. You want to know what's going on. Well, you have been asleep since Friday. I have shaved you and cleaned you. And now it's time for Cinderella to get ready for the ball." He grinned down at her. "Remember I told you about the Epicurean Society and how I wanted you to go with me? Well, I should have explained that we Epicures meet once a year to sample the latest in the culinary arts. And the main course is always human flesh. And you are this year's main course."

Kass's eyes widened. *"No,"* she moaned. It was getting harder to speak.

"Since I can't serve my friends barbiturate-laden meat—it ruins the delicate flavor—I have just administered succinylcholine to you. It's derived from curare. You know, that stuff South American Indians put on their hunting arrows? It's a paralytic. It will hold you nice and still while I work. I've also given you a painkiller, but I'm afraid it may wear off before I'm through. I couldn't give you too much, because shortly you won't be able to excrete it."

Kass was terribly, horribly confused. Her limbs were numb. Bennett took her blood pressure and looked in her eyes again. He smeared something greasy into them.

"This would be a lot easier if I had help, but I can't risk it. Just got to keep an eye on you and make sure your heart and respiration are okay. You know, they use succinylcholine to execute prisoners. They die of suffocation. Bet you didn't know that."

Kass summoned her last bit of strength to croak out, "What are you doing to me?"

"Well, first I have to gut you, and then I have to cook you. I saw in your wallet that you're an organ donor. I have ice chests here, and in about five hours I'll meet my contact. Your organs will be sold on the black market. Maybe I'll buy a Porsche with the profits. If it makes you feel better, I'll get a vanity plate that says 'Kass' on it." He chuckled.

He picked up a bottle of Betadine and washed her torso with it. Kass felt the coldness on her skin. She could smell the sickly iodine odor. She watched him pull on a surgical gown and snap a pair of gloves onto his hands.

"This will take a while. About four hours, I should say. I'll have to concentrate, so pardon me if I don't keep up my end of the conversation." He picked up a scalpel.

The memory of all the dreams she'd had since she first agreed to see Bennett came flooding back into Kass's consciousness. She realized that they hadn't been dreams but premonitions. Bennett was going to carve her up and roast her like a turkey. She was going to die.

Because of the paralytic drug, she could not scream, cry, beg, plead, or even blink.

She felt the pressure of the knife, and in her mind she saw Bennett make a swift cut from the bottom of her sternum to the top of her pubic bone. Blood welled from the incision onto her orange, iodine-stained skin. She fainted.

Pain brought her back. Through the greasy blur, she could see Bennett hunched over her right side. Sweaty strands of hair were hanging in his face, and he was muttering to himself.

"Come, on, come on . . . There. Wow, almost no blood loss. Damn, I'm good." He stopped and picked up the blood pressure cuff. Kass heard the hiss and felt the pressure on her arm. Her entire middle felt like it was on fire. He pulled her eyelid back again.

"BP a little higher. Increased heart rate and respiration. You must be awake. I'm just about done here. See, I just got your liver. That's the hardest part. Lots and lots of blood vessels. Can't have you bleed to death before I cook you." He held up her liver, a great purply-red mass of tissue, so that she could see it.

Kass could not scream. All she could do was look. She was suddenly filled with contempt for a man who would do this to another human being. She focused her eyes on Bennett's. With a level stare, she tried to communicate all that she felt.

For a moment, her eyes reminded Bennett of the look in Lady's eyes after she bit him. An atavistic suspicion hit him.

"I was going to do this after I closed up your belly, but I think I'll do it now," he said coldly. He picked up a tiny metal contraption with hooks on it. He pulled her eyelid back and used the hooks to secure it. He picked up a scalpel.

Five minutes later, Kass was blind. Bennett gently placed her corneas into one of the ice chests. Bloody tears ran down Kass's temples and made pink drops on the table next to her head.

It was Columbus Day. Susie had no school, but Heather had to work. Jess had spent the morning with Susie in Observatory Hill Park. It was a balmy October day, with a sapphire-blue sky and white clouds moving lazily overhead. Susie and Jess sat in silence on the swings. Susie was dejected over her failure to figure out where Miss Becky was, and Jess had no words of comfort for her. They had come home at lunchtime.

"No TV today, Suz. Especially no *Miss Becky*. Okay?"

"Okay," Susie replied. Jess was relieved. She thought Susie might argue with her. Just to be sure, though, Jess unplugged the television.

"Will you read to me? Then I want a sandwich. Miss Becky wants some, too."

"Sure." Jess smiled. She sounds more like her old self, Jess thought with relief. Susie ran to the bookshelf, where Jess kept some of her old children's books, and selected *The Cat in the Hat*. She put her swaddled Miss Becky doll on the sofa, then cuddled close to Jess, and they began to read.

Suddenly Susie began to scream. "Jessie-ka! We're too late! The bad doctor man killed Miss Becky!" She seized Jess's hand in terror and pointed at the TV. Jess looked over. Her eyes widened.

The TV screen was blazing with light. On the screen Jess saw a tall, fair man, clad in a green surgical gown. He was holding a limp Miss Becky in his arms. He placed her in what looked like a tanning bed. But instead of tubes of ultraviolet light, the inside of the bed glowed red-hot. The man closed the bed around Miss Becky and latched it securely. Jess could not see the man's face. There was an exam table and a surgical tray in the room, also. There was blood on the table, and on the instruments on the tray. Coolers were on the floor.

The man pulled off his gown. Jess saw that his left arm was bandaged.

Susie shrieked again. Jess blinked and looked at her. An unwrapped, naked Miss Becky doll lay limply in Susie's lap. The stuffing was gone from the doll's body. So were the shiny black eyes. There were just little holes in the face where the eyes used to be.

"She's hot!" screamed Susie. She shoved the doll off her lap and onto the carpet. As they both watched, the doll's soft, beige plush body began to turn brown, like a turkey in the oven. Instead of burning fabric or scorching carpet, Jess smelled cooking meat. Susie grabbed her again and pointed at the TV. Shaking with fright, Jess lifted her eyes back to the screen.

The man turned and faced them. He had dark-gold, wavy hair, brown eyes, and a moustache. He seemed to look directly into Jess's eyes.

"Just another fun-filled day in Forensics Land," he said softly.

Jess's blood turned to ice water in her veins. She had an urge to vomit.

"Dr. Sykes. Oh my *God,* it's Dr. Sykes! Oh, Susie!!" Jess threw her arms around the little girl and they both wept hysterically.

Kass was in agony. Bennett had lifted her off the table and onto another surface. It was cold and slightly curved. She heard a lid closing over her and the sound of a clamp being locked down.

Am I in a coffin? I can't be dead, it hurts too much.

She thought of Sam and Karen and wondered if they would ever find out what happened to her. A wave of terrible grief surged over her when she realized that she would never see or touch or hear them again. It far surpassed any physical pain she felt.

The surface below her began to get hot. She felt heat radiating down on her, too. She remembered what Bennett had said and realized that she was in an oven. Her skin began to burn.

Dear God, please take care of my babies. Don't let them forget me. Forgive me my trespasses. Into Thy hands I commend my spirit.

Kass knew no more.

Her heart ceased to beat, finally, when it began to cook.

Jess flung open the door when she heard the knock.

"Oh, Mike, I'm so glad to see you. Thanks for coming over." She threw her arms around his neck.

Mike hugged her tightly for a moment, then he released her. "Of course I had to come. You sounded so scared on the phone." He kissed her on her forehead and looked over at Susie, who was sitting stiffly on the sofa, her face chalky with fear.

"Can I have a hug from my best girl?" He knelt down on the floor and opened his arms. Susie ran to him, and he snatched her up. She began to cry.

"Mikey, me and Jess are scared. The bad man killed Miss Becky and baked her in the oven. And Jess knows who he is. It's bad Doctor Bennett Sykes!"

Mike held Susie and patted her back. Jess held up the wreck of the Miss Becky doll for Mike to see. He shook his head when he saw the pathetic rag that used to be Susie's favorite toy.

"Susie, sit right next to me while I talk to Jess, okay? No bad guy is going to get you now." The three of them sat back down on the sofa, Susie in between Mike and Jess.

"Tell me again, Jessie. What did you see?"

Jess repeated what she had incoherently stammered out on the phone. How the unplugged TV had come on. How Susie had grabbed her, and then she had seen it, too—the man putting a body into some kind of oven. And, finally, how she had recognized the man.

"And this guy is Dr. Sykes?" asked Mike.

"Yes," said Jess firmly.

Mike shook his head. Jess saw the doubt on his face.

"Mike, you probably think I'm crazy. Maybe I am. But I know what I saw. Suz saw it, too. Exactly the same thing. And I saw the doll turn brown. I felt it get hot. And then he said 'Another fun day in Forensics Land.' Only Dr. Sykes says that. Mike, I . . ." Her voice trailed off.

Mike reached over and stroked Jess's hair. "Jessie, I know you're not crazy. And Suz isn't crazy, either. I just don't know what I can do. Your story's . . . well, it's really out there, you know? And like I told you yesterday, there's no evidence. I'm only a cop. I can only do so much."

Susie said, "There is so evidence. Look what he did to my Miss Becky."

"Susie-Q, how are we going to make them understand that you didn't do that yourself? Even your mom and Jess didn't believe you at first."

Susie jumped off the sofa and stamped her foot. "Miss Becky is my friend forever. I would never ever hurt my friends like this. Not ever!"

Jess held out her hand to Susie. "Suz, I know that, and Mike knows that. Even Mommy knows that now. But we would have to make the judge believe it. And the judge probably won't."

"It's not fair!" Susie stamped her feet again.

"No, it's not," agreed Jess. "What *can* we do, Mike?"

Mike shrugged. "I don't know," he repeated. "Are you working tonight?"

"No. Tomorrow. And Dr. Sykes is off tonight, too. He's got some Epicurean Society meeting to go to."

"What's that?" asked Mike.

Susie gasped. Her eyes were huge with excitement. "That's where bad Doctor Bennett Sykes was taking Miss Becky! He said he had to get her ready for the Curer's Ball. Except it was Eppy-cure. Now I remember!"

Mike leaned forward suddenly. "You say you saw Dr. Sykes putting Miss Becky into some kind of a machine. Then the doll began to turn brown?"

"And I smelled roasting meat," said Jess.

"What did the machine look like? Was it really an oven?" Mike asked.

"Actually, it looked kind of like a tanning bed," Jess said ruefully.

Mike ran his hand through his curly red hair. He was quiet for a minute. Then he looked at Jess.

"Do you know where they're meeting?" he asked.

"Somewhere in the city, I think. That's all I know."

Mike stood up. "Okay. Let me go home. I'm going to get on my computer and see if I can find out anything about this Epicurean Society. If they're meeting someplace in town, maybe I can find out where. Then I'll just stop by after I get to work and see if there's anything suspicious going on. That is, if I can convince LaVyrle that we need to do this."

"Don't tell her why. Please. Not unless you have to," said Jess.

He shook his head, imagining what LaVyrle would say about this story. After she stopped laughing at him. "Don't worry about that. I'll figure something out. I'll call you, okay?"

"Can't you get a warrant? Search his house?"

"Without a shred of evidence? No way, Jessie. I'm sorry." He put his arm around her as she walked him to the door.

"I know you'll do your best, Mike. Thanks. I owe you."

Mike grinned his little-boy's grin. "Hmm, Jess, sounds good. I got a couple of ideas how you can pay me back . . ."

Jess elbowed him. "Shhh. Tell me later." She looked meaningfully over at Susie, who was watching them with interest.

"Bye, Susie-Q. I'll try real hard to help Miss Becky, okay?"

"Okay, Mike. Are you our friend forever?"

"For sure, little Susie. For sure."

"What's a warrant?" asked Susie. She and Jess were having cookies and milk in the kitchen. Jess marveled at Susie's calmness. After Mike left, Susie was practically back to normal. She herself was a nervous wreck.

"A warrant is permission from a judge to search someone's house for evidence. To see if they are the bad guys," replied Jess. Jess had thought she would be too upset to eat as she prepared the snack for Susie. But the familiar comfort of cookies and milk was irresistible. She ate a fifth Oreo and poured herself some more milk.

Susie unscrewed her Oreo and thoughtfully licked off the filling.

"We're not police persons, so we don't need a warrant," she said.

Jess looked at Susie and narrowed her eyes. "Suz, what are you saying? We can't just go and break into someone's house. That's bad."

Susie returned Jess's stare. "It's bad to cook Miss Becky. Besides, Mommy said it was okay. She said to listen to St. Jude and never mind what anyone said."

Jess was silent for a few moments. She knew she couldn't face Bennett unless she knew for sure, one way or the other, if he was a killer. He was a mentor and a father figure to her. And he wanted to be more to her. Mike, and even Susie, had figured that out. The idea that this brilliant, handsome, kind man could deliberately kill and cook a person was revolting. But what Susie was proposing was very risky and probably very stupid as well.

Suddenly Jess knew it was the only thing she could do. She *had* to do it. It was as if something was pulling her there. Like a moth to a flame, she thought, but even that ominous image could not overcome the compulsion to go.

"All right then, I'll go, but promise me you'll be good while I'm gone."

"No, Jessie-ka. You don't go without me. I know where Miss Becky is, and you don't."

"Pickle, I can't take you with me and break into someone's house. What if we get caught? What will I tell Heather? You have to stay safe, right here."

Susie narrowed her eyes and stared at Jess. "If we don't go together, Miss Becky will die. And Mommy said to believe in myself, and I believe I'm going."

Jess was silent for a few moments, and then sighed loudly.

"Okay, Suz. Go get your coat and your shoes. I'm going to leave a note for your mom. God, I hope I'm not sorry for this later."

"All right! We're going to fight the evil Doctor Sykes!" Susie chortled.

Jess shuddered suddenly, as if an icy wind had just blown through her.

"What's wrong?" asked Susie.

"I think someone just walked over my grave," Jess replied.

"Eeeew," Susie said.

Bennett looked down at the remains of Kasidy Rhodes. Her skin was crisp and golden brown. Juices ran from her pores. He picked up a carving knife and cut into her thigh.

"Medium-rare. Perfect," he said to himself.

He cut himself a small sliver of the meat in order to taste it. He put it in his mouth. It was tender and sweet, the skin crisp and garlicky from basting.

"Mmmmm," he said. As he chewed, savoring the bite, he closed his eyes and saw Kass's smile, heard her musical laughter and smelled the white-floral fragrance of her perfume. All that optimism and beauty were part of his very being now.

After Kass was dead, but before she was fully cooked, he had opened the oven and used a cannula to extract her brain through her nose. He had basted her with melted unsalted butter and pureed garlic, and closed the oven to finish her.

He had taken the brains up to the kitchen and carefully removed the bits of skin and connective tissue from the pinkish-gray, sludgy goo that had come out of Kass's nose. He baked them into a ring mold, seasoned with shallots and minced portobello mushrooms. This would be served with out-of-season asparagus tips as an appetizer.

He also prepared a fine eggplant ratatouille for a side dish and two batches of a Burgundy wine-and-currant sauce. He poured the sauce into a gallon-sized Mason jar to cool and loaded the ratatouille, the ring mold, ingredients for a Belgian endive-and-Dijon-vinaigrette salad, and some fine French bread into the Coleman ice chests. He had earlier purchased a case of vintage French Médoc to accompany the meal.

Bennett had rented a Ryder van for the day's errands. Prior to fixing the side dishes for the evening's banquet, he had delivered three ice chests, filled with Kasidy's organs, to a parking garage near his home. He hadn't wanted to leave while the meat was cooking, but the fat wad of bills he was handed by a man with a hat pulled low over his eyes made it well worth it. The market for black-market organs was extremely lucrative, Bennett decided. He had an appointment tomorrow with a Porsche dealer.

Now he lifted Kass out of the tanning bed oven and placed her onto a sheet, which he had lined with plastic shower curtains. He wrapped her snugly and carried her up the basement steps and through the doors to the street. She was much lighter now. His mouth watered at the fragrance of the roasted garlicky meat. He had parked the Ryder van in front of his house.

He lay her down gently on the floor of the van. Then he loaded in the coolers and locked it.

He went upstairs, showered, and dressed in a tuxedo. He realized he was running late. No time to clean up the room downstairs. He did take the precaution of switching on his computer and deleting all the messages regarding the Epicurean Society meeting. He hurried out to the van and left. The forgotten wine sauce was left behind on the kitchen counter.

* * *

Susie clutched Jess's arm as they stood at the top of Ash-land Street.

"Jessie! This is it—the place that St. Jude took me to!" She let go of Jess and ran, her shoes clicking on the cob-blestones. She stopped in front of the house numbered 315.

"The evil we have to fight is here! But he's gone now. Miss Becky was here, too. But not anymore."

"Three-fifteen," Jess breathed. It was Bennett's house all right. Jess hurried to the door where Susie was standing. She took a deep breath and knocked.

No one came to the door.

Jess knocked again. Susie frowned.

"Why are we knocking if we know he's not here?" asked Susie.

"Just making sure, that's all." Jess was beginning to feel nervous. She could smell the roasted meat out here on the street, as well as other delicious cooking smells.

She tried the front door. Locked, as she had thought. They went around behind the row of houses.

They climbed over several fences, Jess pulling and push-ing Susie over them, listening apprehensively for voices. Finally they were in the tiny courtyard behind Bennett's house. The aroma was even stronger behind Bennett's house. Jess looked up and saw that the kitchen window was open a few inches. She reached up, but she wasn't tall enough to reach the windowsill, much less push the screen out and climb in.

She felt in her pocket for her key ring and pulled it out. She kept a small pocketknife on it with her keys. She knelt down and looked at Susie.

"Listen to me, Suz. You'll have to take my knife and cut the window screen. I'll put you up on my shoulders. Then you'll have to go in through the window and let me in the front door. You have to work as fast as you can so we don't get caught."

"But we're not—"

"Susie, we *are* doing something wrong. We could go to jail for this. But if we don't get caught, and we find what we're looking for, then Bennett Sykes will be the one in jail. I mean it, Suz. You have to work fast if you want to help Miss Becky."

Wordlessly, Susie took the opened pocketknife. She climbed up onto Jess's narrow back then up onto Jess's shoulders.

She poked the knife into the screen and began cutting. Jess trembled under Susie's weight and from her own fear. She listened for footsteps and for cars turning down the street. Susie concentrated on her cutting, the tip of her tongue thrust between her lips.

She put her hand into the slit she made and pushed against the screen. The metal ripped, scoring Susie's hand along with it. She drew out her scratched and bleeding hand and pushed inward. The screen bulged open.

"Push me up, Jessie-ka," she whispered fiercely. Jess grasped her ankles and began hoisting the little girl up toward the window. Susie grabbed the windowsill and pulled herself in. The raw edges of the screen scratched her cheek as she pushed past it.

She fell to the floor with a thud. Jess ran to the fence and climbed back over to the street. She landed on the sidewalk and began to walk nonchalantly up the street as a group of tourists turned down Ashland Street, exclaiming and admiring the lovely little houses. Heart pounding, Jess fought back the urge to run. She didn't want to arouse any suspicion.

She came back to the front of the house. She could hear Susie fumbling with the lock. She tried the door and it opened.

She stepped in and closed the door behind her. Susie hugged her.

"Oh, Pickle, you're bleeding. Let's clean you up." Jess looked at the bloody scratches on the little girl's cheek.

"No, no. I want to see where Miss Becky was first."

"Then just let me get a paper towel or something," Jess said firmly. She went into the kitchen and turned on the lights. Susie followed her, looking around her with her eyes wide. Jess noticed the shiny clean, stainless-steel gourmet appliances in the well-appointed kitchen. She saw the paper towels and took one, dampening it at the sink. Her eyes fell on the big jar of sauce next to the sink. It looked out of place in the immaculate kitchen. Like something forgotten in a rush to leave. Her nerves, already taut, tightened to the screaming point.

Mike leaned back in his chair and rubbed his eyes. They always felt itchy when he sat at the computer for a long time. He stretched his arms out in front of him, fingers linked, and then returned his attention to the monitor screen.

He had searched the police department database and turned up nothing under "Epicure" or "Epicurean." Then he had searched the Web and found more than he ever wanted to know about Greek philosophy and gourmet cooking. Nothing about a society dealing in bloody communions, whatever that was.

He shook his head. Maybe Jess was crazy. Maybe the stress of losing her father and working in such a gruesome place was affecting her mind. As for Susie—well, he was pretty sure she had *some* ability to guess what people were thinking. And she also was facing the loss of her mother. Perhaps Jess and Suz were just feeding off each other's neuroses.

Still—there had been the scorched and mutilated doll. The burn mark on the carpet. Jess's and Susie's stories matched. They had both been terrified, and fear was a tough emotion to fake. And Jess seemed perfectly normal in every other way—intelligent, funny, and sweet. And beautiful. An image of her face as she laughed floated up in his mind. He smiled. After a moment, the smile twisted into a wry grimace.

"Shit," he said. LaVyrle had told him that a good cop must never get emotionally involved with the work. Distance was necessary in order to keep perspective, not to mention sanity. Maybe he was too close to the situation, which definitely sounded like a crock to the casual observer. He pushed his hair back and decided to try one more search.

He typed "Secret societies" into the search field.

"There are 147,824 entries that match your parameters," he read on the computer screen.

"Shit," Mike repeated. He scrolled down through the entries displaying Web addresses for Ku Klux Klan pages, neo-Nazi societies, and survivalist organizations.

Cripes, Mike thought. *How can they be secret societies if they have a freaking web page for the whole world to see?*

One page caught his eye.

He brought up a web page for the Encyclopedia of Secret Societies. *If it isn't in here,* he decided, *I give up.* He typed "Epicurean" into the page's search field.

Bingo.

Mike began reading.

THE HISTORY OF THE EPICUREAN SOCIETY
OF PHILADELPHIA
—From the Encyclopedia of Secret Societies

The Epicurean Society began in Philadelphia in the 1840s. Its members were intelligent, well-educated men, drawn from the upper echelons of Philadelphia and Main Line society. Their philosophy was based upon the discovery that the ancient Aztecs in Mexico engaged in the practice of ritual cannibalism. The Aztecs believed that they would take on the qualities of their victims by ingesting their flesh. They believed that intelligence, courage, honor, and other positive essences would remain in the meat. Eating it would enhance these characteristics in the ones partaking of the body, and also it would confer a kind of immortality on the person being eaten.

In the age of homeopathy and herbal medicine—the concepts of "like curing like" and diluting extracts to the point where the solution held only the memory of the original compound—the idea of flesh retaining the virtues of the person from which it was taken had a perverse logic. The founders of the Society determined to sample human flesh for themselves, to see if the idea had any basis in fact. Over time, its mission evolved into a bizarre gourmet competition, to see who could prepare the most delectable dishes using human meat. Yet the concept of ingesting the flesh of the virtuous to improve one's own virtues remained.

The members met yearly. One member was selected to host the dinner, said host being responsible for securing and preparing the main course. Young women were preferred for consumption, on the basis of their fertility and life-giving abilities, as well as a perception that the meat tasted better.

At first, it was relatively easy to procure victims for the banquets. It was not unusual for poor young women to disappear in the city. Forensic science was nonexistent until the early twentieth century. As detective work improved, aided by scientific and technological advances, it became harder to safely kidnap and murder young women.

Since the Society's existence was a closely guarded secret, no one actually knew who the members were. Identities were concealed. But it was rumored that Edgar Allan Poe, Stephen Girard, and other prominent Philadelphians were once members.

Prospective members of the Society must be citizens in good standing. They are scrutinized closely by other members, usually without their knowledge, before a recruitment effort is made. The most infamous Philadelphia cannibal, Gary Heidnik, who was notorious in the 1980s for kidnapping and eating young women, would never have been considered for membership due to his obvious insanity and negligible social position. Albert Fish would have been disqualified for his preference for small children, and Jeffrey Dahmer for his taste in young men.

Prospects, upon agreeing to attend a meeting, are sworn to secrecy. It is strongly impressed upon them that this oath must be adhered to, or there will be serious repercussions. Prospects are not told exactly what the main course at the banquet is until after they have partaken of it.

If they choose to remain in the Society, they are given a code name (most members know only their recruiter by their real-life name, further ensuring anonymity). They are taught a coded language which they will use when communicating Society business to other members. They are expected to be responsible for at least one banquet in their lifetime. Responsibilities include identifying a likely candidate for the main course, preparing, cooking, and serving it in the most attractive and creative way possible, and selecting appropriate accompanying dishes and wines.

Bennett parked the van in an alley behind the restaurant. The back door was open, and he could see Israel Vega moving around in the kitchen. He got out, opened the back doors of the van, and brought one of the coolers into the kitchen.

"Good evening, Israel," he said. "Thanks for coming to help."

"No trouble, Bennett. It is your first time, after all. I have just finished setting the tables."

They went back out to the van. Israel's eyes widened when he saw the human-sized bundle in the back and smelled the cooling fragrance of the cooked meat.

"Bennett! It is whole!"

Bennett grinned. "Yes, it is. No cute little casseroles for me. Although I did make a nice ring mold from the brains. It's just like a suckling pig, without the apple in the mouth."

Israel stared at him. Bennett looked at his face. "Is something wrong?"

"No, not really. I am just amazed that you would go to such trouble. How did you manage to cook it whole?"

"Converted tanning bed. Look, Israel, if we are going to partake of the blood and body, as it were, I think it's important to remember exactly just what we are partaking of. Don't you?"

Israel nodded, but his face had a strange look.

They brought the body inside and placed it on a table. Bennett carefully unwrapped it. Kass's golden brown, crisped skin and slightly caved-in features made her look like a juicy Egyptian mummy. Israel looked at her face.

"She must have been quite pretty. Where did you find her?"

"I met her on a blind date. I'd been chatting with her on the Internet for a while, stringing her along in case. She was rather pretty. A good woman."

Israel could not take his liquid brown eyes from her face. "So you roasted her."

"Israel, what's wrong with you? This isn't a game, right? I mean, if you're going to eat human flesh, let's not pretend that it's beef or chicken. This is it, my friend. The real thing."

Israel sighed. "You are right. The pupil has become the master." He busied himself unpacking the coolers. "Let's see what else you have here." Bennett thought he detected a shudder pass down Israel's back. A contemptuous smile crossed his face. Apparently Israel was not seeking what he was. He turned back to the counter. Suddenly he stopped.

"Damn it to hell!" Bennett fumed, looking at the dishes laid out next to the body. "I forgot the fucking sauce. It's probably sitting on the kitchen counter right now!"

"Go home and get it," said Israel. "I'll stay here and tend bar for the early arrivals."

"Don't let them get into the Médoc. It's to be served with the meal."

"Not to worry, Bennett." Israel was his light, sophisticated self again. "I brought a case of old Father Dom with me. Champagne always makes the best aperitif, don't you think?"

Bennett grinned and got back into the van.

"Down here, Jessie!" called Susie. She was in the basement.

"Susie, we have to leave. Now!" Jess raced down the stairs.

"No, Jess. Look!"

Susie was standing next to a paneled wall. One of the panels was slightly askew. Jess realized it was a concealed door. Susie pushed at it, and it opened.

"Susie, I think Dr. Sykes forgot something. He might come back for it. We have to go!" She grabbed the little girl and began wiping the blood off her cheek and hand. Then she stopped.

Jess could see the exam table and the IV poles dimly in the light from the basement. The meat aroma was intense in the little room. She stepped in and fumbled for the light switch.

Susie began whimpering. "I saw this place. This is where he cutted Miss Becky's hair. He gave her a bath right here!" She touched the table. "And he hung bags on these poles and poked her with needles!"

Jess's blood ran cold with horror. She saw the empty bags of glucose solution hanging from the IV poles, the IV tubing limp and tangled on the floor. There were blood-stains on the floor around the table. A stained green gown was draped on the table. Her eyes came to rest on the tanning bed, which Bennett had left open. It was smeared with grease and what looked like meat juices. She smelled garlic. She could see that the bed had huge electrical elements instead of UV tubes. Something—or someone—had recently been cooked in it. Susie pressed close to Jess's legs.

"That's it! That's the big oven he cooked Miss Becky in! I saw it."

A wave of nausea passed over Jess. She struggled against it. She had to stay calm and controlled. For Susie if not herself. "I know, honey. I saw it, too. We'll call Mike and tell him right away. But first we have to leave before Bennett comes back."

They started up the stairs to the kitchen. Susie stopped at the top of the stairs.

"Too late, Jessie-ka. He's here."

Jess's head was too full of what she had just seen to really hear what Susie had said. She pushed Susie toward the living room. "Out the front. Run!"

Bennett cursed himself for a fool as he drove the yellow van back to his house. The meat simply could not be served without the wine sauce. How stupid it was to just leave it sitting on the counter. He'd been late and rushing and not paying attention. Of course, it was his fate to hit every red light on the way, and the streets were dense with late rush-hour traffic. He was furious by the time he got home.

He pulled up on Spruce Street, turned on the emergency flashers, and rushed up Ashland Street. He'd just dash in the front door, grab the jar, and run out. As he fumbled with his keys, the door flew open.

A woman and a little girl hurled themselves out the door and into him, almost knocking him down. Instinctively he closed his arms around them. His eyes widened as he looked down into Jess's face. She stared back, too frightened to struggle. His arms circled her tightly, and she gasped for air.

Susie looked up at Bennett. Recognition flickered over her face. She opened her mouth and began screaming.

"It's the bad doctor man! It's him!"

Bennett swept an arm around Susie's shoulders and shoved them both back into the house. He slammed the door shut with a kick. Still keeping hold of Jess, he dragged her over to the sofa and flung her down hard, flat on her back. Susie stood against the far wall, pressing her back against it. Her face was still, but her wide eyes took in everything. Jess lay motionless on the sofa, trembling, her blue eyes dark and searching.

Bennett, elegant and handsome in his evening clothes, looked down at the prostrate Jess, spread-eagled on the sofa. "What the fuck are you doing here?" he hissed at her. His face was dark with rage.

"Unbelievable. This is too weird," Mike muttered.

The text on the Epicurean Society was sketchy at best, but there was enough there to convince him that Jess and Susie were not crazy. Whether divinely inspired or not, Susie had apparently linked her psychic mind with the victim who was to be eaten by these cannibals. And maybe the doll really was a sign from God, or St. Jude, or whatever.

He took a deep breath. Now the problem was finding out where this meeting was going to be. He figured he had enough to get LaVyrle to at least be willing to check it out, although he knew she wouldn't be happy about it. And if they did go, and it turned out to be your average banquet with your average overcooked, crummy food, she'd probably request he be transferred. Preferably to the state mental hospital.

He picked up the phone and dialed Jess's number.

After ten rings, he hung up. He looked up Heather's number in the phone book and dialed it. Susie's chirpy voice requested he leave a message after the beep.

"Where are you, Jessie?" he muttered. Then he groaned.

He knew where they were.

He ran downstairs and got into his car.

Meredith came home from her rounds at the hospital. Her patients had been only a blur to her. She had been restless and unable to concentrate on anything. Mamakass and Bennett had consumed her mind. *Where could the little slut have gone after she left Bennett's?* she wondered for the umpteenth time. A discreet call placed to Holmes Fein & Company had revealed that Kasidy was not at work that day. Bennett was not due in at the hospital tonight, but she knew he had been more or less home all weekend. Alone. She scowled in frustration. She had wasted an entire weekend staking out Kasidy's house, not to mention the money for the car, the flowers, and the gun.

Maybe Kasidy really was gone for good, but Meredith wished she knew for sure. It would have been so much easier if Kasidy had stuck to the script and let Meredith kill her.

As she threw down her briefcase and coat, she glanced out the front window. She reeled back, as if someone had struck her.

There was Bennett, embracing his little med tech Jessica. Jessica's fair hair spilled over his arm like something from a romance novel. Her pale face was lifted to his. A little girl—Heather Troutman's skinny little brat—was jumping up and down with excitement, screaming something in her high-pitched kid's voice. Bennett put his arm around the little girl and hurried them into the house.

He was in a rush to get them in, she thought. *He just*

ouldn't wait, could he? She stared at Bennett's house,
astonished and hurt.

The cool voice of reason crept into her fevered brain.
Give it up, it whispered. *There will always be someone other
than you. He's not for you. Give up and go on.* Meredith
swayed on her feet.

Moments later, this faint plea for sanity was drowned
out by a rising red tide of rage and jealousy and pain.

Jessica. Of all people. His little pet protégée. She should
have *known*. Why, they were always thick as thieves, those
two. The little sneak used her indisputable feminine charms
to seduce him with her wide admiring eyes and her pouty
lips murmuring "Ooh, Dr. Sykes, you're *so* smart." Now she
was there, with her friend's kid. Probably fucking him in the
kitchen while the kid watched TV.

Meredith's head spun. She stood in her living room as if
rooted to the spot. She didn't know how long she stayed
there, watching the images of Bennett wooing Kasidy, and
now Jessica, play over and over in her brain. Suddenly the
air was rent with a scream.

"*No!* He's mine! I'm the only one who understands him!"

She ran into the bedroom to don the black jeans and
sweater she wore on her garbage-picking expeditions. She
was going to claim her man. Once and for all.

Jess stared up at Bennett, frozen with fear. Her mind would
not work. He looked so handsome and perfect in the tuxedo.
So normal. Only the face was different. It frightened her,
badly.

Bennett looked down at the girl, sprawled on the sofa,
her hands raised as if to ward off blows. His sweet little
Jessie had found out about the Society and was off to tell
her cop boyfriend. She'd had such potential, and now she'd
betrayed him. After all he was willing to do for her, after
all he'd invested in her, this was how she repaid him. She

would have to pay for that. But first, he would have to dis
cover exactly how she found out.

He strode over to the sofa and straddled her body, pin
ning her down into the cushions with his weight. He took
her head in his hands and lifted it to his own. She reached
up and grabbed his wrists, trying to pull them away. She
began struggling.

"Jess, tell me why you're here." His grip tightened. Jess
knew he could snap her neck with a twist of his wrists.

She was still, her blue eyes not leaving his. "I saw you
do it. I saw you put Miss Becky in that thing downstairs."

Bennett was momentarily thrown off guard. "Who's
Miss Becky?"

Susie screamed out, "She was my forever friend, and
you cutted her and took her stuffing out, and then you
cooked her. You're evil, and we're going to fight you."

Bennett turned and stared at Susie. "You saw it, too?"

"We're gonna get you, Mr. Bad Doctor Man." Susie
stared defiantly at him from her place against the wall.

Bennett turned back to Jess. "I assume this is Susie."

Jess nodded. Bennett let go of her head. She fell back
against the cushions with a soft thump.

Bennett's eyes never left Jess's. Her hair was fanned out
around her head, and her eyes were round with fear. Desire
stirred in him. He slid a hand under her sweatshirt. Her
skin was velvety soft and warm.

Jess writhed away from the caress. "Don't!"

He brought his face close to hers. "I had plans for you,
my girl. You were special. But everything changed when
you broke into my house and discovered my secrets. You
disappointed me, Jess. Now you'll do what I want. Curiosity
killed the cat, you know." His lips were close to Jess's. She
could feel his breath pass over them. *Please don't kiss me
or I'll throw up,* she thought.

Instead, he slid his hand up her belly and under her cotton
bra. He cupped her right breast, a delectable handful. He

teased the nipple, knowing it would be pink and perfect as a rosebud. Jess squirmed in revulsion. He pinched it, hard.

Jess winced and stared up at his face, so close. His eyes, usually soft and twinkling, had a hard glittery look. She gasped. The skin on his face had gone gray and semi-transparent. Under his skin she could see other faces, vague strange faces. They were all contorted in pain, and shifting as if caught in some kind of current. Bennett's eyes narrowed as he saw the horror etched on Jess's own face. "You've forgotten already, little Jess. You do what I want, or you and Susie will die."

She remembered the basement room, smeared with what had to be human gore. Her gut twisted. She was filled with a cold certainty. Even if she allowed him to rape her, he would still kill both of them. Eventually. His fingers closed on her breast again.

She had been paralyzed by her own fear and disbelief, and even now, pinned to the sofa, his hand under her shirt, part of her refused to believe what Bennett was capable of. He was her mentor, her surrogate father. But, as she stared into the terrible face that was a bare inch from her own, filled with the ghosts of victims, and felt his unwelcome hands on her body, rage flooded her and galvanized her brain into action. Her fear fled, replaced by a powerful determination.

You don't fool me anymore, you asshole. I'm going to get us out of here before you can hurt us. Especially Susie.

Her mind was racing. She kept her face still. Better he should think she was still helpless with fear. But she could not help the color that flooded into her cheeks, and the instinctive clench of her fists on Bennett's shoulders.

He mistook her reaction. "So you like it, you little slut? Like mother, like daughter." He pinched her again, and Jess squeaked with pain. She knew there would be a bruise. "So fresh and young. Untouched. I have some new plans for you, my Jessie. Oh, my, yes." He was rock-hard, throbbing as he thought of all the interesting ways he could take her. And she wouldn't, couldn't say no to him. And, later, there might be a chance to experiment with the mysterious line separating life and death. Jess's life, of course, would be the subject. And then there was the little brat, too. Such luck. His body thrummed with anticipation.

But he had other pleasures to attend to first. He got up and hauled her to her feet, twisting her arm behind her back. Jess cried out as he yanked up on her arm, bringing her nearly on tiptoe. "But right now I have a banquet to go to. A magnificently prepared one, if I do say so myself. Maybe I'll bring the leftovers home for you and Susie." He laughed again, a queer sinister sound this time.

He began pushing her toward the basement stairs. Susie had been watching in silence, taking it all in. The odd, old expression was back on her face. Jess heard her whisper.

"O Blessed St. Jude, help me now in this my hour of need. Show me what to do." She moved ahead of Jess and Bennett, preceding them down the stairs. *Oh Suz,* thought Jess, *I hope he heard you.* But Jess knew she had to help herself. She would kill Bennett before he had a chance to lay a hand on a single strand of Susie's hair. Her lips moved. *Blessed St. Jude, please help Susie and me,* she whispered to herself. *I believe in you. Please believe in us.*

Bennett stopped suddenly and pulled up on Jess's twisted arm. She screamed in pain. Susie turned and looked at them with that same watchful look.

"Your cop boyfriend, Mike. Does he know you're here?"

"No," Jess gasped. "I didn't get a chance to call him."

"Does he know anything about this? Tell me the truth." His grip tightened, and Jess thought her arm would pop out of its socket. Her eyes caught Susie's. *Please, Suz, don't say a word,* she prayed.

"Who would believe anything like this unless they saw it? Let me go. You're hurting me." Bennett accepted her answer and released her. She rubbed her arm and glared at him. He grabbed her again, roughly, and pushed her into the secret room.

Susie followed, still uncharacteristically silent. Susie's eyes fell on the knife by the tanning bed. A thin line of light glittered along the blade, sending out shimmering white sparks. Susie smiled.

"You'll have to wait here while I'm gone." He looked them up and down. "I don't think you can break out of this room if I lock you in, but I think I need some insurance. Don't want you to be in here screaming. Might keep my neighbors awake." He grinned mirthlessly. Jess thought it looked like the grin on a skull. She shuddered.

"Get up on the table." Jess moved toward the table. She noticed Susie edging toward the tanning bed, with its gruesome stains. He walked over to the metal cabinet. "Don't know how much pentobarb I have left here."

Bennett peered into the cabinet. In what seemed a nanosecond, Susie grabbed the knife, smeared with juices from when Bennett checked Kass for doneness. She held it close to her body and sidled over to Jess, pressing the knife into Jess's hand. Jess concealed the knife behind her back.

"Get up on the table, I said." Bennett was drawing pentobarbital out of a vial into two syringes.

"Go on, Suz. Do like he says." Jess looked meaningfully at Susie.

"Okay, Jessie." Susie climbed up on the table. Jess marveled at the child's self-possession. Susie's lips were moving in silent prayer, no doubt to St. Jude. *Well, if Suz can believe, so can I,* thought Jess. She leaned toward the little girl. "I love you, my forever friend," she whispered. A smile flicked over Susie's face and was gone.

Bennett moved toward the table. "Push up your sleeve, little girl."

"No!" Susie said firmly. "You're a bad man, and I don't have to do anything you say."

Impatiently Bennett reached out for Susie's arm. Jess lunged forward and thrust the knife between Bennett's ribs with all her strength. He howled with pain as Jess jerked the knife back out.

"You fucking cunt!" He turned and threw a punch that would have broken her jaw. Jess ducked and the blow glanced off her shoulder. But the force of it knocked her off balance, and she came up against the greasy tanning bed. Her head hit the edge, and the room exploded in a shower of stars. Bennett was on her in a flash, pinning her to the floor with his body. He wrapped his hands around her throat, choking her viciously. She brought the knife up and stabbed blindly at his face. The knife sunk into something. He screamed and then gurgled. But he did not release the crushing pressure on Jess's throat.

She pulled back on the knife and raised it to try again. But she couldn't breathe. The room was darkening. Her neck felt as though it would snap in Bennett's hands. She tried to buck his weight off her body, twisting and writhing against him. The knife flew from her hands, clanging uselessly onto the floor. She felt something hot and wet splashing onto her face. She reached up and with her ebbing strength tried uselessly to pull Bennett's hands from her throat. Suddenly the pressure eased. A few moments later he collapsed onto the tanning bed.

Jess shook her head, trying to clear the purple mists from her brain. She took a long sobbing breath and tasted blood in her throat. She spat onto the floor, and her vision slowly cleared. Susie was standing over Bennett, a hypodermic clutched in her hand.

"I gived him a shot. Right in the heinie," she said gravely.

Jess stared at Susie, uncomprehending. Realization slowly dawned on her. A wave of hysterical laughter surged up inside her. But something in the little girl's face stopped her. Instead she opened her arms and pulled Susie close to her, covering her head with kisses.

"Yuck! He bleeded on you," Susie said. "You're getting me all icky."

Jess staggered to her feet. Bennett's body lay half-in, half-out of the tanning bed. With the heel of her hand, she pushed his head back. She saw that the knife had cut his windpipe. His white shirt and black bow tie were stained with the blood from his neck. She noticed a larger stain spreading from under his arm, where she had stabbed him.

"I trached him," she said hoarsely. "And from the look of things, I punctured his lung." She let out a hysterical giggle and stopped. It hurt to laugh.

"What's so funny? And what does 'trached' mean?"

"Tracheotomy. I cut a hole in his windpipe. He can breathe through the hole but he can't talk. Help me get him into this thing. We'll shut him up in here, and I'll call the police." Her voice sounded like a frog's. Susie giggled.

Together they maneuvered the rest of Bennett's body up into the tanning bed. He lay face down. Jess could hear blood dripping into the metal bottom of the bed. She closed the lid and snapped the clamp shut.

"Come on, Suz. Let's go upstairs. I want to get out of here."

"In a second, Jessie-ka. I want to make sure he's still sleeping." Jess went up the stairs.

Susie looked at the bed. She saw the dial on the side of the tanning bed. It looked like the "time-out" timer Heather and Jess used at home when she was bad. She reached out and twisted the dial all the way up.

"That's for hurting Miss Becky, and for hurting Jessie, and for hurting me, you bad, bad man. Now you can have a nice long time-out." She turned away and followed Jess upstairs.

Inside the bed, the elements began to glow a dull red, then grew brighter.

* * *

Bennett's consciousness struggled up against the barbiturate haze. He felt intense heat and saw a bright red glow, even through his closed eyelids. He realized that he was in agony. The pain was searing. His clothes were on fire. His hair ignited with a sizzling sound. With a sickening stab of nausea, he realized he was in the tanning bed. He tried to struggle, but the bed would not open. He had been locked in. He tried to scream. Air bubbled uselessly out of the hole Jess had made in his throat. A few seconds later his entire body was aflame.

Through the miasma of pain and flames, his burning eyes saw a white light approaching, coming closer. But it was the blinding white of a searchlight, not the comforting iridescence he remembered so clearly. He heard voices, not the sweet murmurs of before, but the shrieks and howls of souls in agony. Still, he pushed himself eagerly toward it. It was the Answer, the Answer he had been seeking for so many years. At the very last moment, he hesitated, suddenly and profoundly afraid. But it was too late. He was pulled into the light, screaming soundlessly.

As the oxygen was depleted inside the bed, the flames went out, but the body continued to char.

Susie stopped at the top of the stairs. "Dr. Meredith's coming," she said to Jess.

Jess did not stop to ask Susie how she knew that. But this time she knew better than to charge out the front door. She threw open the kitchen window and knocked out the torn screen. She vaulted feet first through the window and down into the yard. Susie followed, and Jess caught her as came down.

"Come on, Suz," she croaked. "Let's call Mike."

They scrambled over the fence as someone pounded frantically on Bennett's front door.

* * *

"Let me in! Let me in, you little whore! He's mine!"

Meredith pounded on the door until her hands hurt. She was wearing her black jeans and sweater, and a large raincoat. In the pocket of the coat was the pistol she had bought to murder Kasidy with. Now she would use it to kill Jess, and then herself. That would show Bennett how much she loved him, and what he had missed because of his blindness and his cruel words.

She stopped pounding and screaming when she realized passersby were stopping and staring at her. She listened. Bennett's house was silent. There was a faint odor of smoke coming from the door.

She tried the doorknob. In his haste Bennett had forgotten to lock the door, and it swung open. The living room was hazy with smoke.

"Bennett?" She was suddenly afraid. The house might be on fire. She had to find Bennett and get him out of here. The smoke grew thicker as she made her way to the kitchen. It smelled like burning cloth, and burning meat. "Bennett!" she called again.

The smoke was billowing out of the basement. Meredith made her way down the stairs, barely able to see. A single lightbulb in the basement ceiling gave off a sick orange glow in the murky air. She found her way to the secret room, which was better lit but dense with the smoke.

She saw wisps now, issuing from a tanning bed. A low electrical hum told her it was in use. She had seen no sign of anyone, but someone was in that tanning bed. She reached over to unlatch it.

The latch was blistering hot. She picked up a smock that was on the table, not noticing the bloodstains, and used it to open the tanning bed. A wave of broiling heat struck her in the face like a blow. She saw the electrical elements glowing a dull red. And she saw something else.

It was a man. His clothing had been charred off his body. Scraps burst into flame in the bottom of the bed as the oxygen hit them. His mouth was open in a soundless scream. There was a hole in his neck. His skin was purple and black, and his gray-filmed eyes oozed at the corners. Most of the hair had been broiled off, but there was enough left for Meredith to see it was a dark blond. It was Bennett. Dead. Cooked in some kind of macabre oven.

The corpse smoldered and smoked. Meredith coughed and choked, from her own horror as much as the smoke. She turned to run, then stopped. Bennett was dead. The love of her life. She would never have him now.

She felt like she was falling into a black abyss of nothingness. Everything was gone. Everything was wasted. He was gone. He would never love her. She screamed, a thin wailing cry of grief.

But wait. There was a way, now. A way that she could have him to herself, forever linked with him.

Meredith turned around. She placed her fingertips on his blackened cheek, not feeling the heat burning her. She pulled the gun from her pocket and put it in her mouth.

"I love you, my darling," she said around the gun barrel. "We'll be together forever."

She pulled the trigger and pitched forward onto the smoking mess that had been Dr. Bennett Sykes.

Jess and Susie ran down through the alley and out onto Pine Street. Jess looked wildly up and down the street, looking for a pay phone. She didn't see one on the block.

She grabbed Susie's hand and began pulling her up the street.

"Come on, Suz. We'll find a restaurant or something. They'll have a pay phone."

Susie stopped. "No," she said. "This way."

"Not back past Bennett's? No way am I going there." She tugged at Susie again.

"No, no. Up to the next block, and then over."

Jess's throat was too sore to argue with the little girl. She let Susie lead her. She caught a glance at her reflection in a window and gasped. Blood was smeared on her face and sweatshirt, and purple marks circled her neck. She knew she couldn't go into a restaurant like that without causing a stir. A stir was the last thing she wanted right now.

She wiped her face as best she could on her shirtsleeve.

"Hurry, Jessie-ka!" Susie called. She began to run. Jess ran, too.

As they reached the corner at Spruce Street, Susie stopped and looked expectantly up the street. They heard the wail of a fire siren. Suddenly a car screeched to a halt in front of them, and the passenger door was flung open.

"Get in!" yelled Mike.

They scrambled into his car as the fire truck roared past and turned down Ashland Street. Susie tumbled over the front console and into the backseat. Jess got into the car and yanked the door closed. Her eyes met Mike's. He opened his arms, and she pressed herself into his embrace. He held her tightly as she began shaking violently.

"It's okay now, Jessie-ka," Susie said from the back. "It's over. St. Jude said so."

By the time Jess regained control and told Mike what had happened at Bennett's house, Mike had decided to drive past Ashland Street and see if the police had arrived. The fire department was already there. So was Detective Jay Stanley. Mike saw him standing in the street, which had been cordoned off. He was staring at the house.

Mike parked the car and turned to Jess and Susie. "Stay in the car, ladies. I'll find out what's going on."

He ducked under the yellow POLICE LINE DO NOT CROSS tape and walked over to Detective Stanley. "Hi, Detective. Need any help?"

The detective looked up. "Yo, O'Keefe." Then he looked back at 315 Ashland Street and shook his head.

"No thanks, man. It's all under control." He looked gray-faced, as though he had just awakened from a night full of bad dreams.

"What happened?"

"Damned if I know," Jay Stanley said, shaking his head slowly. "We found a guy who had been cooked in some kind of jury-rigged oven. There was a woman lying across him, apparently a suicide. Gunshot wound to the head. The neighbors identified her as Meredith Shirk, lives across the street. Doctor. The house belongs to Bennett Sykes, also a doctor. We think he's the guy in the oven, but we'll have to get a positive ID from Forensics." He looked sharply at Mike. "What brings you here?"

"I'm off duty. I was just passing by and saw something going on. Thought maybe you could use some help." Mike hoped he sounded smoother than he felt.

"Like I said, we'll be fine. I got enough guys here. Go along now, I got work to do. Press'll be here any minute, and I'll have to talk to them, I guess." Mike could hear the news helicopters flying overhead, shooting footage for the late news. He walked back to his car, where Jess and Susie sat anxiously waiting for him.

He got into the car and ignored Jess's frantic questions. He motioned to her to be quiet and drove a few blocks down to Penn's Landing. He pulled over, stopped, and turned to Jess.

"Mike, for the love of God, what happened?"

"Jess, Bennett's dead."

She said nothing, but her hands began trembling again. Mike took them in his own. Susie smiled to herself in the backseat. Then she leaned in between the two of them. "How, Mikey?" she asked innocently.

"You locked him in the tanning bed, right?" Jess nodded. "Well, somehow, it got turned on. He fried."

Jess gasped. Mike looked at her pale face and the bruises on her neck. "There's something else, too . . ."

"I know!" Susie cried. "That weird Dr. Meredith is there with him. She's all dead, too."

Mike looked at Susie and stared hard at her. "How do you know that?"

"I just know," Susie replied evenly. Jess found her voice. "Don't ask how she knows, Mike. It's just Susie. You saw, yourself, when we called you about the Miss Becky thing. So Meredith is dead, too?" Her voice scaled up.

"Gunshot wound to the head, self-inflicted." Mike looked at Jess and then back at Susie. "What I'm about to tell you goes against everything I've been trained to do. I'm going to take you home. Don't tell anyone where you were this afternoon. Not Heather, not anyone." He sighed. "I want to keep you out of this if I can. Otherwise, you could be in some nasty legal trouble. Jessie, breaking and entering—even if you had a real good reason—is a crime. And if word gets out about little Suz and her psychic ability, they'll never leave her alone. Every wacko in the world will be after her to predict stuff for them."

"I don't think so," Susie said indignantly. "I wouldn't do it."

"It could get so bad for you." Mike sighed deeply. "With any luck it will go down as a murder-suicide. If not—if they find some way to place you there—we'll deal with it when it happens. If nobody saw you two, I doubt they will. But for now, lay low and play dumb. Okay?"

Jess turned to Susie. "Can you do that, Suz? Not even tell Mommy? Or Miss Becky? It will have to be our secret. And we can never talk about it again."

"Miss Becky's dead, Jessie-ka. I won't tell Mommy. I promise." She was silent for a moment. "Miss Becky says it's important to keep your promises."

Mike drove them home. He stayed with Susie while Jess hurriedly took a shower and pulled on a turtleneck to cover the bruises on her throat. Susie sat next to him on the sofa and held his hand. She was quiet, but calm. Almost too calm for a kid who had just gone through what she had.

"You okay, Susie-Q?" he asked.

"Yes, Mikey." She sighed. "I feel bad that we didn't save Miss Becky, but we stopped the evil doctor man. There won't be any more Curer's Balls or unholy communions."

Mike didn't ask how she knew that. He was a fast learner.

Heather came home soon after, and Jess delivered Susie to her. Heather was tired and in need of her pain pills, so she didn't notice that Jess was pale and still a little shaky. Susie was her normal, cheerful self as soon as she saw her mother. Jess used Mike's presence as an excuse to leave, instead of staying at Heather's.

"Nice to meet you, Mike. Be good, Jess," Heather said. She tried to frown meaningfully at Jess, but the frown became a smile. Jess returned the smile.

"I will. Don't worry about me, Heather."

When they returned to Jess's house, she put her arms around him.

"Couldn't you stay here tonight?" she asked.

"No, Jessie. I have to go in. Besides, it'll give me a chance to find out what's going on with the investigation." He hugged her close. "But I'll come here right after work. I promise."

Jess was afraid she would have nightmares, but she slept deeply and dreamlessly. Susie did not come visiting in the middle of the night.

When Mike knocked on Jess's door the next morning, it opened to the fragrance of good coffee and a smiling Jess. She had showered again and put on jeans and another turtleneck. She kissed him and handed him a steaming mug of coffee.

"So. Wanna be boring together today?" she asked.

"Cool," replied Mike.

TWELVE

Jess quit her job one week after the deaths of Doctors Sykes and Shirk. The police never knew that she and Susie had been in Bennett's house. As Mike had predicted, it was ruled a murder-suicide at first. But then it blossomed into a full-blown scandal after the half-eaten remains of Kasidy Rhodes were discovered in a Dumpster behind a vacant restaurant. Mike mentioned casually to LaVyrle that perhaps there might be a link to Dr. Sykes, because of the courier package Kasidy Rhodes had received.

LaVyrle had agreed, and the information was brought to Detective Stanley's attention.

Dr. Singh Pandit performed an autopsy on what was left of Kasidy Rhodes. DNA testing linked her to Bennett's tanning-bed oven. Hospital employees, Jess included, gave statements attesting to the fact that Meredith Shirk was obsessively stalking Bennett Sykes. Kasidy's daughter Karen testified that her mother had just started seeing a doctor she'd met on the Internet. Detectives found e-mails Bennett Sykes had sent to Kasidy Rhodes on his computer, and a lot of research concerning Kasidy on Meredith Shirk's computer. There were also deleted, encrypted messages to and from an Epicurean on Dr. Sykes's computer, but they had been routed through a server that stripped the message of all information regarding the sender. The messages cryptically referred to a meeting, but there was nothing specific to look at.

There was much conjecture as to what happened and why, but Detective Stanley never came up with a satisfactory answer.

The Epicurean Society disappeared. Their link to Kass's and Bennett's deaths was never fully explained.

Heather also quit her job. The lymphoma, with increasing speed, began to lay waste to Heather's body. Jess lived simply off the income generated by the lottery winnings Ramon had invested. As Heather grew weaker, Jess moved into Heather's home and nursed her full-time. Susie was quiet and helpful, so much so that Jess and Heather fretted that she was in some kind of denial about Heather's imminent death. During one of Father Romano's frequent visits, Heather confided in him about Susie's unchildlike behavior.

"It's like she has no clue about what's going to happen. She *says* she knows, but she's so fucking serene. I mean, wouldn't a normal kid be scared?" Heather's eyes glittered with fever.

Father Romano folded Heather's hot, dry hand into his. "I'll talk to her when I see her again. She comes to the chapel quite often now and prays to St. Jude."

"Her and St. Jude," sighed Heather. "Oh, well. I guess it

could be worse. She could be into Britney Spears." She
shifted on the sofa and groaned with pain.

Not long afterward, he saw Susie in the chapel at St.
Laurence's, kneeling in front of the statue of St. Jude. He
waited until she was finished, and then sat down on the
floor beside her.

"Susie, your mother is worried about you," he had said
gently, taking her hand.

"Why?" Susie's eyes were round with amazement.

"She thinks maybe you don't understand what it will
mean to you when she's gone."

" 'Course I do," said Susie indignantly. "Sister Hubert
said that when you die the immortal soul rises to heaven
and dwells with the angels. And I know Mommy won't go
to purgatory, even though she says bad words a lot."

"But doesn't it make you sad to think you won't see
your mom again after she dies? You won't be able to touch
her or kiss her or hear her voice. She won't be here to take
care of you anymore."

Susie put her other hand over Father Romano's. She
looked up at him earnestly. "St. Jude said I can talk to her
whenever I want. And just 'cause I can't see her doesn't
mean she's not there. I'll know when she's there. I'm not
afraid."

He was silent for a moment. "Is St. Jude still showing
you things? About a great evil? The one you and Jessica
were supposed to fight?"

"No," Susie replied abruptly. "The evil is gone. Jessie and
me were brave and strong. And St. Jude helped us. He said
they won't do unholy communions anymore." She withdrew
her hands from the priest's. Something in her direct gray
gaze, and in the set of her sharp chin, dried up the questions
on Father Romano's lips.

Susie stood up. "Tell Mommy I'm okay." She turned
and left the chapel. Father Romano watched her go.

On his next visit, while Susie was in school, Father Romano told Heather and Jess about the first part of the conversation.

"That's an old soul in her body," Jess had said.

"You ain't shittin'," replied Heather as she lit a cigarette with trembling hands.

"Amen to that," said Father Romano with a grin. They all laughed.

A little later, Jess went into the kitchen to get Heather's pain pills. The priest followed her and blocked the doorway with his body.

"I asked Susie if she was still receiving visions from St. Jude. She tells me no, that you and she have conquered this evil. Is that true?"

Jess stared at him. For a moment she saw Bennett's face, hard and angry. Angry enough to rape and kill her. The ghostly images of the countless victims of the sickness that possessed him, moving and shifting in his contorted face. She put her hand up to her throat, remembering the terrible grip of his hands on her neck.

"Are you all right, Jessica?" Father Romano's voice abruptly brought her back into Heather's tiny kitchen. She blinked.

"Father, Susie told you the truth. It's a confidential matter, so please don't ask me anything else." She tried to push past the priest with Heather's pills in her hand. He continued to block the doorway.

"Jessica, there are no secrets from God. I would be happy to hear your confession."

Jess's eyes were icy as she returned the priest's gaze. "Susie and I have nothing to confess, Father. We did God's work for Him."

He stepped aside and let her go.

A few blocks away in the classroom, Sister Hubert rapped the edge of Susie's desk with her ruler.

"Are we daydreaming, Susie?"

Susie slowly lifted her eyes and smiled brilliantly at her teacher. "No, Sister Hubert."

For Christmas, Heather had Jess get a new Miss Becky doll for Susie. Susie's love of the show was unaffected by what she had seen in October, but she had never asked for another doll. The remains of the first Miss Becky doll had been placed in a shoebox, and Jess ceremoniously buried it in the tiny backyard. Susie had cried and cried, then suddenly squared her shoulders.

"Ashes to ashes, and dust to dirt," she said. She wiped the tears from her cheeks and went inside. Susie did not cry again until she opened the box under the Christmas tree.

"Miss Becky's dead. This isn't the real Miss Becky. It's not real, and I don't want it!" Susie pushed the box away with her feet, her face contorted with rage and pain.

Heather was lying on the sofa. When Susie began wailing, she tried to get up and go to her. But before Heather could push herself off the sofa, Jess flew over and gathered Susie in her arms. "Pickle, Miss Becky loves you. She felt bad that you were all alone. So she wanted you to have this doll, to remember her by and to keep you company."

"It's not real," repeated Susie, but with a little less conviction. She used her toes to reach out and pull the box closer. She looked at the curly dark hair, shiny eyes, and red bandanna around the doll's neck. She touched the soft plush body, plump with stuffing.

"Is Miss Becky an angel now?"

"Yes," Jess said firmly.

"So . . . this could be like an angel Miss Becky?"

"Yes, Suz. A guardian angel. For your very own."

Susie considered for a few moments. Then she picked up the doll and held it in her arms, cradling it like a baby. "Okay," she said. "Hi, new Miss Becky. I'm your forever friend."

Jess glanced over at Heather. Tears were running down her cheeks.

"Are you all right, Heather?" Jess asked, concerned.

"No, Jessie, but you will be. You and Suz will be just fine," she said, smiling through her tears.

Through all of this, Mike had been there, a steadfast presence. He accepted from the start that Jessica was a package deal—she came with Susie and Heather—and became as much their friend as he was Jess's. Heather had approved of him immediately.

"Man, that's the kind of guy I wish I'd found, Jessie. Then I wouldn't have gotten involved with Susie's fuckhead father."

"Then you wouldn't have Susie," Jess said, laughing. "I'm glad you like him."

Heather looked at her. "Jess, your dad would have liked him, too."

"I know," she replied. She was a little surprised when no tears came. *I must be getting better,* she realized.

On Christmas, Mike had come over after Susie had accepted the new Miss Becky. He had gifts for all of them. Susie commandeered him immediately to show him the new dollhouse Santa had brought.

"Hey Susie Q, Santa clued me in about the new house. Here's a housewarming present."

Susie unwrapped the package. Inside was a set of exquisitely detailed living room furniture, which fit perfectly into the new house.

"Thanks, Mikey. What's a housewarming?"

"It's a party for your house," he said, grinning.

"Like a birthday party? With cake and ice cream and stuff?"

"Sure."

"Thanks a lot, Michael. Now I have to go make a cake," Jess whispered.

"Not until you open your present." Heather had already opened the box containing a photograph of Jess and Susie in a silver frame. Now he handed Jess a small box. She opened it and saw a simple ring made of three interwoven strands of gold—yellow, white, and rose.

"Mike, it's lovely," she breathed. "But I don't know . . ."

"Jess, I'm not asking you to marry me or anything. You have a lot on your plate right now. I just wanted you to have this . . . like a promise or something. A promise that I'll be here for you." He blushed scarlet, all the way up to his ears.

Jess kissed him with her heart on her lips. "Okay." He slipped the ring on her finger. It fit perfectly. "Now you'll have to make good on it and come help me in the kitchen."

When Heather was finally completely bedridden and needed twenty-four-hour care, he took Susie to the movies and ran errands for Jess. He was always ready to hold Jess in his arms when she was exhausted and drained. He took them to Hahnemann when pneumonia infected Heather's lungs, making her struggle for every breath. And he was there with them in the hospital when Heather died three weeks after Christmas, his arms around Jess and Susie.

Jess had hidden her face on Mike's shoulder, crying soundlessly. But Susie had gone over to the bed and touched her mother's face.

"It's okay now," she said.

Mike took Susie and Jess home that night. Jess put Susie to sleep in her own bed. She couldn't face going back into Heather's house. Susie made no complaint—she was too tired, and she also sensed that memories were better faced in the daylight.

Jess came back downstairs after tucking Susie in. Mike was standing in the living room.

"Well, Jessie, I guess I'll go on home now. You're probably whacked."

Jess looked at him. Her eyes were soft in the dim light.

"Mike, would you mind staying here tonight?"

Mike smiled. "Sure, no problem. I'll camp here on the couch. Just toss me down a pillow and blanket, and I'll be fine."

Jess's cheeks were spread over with a fine pink blush. "Um . . . actually, I meant, stay *with* me."

Mike and Jess had not gone much past kissing, cuddling, and hand-holding. He hadn't wanted to pressure her for sex, and she had never brought it up. Until now. He stared at her.

"Jess, we don't have to do this if you don't want to," he replied. Suddenly he was nervous. He put his hands in his jeans pockets and dropped his eyes.

"Mike, I do want to. Heather told me I should get a life, that I have to stop hiding in my house, hiding behind Suz." She walked over to him and stood very close to him, looking up into his face. "I want you to be part of my new life. I want you to help me start."

Mike put his arms around her and rested his cheek on her soft hair. They held each other for a few moments. Then he straightened abruptly and stepped back.

"Jess, I can't. I don't have any protection on me."

Jess blushed again, this time a fiery red. "I got a box of . . . protection. Last week. It's upstairs in the front room."

Mike grinned. "A whole box? Are you planning a long-term relationship? Or do you just think I'm Superman?"

Jess laughed and hugged him. "Both," she said. Then it was her turn to feel nervous. "There's something else you should know," she whispered.

"What?"

"Um . . . I never did this before. So I might be a total moron. I'm also kind of scared."

"Me, too," he whispered. "Kind of scared, I mean. Don't worry, Jessie. You could never be a moron. I love you."

Jess kissed him. They let their hands roam over each other's bodies, exploring each other. Then Jess led him upstairs.

Mike tangled his fingers in Jess's tousled hair and kissed her for the hundredth time.

"Well? What do you think?" he asked.

"A little weird. A lot of it felt good. Then it hurt, a little. But it felt right."

Mike laughed. "I've never heard anyone call it weird. But I guess it is, kind of."

Jess turned toward Mike and propped herself on her elbow. They were in the big bed that Ramon had shared with Ingrid twenty years ago. Moonlight filtered though the frosted windows and gleamed along the curve of Jess's hip and legs. Mike ran his hand over the silken warmth of her skin.

Jess remembered how Suz had called it weird when Bennett Sykes had done things to Miss Becky in her dream. Suz had also called it icky, but being here with Mike definitely wasn't icky. Not even close. "I guess you must have had lots of experience, then," she said. Her eyes were black in the ghostly light.

"Not a whole lot. I'm kind of picky about my women."

"Jeez, should I be honored or something?"

Mike stopped stroking Jess's hip and put his hand against her cheek. "No, Jessie. I'm the one who's honored. Being the first for you."

Jess covered his hand with her own. "Daddy was really strict about me and my boyfriends. He'd grill them up one side and down the other when they came to pick me up.

And I didn't want to disappoint him. I knew he'd want me to wait until I was really sure about someone. So I waited. And then, after he died, I just wasn't interested in a boyfriend." She lay back down against the pillows.

"But you are now. Interested in a boyfriend, I mean."

"No," she replied.

Mike was silent. After a few moments, Jess sighed. She reached over and pulled him toward her, bringing him across her body, feeling the heat of his skin and the whorls of his chest hair against her breasts.

"Michael, you dope, I'm not interested in a boyfriend. I'm interested in *you*."

"Don't scare me like that, Jess. Or I'll . . . I don't know what I'd do."

"I can think of something you can do. Right now."

"Like what?"

She whispered in his ear.

"Cool," he said and reached for the box of condoms.

"Hi, Mommy. It's me, Susie. Are you an angel yet? Me and new Miss Becky got you some flowers with my allowance."

Susie knelt by the granite headstone and sat the Miss Becky doll down beside her. She carefully placed a bunch of red and white carnations against the polished surface.

"Heather Elizabeth Troutman," Susie read aloud. "I read good now, Mommy. Jessie-ka takes real good care of me. Mikey does, too. We're going to go look at a new house after I finish talking to you." She tucked her sun-streaked brown hair behind her ears. "We went down the shore this summer, Jessie and me. We rented the same place we used to, right there on Pleasure Avenue. The waves were real big. Mike taught me how to bodysurf, except I kept getting water up my nose . . ."

Jess and Mike stood silently a few feet away, holding

hands as they watched Susie. Jess blinked back her tears. Mike glanced over and squeezed her hand.

"She's a tough little kid, Jessie. She'll be okay."

"That's what scares me. She's seven going on fifty." Jess smiled tremulously at him. "I wish I had some of her strength. I can't believe how nervous I am about this house thing. I mean, Mike, I'm not old enough to buy beer yet, and I'm buying a house!"

Mike laughed. "It's just like buying the car. It takes longer, that's all. And there's tons of papers to sign."

"Great," groaned Jess.

After Heather had died, Jess had moved Susie's things over to her house. She decided to put Heather's house up for sale. It was Mike who suggested she sell both of them and move out of Upper Darby.

"But if I move, I'll need to get a car," she had said.

Mike laughed. "If that's the only thing holding you back, well, let's get you a car."

At first, Jess, feeling her responsibility to Susie, decided she had to be practical. She looked at frumpy family sedans and boxy minivans. She hated them all.

"I know I need a car, but I hate spending all that money on something so ugly," she complained. Then, one gorgeous spring afternoon, Mike had pulled up in a gunmetal BMW 328i convertible. Jess spotted him from the front window. He had the car top down and a huge grin on his face. She ran down the front steps, her eyes alight.

"Michael! Where did you get that car?" she asked. She put her hand on the hood and listened to the purr of the finely tuned engine. "It's so beautiful." She looked at the black leather upholstery and the dashboard that curved in toward Mike, giving him complete control of the car at the touch of a finger.

Mike shut the engine off and got out. The door shut with a satisfying thunk. He looked at Jess, who was still admiring the car.

"You want it?" he said, smiling slyly.

She met his eyes, puzzled. "What do you mean?"

"Look, Jessie. You've been hemming and hawing over those family cars. Sure, you have Susie now, but honey, live a little. I saw the way your face lit up just now. I took this off the dealer's lot. Said I was going for a test drive. Well, you passed the test. Grab your purse, we'll go sign the papers, and it's yours."

Jess stared at him. Then she began to laugh. She could not stop. It was as if something had finally let go inside her. Tears ran down her cheeks. Mike took her slender body, shaking with emotion, into his arms. "What's so funny?"

"I don't know. All I know is that it's exactly what I want, and I'm going to buy it." She turned her blue eyes up to his green ones.

"Jeez, Jessie, it's so good to hear you laugh again. You're always so freakin' *serious*. Like a nun or something."

"Yeah, well, I don't think nuns do what I do with you at night." She grinned wickedly up at him. "I think it's against the rules or something. Their loss."

He reached down and touched her cheek. "You haven't laughed like this since we went to the zoo. Remember?"

"I sure do. Man, it feels so good, too." She giggled again, then met his eyes. "Know what else?" Mike's heart skipped a beat as he looked down into her shining blue eyes.

"What?"

"I love you, too." She drew his face down to hers and kissed him right there on the sidewalk. They stood there for a long time, embracing.

Mike and Jess brought the car home. A few days later, Mike moved in with Jess and Susie.

* * *

Jess grinned, remembering. She glanced affectionately at the car, parked in a shady spot on the gravel path that wound through the cemetery. She tightened her grip on Mike's hand. He grinned down at her, and she knew he was remembering, too.

"I think you moved in with me for the car," she whispered.

"Yeah, right," he snorted.

Susie came running up to them, new Miss Becky flopping from her hand. "Mommy's fine. She liked the flowers. She sits on the clouds and watches us, you know."

Mike stroked Susie's hair. "Of course she does, Susie-Q. She's proud of you."

"She says learning how to play the harp is a real bitch."

"Susie Troutman!" exclaimed Jess. "Don't you use that word again."

"Well, that's what she *said*," replied Susie in an aggrieved tone. "What's a bitch?"

"A female dog," Mike answered promptly. Susie looked mystified.

"Let's go. We don't want to be late," said Jessie. They walked back to the car and drove away. Susie watched out the back window as the headstone and the bunch of carnations grew small and disappeared.

They drove along Spruce Street. The homes were lovely old eighteenth-century town houses, with marble steps, Grecian-style pillars, and wrought-iron railings. Fall color was just beginning to touch the leaves on the trees planted along the street. In another three weeks this street would be blazing with reds and golds.

Susie looked around, excited. "It's so pretty here, you guys. Are we going to live here? Which one is our house?"

"We're just looking, Suz." Jess was nervous. The thought that she could actually afford to buy one of these elegant homes, after living all of her life in a cramped, slightly shabby twin home on a busy street, was almost over-whelming.

Mike was driving, and he pulled up in front of a home with black shutters. A FOR SALE sign was in the front window. It read 5 BR, 2 BA, PRKG. A pearl-white Cadillac was parked in front of it. A meticulously groomed middle-aged woman in an impeccable business suit waved to them from the sidewalk in front of the house.

"This must be the place. And that's got to be the real estate agent. Wow, business must be good," Mike said, admiring the car.

They got out of the car and walked up the steps. A planter full of chrysanthemums adorned the entry.

"I'm Virginia Harman," the agent said in a friendly yet professional way. "Let me get this door unlocked, and we can go right in." Jess looked around. She saw the old homes, lined up tall on either side of the street. They looked warm and welcoming, as they had been for almost two hundred years. She felt a sense of peace steal over her, as if she belonged here.

Susie slipped her hand into Jess's and squeezed it. "I like it here, Jessie-ka," she whispered.

"Me, too, Pickle." She returned the squeeze.

Virginia Harman opened the door and motioned them inside. She shook her head. Jess caught it out of the corner of her eye and knew what the woman was thinking. How could someone as young as she was afford a house like this? And was she Susie's mother? Jess smiled to herself. *Let her wonder.*

They looked around the living room. The house had a forlorn air, like a lost child. Most of the furniture was still there, but the photographs and collectibles and bric-a-brac that make a house look lived in were gone. The hardwood floor needed dusting. The big marble fireplace was empty.

"The owner is interested in any offers you may care to make on the furniture and rugs," said Virginia.

"Why are they selling?" Mike asked.

The room felt very cold, even though it was a warm day. Susie suddenly clutched Jess's had hard enough to make her wince. She looked down at the little girl. Susie had her head cocked as though she were listening, and an intent expression on her face.

"This was Miss Becky's house. The Miss Becky on TV. The one bad Doctor Bennett Sykes killed." Susie's voice was level, but she was beginning to tremble.

Jess began to tremble, too. Was this Bennett's victim's house? "Oh, Suz, are you sure?"

"Yes, Jessie-ka. She's here, right here."

Virginia had gone white. Jess knelt and put her arms around Susie. Mike knelt down next to Jess and put his hand reassuringly on her shoulder.

"How do you know, Suz?"

"I can hear her. She's trying to tell me something. Except her name is Kassie, not Becky."

Virginia cleared her throat. "I'm not supposed to say anything to buyers about this, but it seems that you already know. A woman named Kasidy Rhodes owned this house. She was murdered almost a year ago. They found her body in a Dumpster. It seems that some doctor murdered her in his basement and then cooked her." Virginia shuddered. "The house is being sold for the estate. She had two children, who live with their father and stepmother now."

Susie was still listening, but not to Virginia. Her body relaxed.

"It's okay. Miss Bec—I mean, Miss Kassie—wants us to have this house. She's an angel just like Mommy. She's my forever friend, too. Maybe I should ask her to help Mommy learn the harp."

Jess stood up, keeping one arm around Susie and another arm around Mike. She looked at Mike, her eyes questioning.

"Jess, baby, it's your call. But if you like the place . . . I don't know why we shouldn't buy it. It's not like it's haunted by an evil spirit or something."

"No, Miss Kassie is a guardian angel. Like Mommy and new Miss Becky." Susie paused. "She has to go now, but she said to go see the bathtub upstairs. It has claw feet on it. She said it's really cool."

"How could she know about that?" muttered Virginia.

"You could do worse than a house with a built-in angel. Beats a built-in microwave any day," said Mike, smiling at Jess.

"I want to see the bathtub!" said Susie.

"Okay, Pickle, lead the way," said Jess.

They all followed Susie up the stairs.